CAITLIN SWEET
THE DOOR IN THE MOUNTAIN

CHI
TEEN

An Imprint of ChiZine Publications

FIRST EDITION

The Door in the Mountain © 2014 by Caitlin Sweet
Cover artwork © 2014 by Erik Mohr
Interior design © 2014 by Erik Mohr

Distributed in Canada by
HarperCollins Canada Ltd.
1995 Markham Road
Scarborough, ON M1B 5M8
Toll Free: 1-800-387-0117
e-mail: hcorder@harpercollins.com

Distributed in the U.S. by
Diamond Comic Distributors, Inc.
10150 York Road, Suite 300
Hunt Valley, MD 21030
Phone: 1-443-318-8500
e-mail: books@diamondbookdistributors.com

Library and Archives Canada Cataloguing in Publication

Sweet, Caitlin, 1970-, author
     The door in the mountain / Caitlin Sweet.

Issued in print and electronic formats.
ISBN 978-1-77148-191-5 (pbk.).--ISBN 978-1-77148-192-2 (pdf)

     I. Title.

PS8587.W387D66 2014   C813'.6   C2014-900784-1
                                             C2014-900785-X

CHITEEN
Toronto, Canada
www.chiteen.com

Edited by Sandra Kasturi
Copyedited and proofread by Christie DiIorio

 Canada Council   Conseil des Arts
for the Arts   du Canada

We acknowledge the support of the Canada Council for the Arts which last year
invested $20.1 million in writing and publishing throughout Canada.

 ONTARIO ARTS COUNCIL
CONSEIL DES ARTS DE L'ONTARIO
50 YEARS OF ONTARIO GOVERNMENT SUPPORT OF THE ARTS
50 ANS DE SOUTIEN DU GOUVERNEMENT DE L'ONTARIO AUX ARTS

Published with the generous assistance of the Ontario Arts Council.

Printed in Canada

I remember listening to my father's voice
in the dark, years before I could read.
I remember him saying
"Ariadne" and "the Minotaur" and "the labyrinth"—
words that were magical and mysterious then,
and still are.

This book is for him.

— BOOK —

ONE

CHAPTER ONE

It was no use: the water didn't move. Ariadne bit her lip and watched her reflection do the same. She dug her fingernails into the basin's sides and leaned forward so that all she could see were her own wide brown eyes.

"Ariadne—no—let go." Her mother's hands lifted her off the stone. Just before they did, Ariadne saw the water fill with sky. "Do not try so hard; it will not make the god think any more kindly of you. Wait, and breathe . . . Good. Now look again."

She stepped back onto the stone that brought her upper body to the edge of the basin. She didn't look at the queen, but she could see her shadow on the water. The smooth, still water that refused to ripple.

"It won't work." Ariadne's voice sounded high and wavery and she coughed a little, to hide this.

"It will. You are a daughter of Poseidon, the Bull. Here—watch me one more time and see how I call up his power."

No, Ariadne wanted to say, *I've watched before and I've tried before and nothing ever happens for me, even though I'm a princess and already five*—but then Pasiphae tilted her head toward the basin, and Ariadne did watch.

For a moment there was only more stillness. Small things moved—the golden rings that dangled from her mother's ears, and the wispy clouds above the palace's walls—but Ariadne hardly saw them, just as she hardly heard the voices that sang and shouted in the corridors beyond the altar. It was the quiet that consumed her.

Pasiphae's green eyes were on the water, yet they seemed to be gazing through it, too, into a place Ariadne couldn't see. For a few breaths the queen stayed like this— like a statue or a bird carried motionless on a river of wind. She curved her fingers. The gems on them winked, and the copper wrapped around her wrists glinted, and one black ringlet slipped down over her shoulder and bobbed just above the water.

The queen smiled. *Now*, Ariadne thought, and there it was: a circle in the centre of the basin; a silent ripple that rose and broke like a miniature tide against the stone. The queen lifted her hands, which had begun to glow silver. The ripple became a wave, and the wave leapt out of the basin.

Ariadne sucked in her breath. She knew what would happen; she had watched her mother draw swells from a calm sea and turn a stormy one mirror-flat. But she gasped now, as Pasiphae held the ring of water in mid-air. It shone as her gems did, struck by shifting sun and cloud shapes. It pulsed a bit, as if it too were breathing.

"My thanks, Lord Poseidon," Pasiphae whispered. She smiled another, even more dazzling smile and brought her hands slowly down. The water flowed back into the basin and was a smooth, still pool again, and the silver faded from her skin.

"And so you see," Pasiphae said briskly as Ariadne blinked, "you must not strain; you must be quiet, open to the bull god's gift. I learned this from my own mother and was marked by the god by the time I was three. It is past time for you. Now. Try."

Ariadne leaned forward. She stared at her eyes and brow, which were frowning. She tried to ease away the frown, and did, but then she realized that her hands were clenched. *Please*, she thought, *Lord Poseidon, come to me like you come to her—I'm going to be six soon, and you still haven't come to me, and I'll never be queen if you don't, and even the cook's child has a mark—*

"Stop!" cried a new voice, so loudly that the water seemed at last to quiver. Ariadne stumbled backward off the stone. She felt her mother's fingers dig into her shoulders before they pushed her away.

"Husband." Pasiphae's voice was flat but somehow also sharp, like the shell Ariadne had cut her knee on the summer she was four.

"Wife," Minos said. His teeth showed through his beard; they were bared like an angry dog's. A smile, Ariadne knew. Her father's smile. She smiled too, a little, and her heart thumped in her chest.

"I see you are still attempting to prove that the child bears your god's blessing," the king said. "You are very sweet, my dear, when you are desperate."

"She bears his blessing because *I* bore *her*."

The water in the basin began to bubble and froth. Ariadne smiled even more widely as red-gold light shot through with silver bloomed beneath her father's skin.

"Admit the truth at last," Minos said. He was rubbing the tips of his first two fingers against his thumbs; Ariadne watched sparks kindle and spin. They turned to cinders as they fell. "Her gift may well be from Zeus—for she is also my child."

Pasiphae took a step toward her husband and now Ariadne could see both of them, standing very tall, a forearm's length between them. "*She* may be your child," the queen said in a low voice, "but this one, at least, is not."

She put her hands on either side of her belly, which was a small round lump beneath the green folds of her dress. She pulled the folds taut so that the lump was very clear.

Minos made a sound deep in his throat. He raised his

11

hands and held them flat; bronze and copper fire licked along the seams in his palms and up into the air. The flames stretched and shimmered and crackled, and Ariadne lifted her face up into their heat. Behind her the water hissed and churned; it spattered cool against the back of her neck.

"If you continue to flaunt your union with the bull priest, I will cast you out as I did him." Smoke coiled from Minos's mouth as he spoke.

Pasiphae laughed. Her cheeks and arms were beaded with moisture. Ariadne knew that soon her mother's dress would darken and cling to her, as if she'd been swimming, and that her father's tunic would be bored with blackened holes.

"You will not cast me out," the queen said. "When you banished him, my people rioted—they shattered Zeus's altar—imagine, Husband, what they would do to this island if you did the same to me. No." She laughed again, and the water tinkled and sang. "I will bear Poseidon's child here."

Minos thrust his arm out. It was bare, coursing with light that was gold now, and so bright that Ariadne had to look away. She saw a tongue of flame dart out and attach itself to her mother's cheek. It slithered and lashed but couldn't cling, for Pasiphae's skin was slick with water. The queen closed her eyes, and Minos cried out a deep, ragged word that Ariadne didn't understand because his open mouth was awash with smoke and rippling with heat.

"Mama!" Ariadne cried. She wasn't afraid; she just wanted them to look at *her* now, not at each other. "Papa!" But they didn't look at her. They stared and stared, only the two of them in the world, so far away from her.

She reached out and raked her nails along Pasiphae's arm. The queen rounded on her, water spraying from her mouth, and from the palm that struck Ariadne across the face. "Go—go *now*," the queen snarled, but Ariadne was already running.

"Hush, Minnow. There, now—hush . . ."

Naucrate's skirt smelled like lemons. Ariadne burrowed into it as far as she could, until she felt Naucrate's knees pressing against her forehead.

"You ran very fast," Naucrate said. Her hands stroked Ariadne's back, which was still heaving.

Ariadne nodded into the cloth. She *had* run fast, and far—all those corridors and courtyards, their walls just blurs of paint. She hadn't even slowed when she passed the dolphin fresco that had a tiny figure of her in it, beneath a curling wave. She'd been too angry.

"Look at me."

Ariadne did. Naucrate's head was angled a little; the sun slanting in from the doorway was playing over her dark hair and the bronze clasps that held her bodice jacket closed. Her lips weren't smiling but her eyes were. *Good*, Ariadne thought. *She'll listen, and then she'll give me a treat. She always does, when I cry.*

"Tell me what's wrong."

Ariadne swallowed. *They weren't looking at me* didn't seem right, even though it was true. "They were fighting," she said instead, and snuffled.

"And what were they fighting about this time?"

"Their gods. And the new baby."

"Ah. What were they saying about the new baby?"

The words came quickly, now that she knew which ones to speak. "My mother said that the king isn't its father, but I don't understand—he's *my* father, and Deucalion's and Glaucus's and Androgeus's—why isn't he this baby's, too?"

Naucrate straightened. She seemed to be gazing at something above Ariadne's head. The smile was gone from her eyes.

"There are rites—the gods inhabit the bodies of priests . . . but you are too young to understand." She blinked and looked back at Ariadne. "Your mother thinks that Poseidon came to her and is the baby's father, and your father does not want to believe this."

"He was so angry," Ariadne said in a rush, glancing up under her eyelashes to watch Naucrate's face, "I think he hurt her—the fire was all over him, especially in his hands, and he was trying to touch her. . . ."

Naucrate smoothed the damp hair back from Ariadne's brow. "He did not hurt her. I know the king. He used his fire on me once, when I . . . displeased him. But even though it crackled and smoked and made me very hot, it never hurt me."

Ariadne shuffled backward, away from Naucrate's stool, and crouched with her arms around her knees.

"Little Princess—was there more?"

"It's just . . . they were angry about me, really, at first. Because they both want me to have their godmarks, but I don't—I'm unmarked and I always will be." She hadn't expected *these* words, which made her want to cry real tears. "I hear the priests and priestesses talking to my parents: they say royal families have to keep having godmarked children. They say our family has been great since the earliest days, when we were commoners whose marks were better than the king's, but now I'm not marked and I never will be and I'll bring shame to everyone and some other family will rule instead. . . ." She bit the inside of her cheek so hard that more tears came.

Naucrate rose and went to the table that stood beside the inner door. "You should not listen to priests and priestesses," she said as she plucked the lid off an alabaster jar. Ariadne straightened, real and false tears forgotten. "They sometimes speak more for their own glory than they do for the gods'. And Minnow: I was seven when I was marked, but after all my yearning, my gift was slight. Who could be impressed by a girl whose whistling sounded like birdsong—even if she could imitate any bird on earth? No, in the end there was so much teasing that I thought I would have been better off unnoticed by the gods."

She came back to Ariadne and knelt, holding the open jar. Inside its smooth, purple-veined white were three honey cakes.

"Take one," she said, and Ariadne did. "See: they're fresh, and even sweeter than usual. Icarus will be hungry by now; will you take him one, too?"

Ariadne nodded, her mouth already so full of honeyed oats that she couldn't speak. Naucrate put another cake in Ariadne's palm and closed her fingers around it.

"Good. You know where to find him."

Ariadne didn't run this time. She walked slowly, drawing her free hand along the stone walls, feeling where they were sun-warm and where they were shadow-cool. A line of tiny bulls led her around corners and up steps; Daedalus's bulls, which he had painted low enough that a child could see them. She knew when she came to the one with the golden bird perched on its horn that she was nearly there. Three steps down, and then she *was* there, in the first of Daedalus's workrooms.

This one had no roof: it was a courtyard, bounded on all sides by blue-washed walls and scarlet columns. Ariadne could see the three entryways to the other workrooms; the one with the paint pots and walls covered with brushstrokes that never seemed to be the same the next time, and the one with looms that clacked all by themselves and other machines of metal that whirred and clanged, and the one deep beneath the ground that held sea creatures captive in pools fed by salt springs Daedalus had coaxed from rock. This courtyard was wondrous too, with its towering blocks of marble, some already carved in shapes of men or beasts, others shrouded in cloth and surrounded by wooden ladders and platforms. Vines crawled up the walls and over patches of ground. Tools lay upon them, and models of ships and cities, and even a tiny Knossos, with all its corridors and rooms, and painted clay figurines that were its people. Beside Knossos was a many-pillared temple, which she knew was in Athens, far away over the sea, and which Daedalus never spoke of, though Naucrate had told her that he'd come from there.

He was crouched before the little temple now, with his back to her. She crept up behind him until she could see over his shoulder. He was holding two figurines in his hands: one as long as his forefinger and one half that size. The figurines glowed silver because he was touching them, with his godmarked craftsman's skin. His head was bent. She could see white strands in his close-cropped black hair. His cheeks and chin were as hairless as a boy's.

"Ha!" she cried. She lunged forward and wrapped her arms around his neck. She felt his muscles bunch and tense and saw him drop the figurines onto the ivy. When he turned to face her, he was laughing.

"Again, my Minnow!" he said, disentangling her arms and rising at the same time. "How do you do it?"

"You're always thinking," she said, craning up at him. "So it's easy to surprise you."

He smiled. His teeth were straighter and whiter than her father's.

"Today I am thinking about what must lie beneath our feet," he said. "Fire, I believe. An ocean of fire that turns rocks to gold. If only I could pluck them free."

"You're silly," Ariadne said, scuffing her sandals against the ivy and the stone. "My feet aren't hot at all."

Daedalus nodded at her. "Of course I am silly. And I am

glad I have you to remind me of it, Princess. Now, then: what are you holding onto so tightly?"

She held up her hand. "It's for Icarus." The honey cake was lumpier than it had been, and her fingers were sticky. All of a sudden she wished she'd eaten this one, too, and gone back to her rooms.

"Ah," he said. "You are kind as well as regal. Can you guess where he is?"

She didn't want to look. But she did: she glanced up to the scaffolding around the tallest slab of marble. He was there, a hunched shadow moving back and forth: she could see this even from so far below.

"Icarus!" Daedalus called. The shadow head turned sharply and cocked down. "Look who's come to see you!"

Icarus was still for a moment. *Good*, Ariadne thought, *he'll stay there*—but then he spread his arms wide and let himself fall from the platform. She caught her breath and stepped back, even though he was nowhere near her, and she'd seen this before. He fell sharply, righted himself and fanned his arms up and down until his feet struck the ground. He crumpled there, knees to ivy, hands skidding out in front of him. Then he rose and stumbled toward her.

His arms bristled with short white feathers, she saw as he approached. Again she tried not to look, tried not to care that there were more than last time, or that his nose was thinner and longer.

"Highness." His voice was high. He was taller than she was because he was already six, but his shoulders were still rolled forward, so his eyes were level with hers. His pale eyes, silver-white-blue, with round nubs of black within.

"Here." She thrust out her hand. The honey cake felt sodden and heavy.

One of Icarus's hands darted out. His fingers grasped the cake—only they weren't blunt fingers: they were sharp.

17

Ariadne glanced down and saw translucent points shining from his fingertips. She remembered the owl she had seen at the mountain shrine where her father had taken her last summer, with her brothers. An owl with talons that had curved around its perch.

"My thanks." His hair looked more layered than it had a few days ago. Shades of bronze and gold and brown brushed against his cheeks and neck. She wrenched her gaze away from it, but then she was looking at his mouth, with its cleft upper lip, all twisted and purple in the middle.

"Your mother wanted you to have it," she said, staring at his bare feet. His toes were splayed too wide, but otherwise his feet looked unremarkable.

"Yes." Daedalus put one hand on her head and one on Icarus's. "And we thank you, Ariadne, for delivering it. Now Icarus must eat and rest."

Icarus cocked his head and shifted from foot to foot. "Papa—I want to show Ariadne the new string you gave me—please may I?" His voice was a bit deeper but still sounded like it came more from his nose than from his mouth. Only a few of the feathers remained on his arms. Ariadne couldn't recall having seen the others vanish. The flesh where they had been was pocked with red circles.

"Very well," Daedalus said, and ruffled his son's hair. "But then you *must* rest. If you tire yourself out with changing now, you will never learn to fly—and you will not want to use that string forever, will you?"

"No!" Icarus was already running back toward the tallest slab. "But watch, Princess—look—I don't need to climb, anymore!"

He was at the base of the marble, swinging something in wider and wider circles. Whatever he was holding (the string, Ariadne supposed) looked silver in the sunlight. When he let it go, it slithered up and up like an eel swimming for the surface of the sea. She heard a long whine and a snick as it caught the top of the marble.

"But how?" she whispered. "He's so small—how did he throw it all the way up there?"

Daedalus chuckled. "Mysteries, Minnow, that only my god and I may share. Look, now. . . ."

Icarus hardly seemed to be moving his arms and legs, yet he was ascending, smoothly and swiftly. *A spider* and *a bird*, she thought, and shuddered. He pulled himself onto the top of the stone, unhooked the string, and wound it up into a ball, which he waved in blinding silver arcs.

"See?" he called. "Isn't it wonderful? Come back tomorrow, Ari; I'll show you how it gets me to the roof!"

She swallowed. *No*, she thought, *I won't come back; you're too strange*—even more words she couldn't speak aloud, if she was to continue being the favourite of the great Daedalus. Before she could say anything at all, though, voices and footsteps sounded from behind her.

"Master Daedalus—we've brought the new hammers for the forge."

There were five men, their bare chests shining with sweat. Two were pulling a wagon, or something like a wagon (it seemed to have too many wheels; Daedalus had probably designed it as well). Ariadne turned and darted away from them. She didn't look back, not even when Icarus called her name from the sky.

CHAPTER TWO

"Princess—wake up!"

Ariadne thrashed in her sheets and thrust with both hands at her tangled hair—and then someone was drawing her up and out of her bed.

"Is it morning?" she mumbled, but even as the words came out she knew it wasn't. She could feel cool air sliding over her arms and legs—and the sky outside her doorway was very dark.

"No." Her mother's night servant—Pherenike. "The queen wants you. Come."

The palace was silent except for the scuffing of Pherenike's sandals on the stone. (The woman hardly seemed to be lifting her sandals at all, in fact; Ariadne thought that must be because her belly was so swollen. All the palace women, even the slaves, seemed to be having babies.) Ariadne's bare feet made no sound at all. She followed Pherenike and her bobbing lamp, and as she did her head filled with a tired, knotted string of words: *The god came to my mother because I was sleeping and he couldn't wake me and he couldn't wait so he had to tell her: he's finally chosen my godmark—and now* she'll *tell me. . . . Or maybe she'll say something else—maybe she realizes I'm special in another way; even more special than the baby that's inside her. Yes. She'll be in her bed combing out her hair and that's what she'll say. . . .*

But they didn't go to the queen's chambers. Instead Pherenike took them between the pillars and through the doorways that led to the central courtyard. It looked much bigger at night, and the shapes of the sacred horns on the walls so far above lay long and stark in moon-shadow.

Ariadne felt a stab of fear that pushed her sleepiness away. *Why are we here? Where is my mother?* She nearly whimpered, but thought, *No—Glaucus would make a noise like that; I mustn't.*

She and Pherenike crossed the courtyard and went down a shallow flight of steps into a chamber Ariadne knew well. But now there was no sunlight to slant across the floor, the stone bench, or the red, blue, and pink spines of the painted anemones, and there were no people sitting on the bench either, beneath the watchful eyes of priestesses of the Great Mother. This room was as silent and empty as the others they had passed through, though it wasn't quite as dark. A pale strip of moonlight fell to just past the doorway, and an orange glow wavered behind the row of pillars within.

"Stay close to me, Princess," Pherenike said, very softly, as she drew Ariadne forward.

Two braziers set on either side of the inner door washed the chamber beyond in light. It flickered off the rectangular column in the chamber's centre. Ariadne leaned against Pherenike's lumpy belly and stared at the little wriggling shadows that were the shapes of double axes, cut deep into the column.

"Pherenike—is that you? Have you brought her?"

Ariadne hardly recognized her mother's voice: it was thin as thread, a winding echo.

"Yes," Pherenike said, and pushed at Ariadne's shoulders so that she had to take a step.

Pasiphae was squatting at the foot of the pillar, between the sunken altar basins. She was naked. Her flesh glowed: her shoulders, her breasts (even her nipples, which looked huge and black), her stomach, her thighs, which she was gripping. Her hair was unbound; it was a mass of snakes in the orange-dark, twisting, alive.

"Mother?" Ariadne's own voice cracked.

"Come closer, child—come *here*." The queen reached out and gripped Ariadne's hands. She tugged until Ariadne was crouching too, and placed them flat on the swollen mound of her belly. It was slick—with olive oil, Ariadne realized as the scent of it surged over her. Beneath her right hand, her mother's skin felt taut; beneath her left it was soft and yielding. A moment later the soft part went taut too, and a moment after this her entire belly was as hard as metal or marble.

"He is coming," Pasiphae breathed. Ariadne smelled wine and honey.

"The god?" she said, because her mother always talked about the god, so who else could it be?

The queen threw her head back and made a sound that was part laugh, part moan. The long line of her throat glistened with oil. "Oh, my girl, the god is already here. He is . . . always here. Lord Poseidon—let me speak of him now, so the babe may hear it too . . . Lord Poseidon: though when he first emerged on our shores he had a different name, one only the Great Mother still knows . . . We no longer speak his language, and some, like your father, believe that Zeus has grown stronger—and yet Poseidon is still . . . our master. And he rewards those of us who love him most . . . with the fish that feed us and the storms and volcanoes that raise islands like ours out of the depths . . . and also, sometimes, with children. With babies who are half blood and half sea."

She rolled back on her heels and quickly forward again. She leaned into Ariadne, her nails clawing and digging at the princess's hands. Ariadne could feel her mother's moan as clearly as she could hear it.

"Babies," Pasiphae hissed when she had finished moaning. She opened her eyes. They were as black as her nipples and her hair. "Like this one. This one—and *he* is the one who is coming, child. He is nearly here. Now go"—and she wrenched Ariadne's hands away, shoved her so abruptly that Pasiphae ended up on all fours, panting and rocking— "go and . . . pour libations to the Great Mother and the Great Bull, so that they will . . . look kindly on us all."

Ariadne scrambled backward and into Pherenike's legs. The servant pulled her upright and leaned down to her, at the same time. "There will be no priests or priestesses here tonight," she murmured. "The queen said to me, 'This child is different, and so shall his birth be.' So it is just us, Princess. You must do as she says."

Just us. Just me—*she wanted* me. These words were enough to make Ariadne forget the ones her mother had spoken—the ones about the god and his precious baby. Ariadne looked beyond the pillar and the basins, to the stone table that stood by a wall she couldn't see. The table was clear in the firelight, though; its three squat legs, and the pitchers and offerings that sat upon it. She walked over to it and stood up on her toes. Her hands were steady when she reached among the rows of shells and tiny bronze double axes and picked up the pitcher with the slenderest neck. *Help me,* she said silently to the goddess who was there on the table; the goddess who was smooth, fired, painted clay, but whose pleated skirts seemed to ripple in the light. The snakes coiled along her arms lifted their heads—Ariadne was almost sure of it—she saw the darting of their wet forked tongues.

"Now, Ariadne!" Pasiphae cried.

The basins were set deep into the floor. When Ariadne stood over the first, she couldn't see the bottom—only a dull sheen of liquid. She tipped the pitcher and a thick stream of oil fell. "Great Mother," she whispered, "aid us now—please."

"Again!" The word was shrill, and it sent Ariadne scurrying back to the table. She set down the oil pitcher and fumbled for another. This one was short and round, and the octopus painted on it seemed to undulate just as the Great Mother's snakes had. Ariadne carried it to the farther basin. Her eyes were on the wine that sloshed about within it, but she could still see her mother, swaying beside her.

The wine came out much more quickly than the oil had. It made a splashing noise and sprayed up and over her legs and Pasiphae gasped, "Clumsy, graceless girl—now you must . . . offer something else."

"But there *is* nothing else!" Ariadne said. "Just the oil and wine."

"Back to the . . . table. Bring me one of the axes. Metal, not . . . clay. Sharp."

Ariadne chose the one closest to the table's edge. It was bronze and its haft fit perfectly into her fist. She tried to hold it out to the queen at arm's length, but again Pasiphae gripped her hand and pulled her close. "Give it to me." Ariadne let go, and Pasiphae straightened into a squat, clutching the miniature axe in one hand and her daughter's fingers in the other.

"We should offer a . . . calf. We cannot, here, now." She shuddered then, and closed her eyes, and growled deep in her throat. Blood spattered the stone beneath her. Ariadne saw that the insides of her thighs were already smeared with it.

After the shuddering had passed she opened her eyes and said, all in one breath, "Blood is what we must offer, and see, the baby has drawn mine already—but we need yours, too, child—yours"—and she tugged one of the axe edges sharply along Ariadne's palm.

She didn't cry out. Glaucus would have. Even Deucalion might have—but Ariadne only flinched, and only a very little bit, as heat lanced along her palm and up her arm. Prickly, numbing cool came after it. She watched her own blood drip onto the edge of the basin.

Pasiphae pressed Ariadne's hands against her belly. She rubbed them in sticky circles, around and around, until her flesh looked like one of Daedalus's inky maps. When another long shudder took her, she held Ariadne's hands down even more firmly. Her skin hardened and stayed that way for long moments. She was breathing very fast, between her teeth. When the hardness finally eased, Ariadne felt something move—something both pointed and round. "See, daughter," the queen said, "he is . . . greeting you!" The knobbly thing beneath Ariadne's hands thrust at her once more and subsided.

The queen threw back her head in a blur of dark curls. "Pherenike!" she called. "Go and tell the king—say that Lord Poseidon's son is coming."

"My Queen, I do not think—"

"Go to him *now!*" the queen shrieked. There were other words too, but they were lost in a rumbling that shook Ariadne free and sent her sprawling. The basin's oil and wine churned and the brazier's glow trembled wildly on the walls. She stared at the walls, as she thrust herself onto her knees. They looked different, wrong—and after she'd blinked at them a few times, she understood why. Water was coursing down from the ceiling and from all the seams between the stones, and it was bubbling up from the floor, white with foam. It washed over her legs and hands, warm, so salty that the cut on her palm stung. Almost as soon as she felt it, the sensation faded. The water bubbled and poured, silently, touching nothing, shining with the silver of Pasiphae's godmark.

She twisted around to look behind her. Pherenike was gone.

"Ariadne. Need you."

She had to crawl because the ground still seemed to be tipping. The queen was squatting facing the pillar now, her brow and forearms leaning against it. "Help me." Her voice was muffled and low. "Help him. He is here."

There was a dark, wet thing between her thighs. It moved down a bit—it was round, and the dark was *hair*—and then back up. The queen panted. Her silver-sheened limbs trickled water that beaded because of the oil. "My Lord," she said. "Lord of the sea; bull from the sea." She moaned, and Ariadne watched the muscles in her legs and shoulders and sides clench. "My Lady, Mother of us all . . ."

The wet round thing moved again, farther down. Ariadne saw crumpled folds of skin that smoothed, as she watched, into a chin, cheeks, a pair of scrunched-up eyes—all upside-down and pointed toward her. Pasiphae cried a long, rising, giddy cry and the thing inside her slid out. Ariadne put up her hands. It slid right into them and almost through; she clutched it as she once had a wriggling soaked puppy she'd wanted to hug. It—her brother—*he* squirmed, and she held him more strongly yet, even though the cord that started inside her mother and ended in his belly was looping over her hands and making them slipperier.

"Cut it," Pasiphae said. "Use the axe." Her words sounded matter-of-fact, as if she'd just demanded a fig, or told Ariadne to brush her hair.

Ariadne laid the baby down carefully on his side. He rolled his head back and forth; his tiny plump shoulder rolled too. There were creases in his arms and drawn-up legs. She reached behind her and found the axe. She pinched the wound-up cord near his skin. It pulsed twice between her fingers and stopped, and she sawed at it. It was tough and spurted blood, but she didn't pause because he didn't cry. He gazed up at her with wide black eyes and waved one balled-up hand.

Pasiphae turned herself around. Ariadne thought she would surely lie down now but she didn't: she continued to squat, and she grunted, and another thing slipped out of her. It wasn't a baby; it was round and flat, and it looked like something the priestesses would cut out of a calf at an altar. The queen nudged it with her foot until it fell into the wine basin with a *plop*.

"Pass him to me."

He was still slick, but this time he seemed to cling to Ariadne. He wrapped his arms and legs around her hands and made a mewling noise.

He doesn't want to go to her; he wants me. Pasiphae reached over and disentangled him. She put him to her breast. *No— his mouth is too little for there*—but apparently it wasn't. He suckled and coughed and suckled, both fists waving until Pasiphae grasped them and held them to her lips.

"Asterion," she murmured.

Ariadne stood up. The room had stopped rumbling, and the last of the silver water was sluicing away. She looked down on the baby's head, with its dark hair (tufty, now that it was drying) and saw two bumps in it. Two nubs with rounded-off tips pushing out from the hair on either side of his brow. She bent and touched one; she had to—it was so strange. Her mother's hand came down over hers and kept it still.

"You see? Already he shows his father's mark. Imagine, Ariadne, how these horns will grow."

Pasiphae might have said Ariadne's name, but it didn't sound as if she were really speaking *to* her. Ariadne glanced up and followed the direction of her mother's eyes. Pherenike was standing just inside the pillar by the doorway, but Ariadne didn't look at her; she looked instead at her father. Minos was framed in the doorway itself. It was lighter behind him, so she couldn't see his face, at first.

She felt her stomach lurch, waiting for his features to get clearer—but when they did, there was nothing frightening about them. His eyes were steady and his mouth was a bit open, neither frowning nor smiling.

"Yes," Pasiphae said, "look at how fine and strong Poseidon's son is."

Ariadne shrank back against the column. She wished suddenly that she could do things over—that she could drop the baby on the ground, this time, or cut the horn-nubs from his skull with the bronze axe. For she was nothing now—nothing, next to the bull god's son. She pressed herself against the stone so hard that she could feel the edges of the double-axe carvings, even through her sleeping shift. The baby's suckling sounded very loud.

A shadow-smile curved Minos's lips. He stayed still a moment longer, and then he turned and walked away. Smoke and sparks flowed out into the dark behind him and were gone.

dipped and climbed. Androgeus's hand was light and sure on the animal's neck.

"Amazing," breathed the same bearer. "Such a size—the biggest yet . . ."

Androgeus's first animal had been much smaller: a swallow, brought down by a servant boy's slingshot. Ariadne had heard their father tell the story countless times: Androgeus, four years old, had taken the wounded bird in his hands and bent his head down to it and it had stopped its frantic flapping. Its tiny brown eye had fastened on the boy, who whispered words no one else could hear. It had died quietly, bathed in a silver light that seemed to come from his cupped palms, and everyone watching had known: Artemis had marked him. It had been proven time after time, over the years: he touched animals and spoke to them and they understood; they *followed* if he led. Men had tried to use his gift in the hunt, but from childhood he refused. "He only leads beasts to death for the gods' glory, or the goddesses'," Minos would say. "He is the purest of all their children."

I hate him, she thought, every time she heard the story— and she thought it now, too, watching everyone watching him.

This beast's eyes rolled back, the closer it came to the group on the plateau. Androgeus stroked the stag's thick, burnished neck. Ariadne watched his lips move and heard the lilt of his marked voice, though, as ever, she couldn't make out the words.

"My King." These words she did understand; Androgeus spoke them very clearly, when he and the stag reached Minos. "Father. The goddess has blessed us."

Minos looked solemn, but his eyes were bright. Pasiphae stood beside him, smiling. Ariadne saw with another lurch of her belly that Asterion was asleep on the queen's shoulder. She was swaying a bit, tracing circles on his back.

"She blesses us through you, my son," said Minos. "Now come—let us sacrifice to her so that she will know the strength of our devotion."

Ariadne's heart began to pound as she followed her family down the slope again. This time was different—this time they walked past the squat, twisted tree and the owl, and past the priest who stood beside them. They walked from sunlit, springy grass to shadowed rock. The stag's hoofs rang, and its snorts echoed from the walls and low ceiling, but still the party walked. She saw that Deucalion had his hand on Glaucus's shoulder, but she was too full of frightened wonder to mock.

The king and queen stopped where the last spear of light fell. It was wan and wavering, hardly made of sun at all, but it was enough to illuminate the pillar of stone that rose toward the cave's roof. The pillar shimmered with crystal— bumpy jewels that made strange shapes and angles—and Ariadne knew that it hadn't been carved by men.

"The gods and goddesses of this place bid you welcome," said a priestess. She was almost invisible against the air beyond her; her dress (tight bodice and a cascade of skirts, Ariadne saw when she squinted) looked black. One of her hands was resting on a side of the rough stone wall that enclosed the pillar. Her other hand was raised, its fingers spread wide. "I see you have brought a sacrifice."

"We have." Androgeus's voice leapt from the rock. He sounded like he should be a giant; Ariadne imagined his curls pressing against the cave's top.

"Then make it now, and well," the woman said, and stepped away from the low wall with a rustling of cloth against earth.

The stag tossed its head once as Androgeus drew it forward. He murmured and cupped his hand around the animal's ears, and it lowered its head so far that its antlers scraped the broad, flat stone that lay inside the wall. It stepped once, twice, and blew out its breath. Ariadne thought she understood her brother's words; she thought she heard, "Gently, gently; don't be afraid . . ." It bent its front legs and sank to the stone as if it were bowing. Androgeus touched its neck; his hand trailed silver which pulsed and vanished with each stroke. His other hand came up. The knife in his fingers was bronze; Ariadne wasn't sure which light was stronger. She looked up at her parents and saw that their faces were rippling, and her own hands and arms were, too: silver and bronze, silver and bronze.

The stag angled its head so that its antlers were pointing away from Androgeus. He closed his eyes, for a moment, then opened them and drew the blade in a long, smooth arc across the place he'd been touching. The beast fell slowly, its antlers and hide and spouting blood lit by one last flare of silver. Ariadne smelled something sweet, as cloying as rotting apples. A few breaths later she smelled smoke. She turned and saw it coiling into the air past the wall. The priestess was there, both hands raised. The smoke twisted along her arms and through her fingers; Ariadne thought she looked like the clay goddess with her snakes.

Androgeus slung the stag across his shoulders. Ariadne didn't see him do it; she saw him only when he was past her, walking toward the priestess. His head was bent a bit, but just because it was so close to the sloping roof. His back was straight, the muscles in it bunched and firm. *Glaucus won't ever look like that*, Ariadne thought, and felt a surge of triumph.

Minos followed Androgeus, and Pasiphae followed Minos, and the rest crowded after—even Glaucus, though Deucalion's hand on his arm was probably what made him move. They walked until the smoke stung Ariadne's eyes and throat. When she had blinked away some tears, she saw Androgeus standing at the edge of the deepest darkness yet. She'd heard her father speak of this place, last summer— "Down there, yes, down even farther, there is a pit for the burning of sacrifices; a wide, deep pit stacked high with wood"—but his words hadn't prepared her. It was a mouth in the ground: a great, gaping mouth with jagged wooden teeth and a black throat with no end.

Behind her, Glaucus made a strangled sound. She craned over her shoulder at him, whispered, "Quiet, Glaucus, or I'll push you in." She caught just a glimpse of his streaming, blinking eyes before Deucalion poked her in the side, hard enough that she sucked in her breath.

"Leave him alone," Deucalion whispered back at her. "He's—" but then his voice disappeared beneath the priestess's.

"Flesh to fire and bone to ash!" she cried. Androgeus eased himself into a squat. At the very same time, it seemed, the stag slid from his shoulders and into the pit.

Fire? Ariadne thought as he straightened. *Where?*—but it was already there, leaping and dancing, plucking cracks and crystal veins from the rock.

The priest walked to the pit's edge, holding two torches high. He handed one to Minos and the other to Androgeus.

"A loving death," the priestess said, more quietly. Minos threw his torch, which flew and fell, trailing flame.

"A death of honour." Androgeus drew his arm back and his torch traced its own bright, smoky path into the pit. Ariadne heard them both land: wood against wood; crackling pops and hissing.

"Accept our offering, lord of sky and lady of the earth."

Ariadne glanced up at her mother—*She won't like that: Zeus but not Poseidon*—and saw that she was leaning her head against Asterion's, stroking the nubs of his horns with her thumb and middle finger. The firelight made her eyes into wet, glinting pearls. She was still smiling.

The flames grew and grew, blurring the lines of the pit and the stag, but the smoke soon hid all this—hid everything in a thick, grey pall, speckled with sparks and ash. Ariadne felt a hand tugging the cloth of her bodice; she half-turned, saw Glaucus, shook his hand away with a cry that was supposed to be "Let go!" but which came out as a cough. She wrenched herself away from his grip and doubled over. The smell wrapped around her now: burning wood and hair and flesh. Glaucus's hand was there again, pawing at her; she thrust herself toward him and felt their foreheads knock together. "Coward!" she shouted. "Find Deucalion and leave me alone!" His hand fell away, and the smoky blur of him vanished before she could pull him back—she *wanted* to pull him back, because she was beginning to be afraid too.

The smoke billowed around her, smothering and tight. She saw shapes in it: legs, a sandal, the pleat of a skirt—and though this last was as grey as everything else, she knew it was her mother's and she lunged toward it. She whimpered as her fingers tangled in cloth, and she coughed, and then she was up above the smoke, lodged on Pasiphae's hip. Asterion was on her other shoulder, writhing and grinding his head against her. His eyes were very wide and rolling in their sockets—up and around, their black centres enormous—but he wasn't crying. (Pherenike's baby was, though; Ariadne could tell that was who was making the noise, even without looking. Chara, the child's name was—and she seemed to do nothing but whine.)

Ariadne stared at his eyes and at the top of his head, where two points of light had begun to glow. Bronze light, dull because of the darkness and smoke, but still visible. *His horns*, she thought. She glanced up at Pasiphae, who was looking at the ground ahead and not at him. Ariadne wouldn't be able to bear it if the queen did look at him because she'd give a joyful cry and thank Poseidon and the Great Mother for their continued blessing, and people would crowd round him and be amazed, just as they had been when Androgeus came up the hill leading the stag.

"Mama," Ariadne whimpered. "Mama, I'm so afraid"— though she wasn't anymore.

"Hush," Pasiphae murmured. Her eyes darted from the path to Ariadne. She didn't look at Asterion at all until she set Ariadne down by the owl's tree, and by then his horns were no longer glowing. He started to cry—a thin mewling sound with nothing of the god in it.

She didn't see, Ariadne thought. *Only I did, so it's my secret.* She was so light with relief that she hardly even noticed when Glaucus kicked her shins as he passed.

CHAPTER FOUR

When she turned seven, Ariadne still had no godmark—but Daedalus made her a dancing ground. Minos commanded him to do it one evening after she'd danced for a gathering in the throne room. She'd whirled around the wide round hearth before the throne itself and in the narrow spaces between the hearth and the people watching her. She'd leapt head over heels as she did when she performed the bull-dance in the ring before the palace's western doors— only now there was no bull to draw the onlookers' eyes from her grace and daring.

When she was done (collapsed artfully at the hearth's edge with her hair spilling over her face and arm), Minos leapt from the throne and cried over all the other cheering voices, "The princess is a wonder—she must have a larger space in which to reveal the extent of her skill. Daedalus!"

Daedalus stepped forward from his place by the outer door. He looked as distracted as he always did: gaze unfocused, hands plucking at clothing, feet lifting and falling as if he were about to spring away from where he was. "Minos King?"

He didn't *sound* distracted. Ariadne thought, *He sounds like he's going to be angry, in a moment.*

"Do this thing for me, Master Craftsman. Build me a dancing ground for my daughter and you will be closer to the freedom you claim to desire."

A few people murmured to each other, because how could

a man—an *Athenian* exiled from his city—possibly want to leave Crete? Why, when he was given all the marble, metal, wood and paint he wished?

"I will do it," Daedalus said in his cold, flat voice. "For Princess Ariadne." He turned to her then, and smiled at her, and she lifted her chin and smiled back at him.

It took him many months. Some days he just stood on the broad steps, overlooking the place he'd decided on: a flat, empty spot that had only been meant to awe visitors to the palace as they approached. He stood and gazed, and paced and gazed. Once Ariadne saw him lie on his belly with his cheek against the dusty ground, as if he was listening to whatever was beneath it. Other days he strode about flailing his arms and shouting orders to the men below him; still others he was on his knees among them, setting small stones in the earth or patting at mortar with a trowel. Sometimes Ariadne herself walked among the workers, who stopped as she passed and made the sign of the horns to her. Sometimes she sat on the highest of the broad steps and watched them with her chin in her hands. *Mine*, she thought at all these times.

She first danced there on a morning in midsummer. It was already very hot; in a few more hours everyone would disappear indoors to sleep away the heaviest part of the afternoon.

"Wait," Naucrate said to Ariadne. "There's no need to dance now—it may be cooler tomorrow."

"No," Ariadne said. There were already people thronging the staircase and the spaces between the second-storey pillars. "Daedalus said I could start today and I will."

She ran down the steps and stood with her bare toes touching the edge of the dancing ground. It was marked by a ring of stones set into the earth—tiny ones that seemed to flow from the outside into the centre in swirling shapes like octopus arms. She looked up and over her shoulder, saw her parents and brothers standing in a gallery over the entrance columns, and Daedalus pacing behind them. Icarus was above them all, crouched between two massive sets of horns on the palace's roof. Even from so far beneath, she could make out his thin, twisted smile and the glint of the metal string at his belt.

She lifted her arms and the audience hushed. A flute began to trill but no one looked at its player—they gazed at her instead. She felt their eyes on her. She smiled and closed her own. Her feet were already shifting, but only a little; she wanted to imagine how the flute's notes would lead her before she danced. So she stood, perhaps a bit longer than she needed to, while the palace waited.

The pebbles were cool. She lingered on them at first, drawing her soles over them as if she were wading through water. Soon she was moving faster, spinning as the music did, tracing patterns over stone and dust. Her dancing master had taught her these steps, and yet she felt others among them that were her own and the earth's. *Maybe this time*, she thought as she leapt and whirled. *I'll be surrounded by a silver light and everyone will know that I've finally been marked.*

But there was no light except the sun's. She knew this as she folded herself onto the ground in the very centre and the last of the flute's notes faded. For an instant, her heart broke again—but then the cheering began, and she straightened and smiled at all the people who loved her.

———— · ————

That afternoon, Ariadne couldn't sleep. She lay as motionless as she could atop her sheet, her arms and legs spread wide, but sweat still seeped from her skin and flattened her hair. She imagined her mother lying in *her* bed, one corridor away. The same sunlight would be oozing between the round pillars up near the ceiling; the same heat would be pulsing through the walls. But Pasiphae would probably be sleeping, her own skin beaded with water, not sweat.

Ariadne groaned and sat up. The paint on her walls seemed to swim: the green coils of plants and their crimson flowers; the brown of fawns and hares. "Deucalion," she said, and reached for some hairpins. He would help, she thought as she stuck the pins into her sodden curls—he'd summon a small, fresh wind that would soothe them both. But he was asleep, curled up like a cat in the chamber beside hers. Glaucus was asleep too; even the children's slave was sleeping, sitting cross-legged with her back against the square pillar that separated the boys' rooms.

Ariadne almost woke her brothers (with a single, piercing scream, right in Glaucus's ear), but then she thought, *No— it's so quiet, and I'm alone—I'm the only one awake, and I could do anything I wanted . . . If only Phaidra didn't have a nurse, I could creep in and put a lizard in her cradle. But Asterion—he's just moved into his own chamber. Yes—Asterion . . .*

He wasn't alone: that girl, Chara, was asleep on the floor at the foot of his bed. She was lying on her back with her limbs splayed, as if she were on the finest of mattresses and not stone. Ariadne ground her teeth in annoyance. The child was always with him when her mother, Pherenike, was attending to the queen—a small, thin, dark-haired little shadow whose grey eyes were strangely solemn, when they were open. Now, though, they were tightly closed.

Ariadne looked from Chara to Asterion. At first she thought he was awake because his arms and legs were twitching. He was facing the doorway but his chin was tucked against his chest and she couldn't see his eyes. He twitched and twitched, and his limbs made hissing sounds on the cloth. She stepped

40

through the doorway and walked slowly toward the bed, her bare feet silent on the stone. When she was close enough to touch him, he sucked in his breath and flung himself onto his back. She froze and held her own breath until she saw that his eyes were closed. They rolled beneath their lids, up and down and around. She remembered this rolling from the cave, nearly two summers ago; the very same movement, though his eyes had been open that time. She also remembered that his horn nubs had glowed like molten bronze, before. Even though his hair was much longer and thicker, she could see that it was the same now: two points of light were throbbing on either side of his head.

It was very hot in the cave, she thought. *And it's very hot in here.* She pressed a stray curl flat against her forehead, wound it tighter with her fingertip until it was like a whorl of seashell. *What would happen to him if it got hotter?*

Getting the lamp was easy. There were only a few slaves about between the family's quarters and the underground storerooms, and all they did was raise their hands to her in the sign of the Bull and continue about their business. She paused in the grain room, which was dark except for the flickering of oil lamps. The rows of jars soared above her head. Their shadows were taller yet. She drew in gulps of cool air, but just for a moment—soon people would be stirring.

The lamp's base was metal and she had to shift it from hand to hand as she walked so that her skin wouldn't burn. She set it down quickly on the floor beside Asterion's bed; it clanged against the stone and he grunted and thrashed, but his rolling eyes didn't open. Chara didn't move at all.

Ariadne stared at his walls for a bit while she thought. The paint on them was all blues and whites: water, sky, the god-bull forming out of a foaming wave. The god-bull on the wall and the god-boy on the bed—she scowled and turned back to the lamp.

The hem of Asterion's sheet caught fire almost as soon as she touched it to the lamp. The cloth melted black behind the flame, which widened as it climbed. When it reached the bed frame it was nearly as long as Asterion was, from glowing horns to scuffing feet.

No, she thought as she stumbled backward, *I was wrong; I shouldn't have. . . .*The fire was flowing under the arm and leg closest to the edge; it was around them, over them, in the space of a single heartbeat. He woke with a cry and lurched up on the bed, and the fire was eating at his loincloth. He cried out again; his voice sounded too low, as if he were a man, not a two-year-old boy. He threw himself off the bed, straight at Ariadne. She leapt back and he fell at her feet. Sparks caught in her skirt and she smacked at them with her hands until they died.

He gazed up at her, and in the space of one more heartbeat his eyes widened and rounded until there was no more boy in them. He heaved himself onto his hands and knees. His loincloth fell away in gobbets of black and embers and his spine arched. Blisters unfurled on his skin and turned almost immediately to coarse brown hair that bloomed along his back and sides in patches that joined. His golden head had gone dark and matted too, and his horns were longer, curving out and up above folded-over ears. He scrabbled at the ground with fingers and toes that fused as Ariadne watched, their nails spreading and yellowing into cloven halves.

He turned his head—sideways, because his neck was so thick that he couldn't lift it up. The fire was only sparks now, spinning and settling on his furred body and on the lashes clustered around his eyes. His eyes were rolling again, white and brown and black. She lowered herself slowly into a crouch, too fascinated to be afraid anymore.

She thought, *He can't see me.* "Look at you, Brother," she

said, loudly enough to be heard above the *whuffing* of his breath. "Look at what you are—and I'm the one who found out. I'm the only one who knows. So if you change back now—if you can just do that, no one else will—"

The beast that had been Asterion bellowed. This wasn't the low cry of before but a full-throated roar that startled Ariadne back onto her heels. The roar didn't stop. She heard another sound—a scream, behind her—and began to scream herself because she knew she should, and because she was afraid again. The children's slave ran past her. She flapped her skirt against the sheet until the flames died and then hovered a few paces away from the bull-thing. She raised her hands to her mouth but they muffled nothing. Her scream trailed into a sort of whine, while Ariadne's continued. Footsteps pounded along the hallway, closer and closer (Ariadne heard them when she paused to breathe). She squeezed her eyes shut.

"Quiet—*quiet*, Ari!" Deucalion, shaking her by the shoulders but not looking at her. Glaucus was clinging to the doorframe. He was already crying, Ariadne saw. Androgeus strode past Glaucus. He stood above the bull, who was on his side, kicking as he roared. Androgeus knelt. He placed one hand on the creature's flank and one on his head, between the horns. He leaned close and spoke his godmarked words again, which Ariadne could never understand. The coarse hair beneath his hands turned to silver.

The bellowing and kicking stopped. The rolling eyes went still and changed shape—everything did, from hoofs to legs to flanks to barrel chest to damp, flaring nostrils. It happened in the time it took Ariadne to blink three times (she tried not to blink at all, but there'd been tears with her screaming), and when it was done, Asterion the boy lay on his belly on the stone. His slender arms and legs trembled. They were covered with blistered welts, but his back was the worst: red and raw like the insides of a flayed animal. Androgeus drew Asterion's head gently onto his lap. He stroked his damp golden hair and murmured more words as Asterion gasped and sobbed. *He's in such pain*, Ariadne thought, and felt a rush of horror and pleasure that sent blood dizzily to her head.

Someone was laughing. Ariadne turned and saw Pasiphae standing in the doorway. She was laughing and maybe crying—it was hard to tell whether the moisture on her cheeks was sweat or godmarked water or tears. She walked slowly to her sons and knelt by Asterion. "My little god," she said. "Poseidon's little bull—I saw him in you, just now, and I heard him in your voice." She held her palms above his back. Water dripped from them and fell on his raw skin like a mist. All his muscles bunched when it touched him, but as it seeped and spread he went limp.

"I look on you now, and I rejoice in your godhead, and yet," she went on, each word harsher than the one before it, "I hate your pain. I hate it, and I wonder what caused it. Who caused it."

The slave gasped, "My Queen, it—" and Ariadne leapt to her feet.

"It was her!" she cried, pointing at the slave. "I came because I heard him shouting and she was already here with the lamp!"

The queen's green eyes shifted. The brows above them arched.

"No!" The slave's hands were still over her mouth. "No, that's not true! Why would I bring a lamp on such a hot day? My Queen, *I* came when I heard the prince shouting, and it was *she* . . ."

The slave was fat. She was fat and her hair was lank and her eyes were small and darting, like a sow's—and yet Pasiphae was gazing at Ariadne now, looking her up and down as if she might actually believe the woman.

"Daughter," she said. "Tell me once more what happened."

Ariadne swallowed. She drew herself up tall. One of her hairpins was slipping out; she felt its metal tines and a wayward curl tickling her neck but she didn't fidget at all.

"I heard Asterion. I was too hot to sleep; I heard him and got here very quickly. He was on the floor and *she* was kneeling by him. The sheet was still on fire so I put it out with my skirt—look!—there are holes in it, and my hands are all pink and burned! I screamed so that someone else would come."

Asterion coughed, and froth came out of his mouth. He was staring at her. *He can hardly speak*, she thought. *He's only two. So there's no way he can understand me, either.* And yet he stared at her. Chara was staring, too—how long had she been awake? She was crouched with her arms wrapped around her knees, a thumb in her mouth. Her sea-mist eyes were almost as round as his had been.

Before Ariadne could say anything else, hands came down on her shoulders. They were large and blunt-nailed and covered with black hair. She knew they were her father's even before she craned up at him.

"I have only just come, and yet I think I understand this much: a slave is telling the royal family that the Princess Ariadne lies."

The slave bent her head. Her hair fell in sweat-clumped strands around her face. "I am," she whispered.

Fool! thought Ariadne, but as she did, a sick shudder rose from her belly to her throat. (Had she really been dancing in front of everyone, just this morning? Had everyone really just been cheering for her?)

"Leave this room," Minos said to the slave. His voice rumbled through Ariadne and she felt heat—flame stirring beneath the skin of his fingertips. The sickness had already gone. "Leave this city. And tell everyone who asks that Minos King was merciful enough to let you live."

The woman shuffled toward the doorway. She paused and moved her hair aside with one fat-fingered hand when she reached Ariadne. Her beady brown eyes found the princess's and held them.

"*Now*," said the king. The slave shuffled on, and out.

Pasiphae was looking down at Asterion, drawing her weeping palms gently along his burns. Deucalion was standing with his head against the painted bull-god's flank, facing his mother. The only eyes Ariadne could see were Androgeus's and Asterion's, and they were on her, steady and knowing. *Androgeus can talk to animals*, she thought, and the sickness was in her throat again.

"He is monstrous," Minos said.

Pasiphae smiled and smoothed a lock of hair behind Asterion's ear. "He is my god's, and he frightens you. Shames you, too—for your own family came to kingship with marks far weaker than his. Conjurors of light and thunder; the gods were hardly even trying when they marked *your* line."

Minos gripped Ariadne's shoulders even more tightly. The heat in his fingers made her want to wriggle, but she didn't. She waited for him to growl a curse or shoot bolts of fire at her mother, but he only stood and stood, breathing heavily—and then his hands were gone and he was walking swiftly down the hall, in and out of the light that fell between the pillars. "No!" Ariadne wanted to cry after him. "Come back; *do* something!"

"My son," Pasiphae crooned. "My little lord."

Ariadne felt blood surging up into her head again. There were voices, too, her own and ones she didn't know: *You should've been the only one to know about him no one's looking at you no one's paying you any attention at all not the gods and not men even though you danced for them only this morning run away run away and they may notice. . . .*

She ran, but no one called after her and no one followed. All of her hairpins fell out; by the time she came to a panting halt in Naucrate's outer chamber, her curls were hanging against her neck and back in a tangled mess.

"Princess! What is it now? Come here and sit by me. . . ."

Naucrate smelled like lemons, as always, and her hands were as firm and gentle as ever, tracing long lines on Ariadne's back, but the voices and blood didn't stop their pounding. Ariadne pulled herself free of Naucrate's arms and ran to the table. She swept everything off it—all the tiny jars and vials and boxes. Kohl, perfume, figs, and glass rained down onto the stone.

"Ariadne," Naucrate said, into the silence that followed. "Oh, Minnow, what's wrong?"

———— • ————

Chara waited for the voices to stop. The screaming and shouting frightened her—and she'd already been afraid because of the fire. She crouched down as close to the floor as she could and put her hands over her ears. But she couldn't leave because he was in the fire, he was screaming, he was growing fur and horns and falling down, and she just couldn't get up and run, even though her feet wanted her to.

So she waited on the floor at the end of his bed. The fire went out and the first people left and others came. One of these others spread oil over his body and then wound him in long strips of white, which made him look like the doll her mother had given her to sleep with: a hard, fat thing with arms that always stuck out, and no eyes. She could still see his eyes, though. They shone in the light of the lantern the other people brought—more fire, but this time it stayed where it should, and he didn't seem afraid. The sky got darker. The room grew shadows—but she knew that he could see her, too, squeezed into the space between a pillar and a wall. He blinked at her, over the shoulders of the people who knelt to help him and talk to him. Talking, talking; Chara wanted it to be quiet.

At last only Chara and one old person were in the room. The old person was always here, and hardly ever spoke, and never tried to make Chara go away like other people sometimes did. So Chara crawled to his bed, around the old person who was slowly washing the floor. She put her hands on the edge of his bed and stood up on her toes. He was crying; she hadn't seen that from the space between the pillar and the wall. His cheeks were wet and he was making little noises. She patted his arm, which was hard and fat with all the white strips. She wiped at his cheeks with her own sleeve, the way her mother did with her.

He smiled at her.

CHAPTER FIVE

No one in the altar-room was paying any attention to Chara. People hardly ever did, except when they wanted her to fetch something: sealing wax or cleaning sponges, or amphorae of wine that were very heavy, but that she carried without shaking. She was nearly eight, unmarked by the gods, and the daughter of a slave; no one except Asterion really saw her, even when they looked right at her, and she didn't mind this at all. Being invisible had its uses. She could go almost anywhere she wanted in the palace; she knew all its corridors and corners, and the deepest and highest of its rooms. She could run in the dark without stumbling because her hands recognized each column and wall by its carvings, and even the texture of its paint. (The scarlet parts of the olive storage-room walls were pebbly, and the white parts felt like sand ripples. Daedalus's bulls were lumpy, and the gold of their tiny horns was cool and smooth.) She could press herself into the shadows and watch things—as she was doing now, in the altar-room of the Great Mother.

Asterion was standing before the double-axe pillar. He was naked and glistening with oil; he looked like a golden creature that had just pulled itself out of the sea. A priestess was kneeling before him, holding up a lamp. He lifted his hands. Chara bit her lower lip; she always did at this point in the rite because the first time she'd seen it she'd gasped, and the queen had glanced over at her. Yet maybe it hadn't been the first time? Because whenever she watched Asterion change, Chara felt something like a memory, tugging at her—but she couldn't ever see it clearly enough to understand it.

He passed his hands slowly through the shuddering tip of the flame. He didn't flinch. Just this one pass was enough: he fell forward onto his hands and knees and changed, swiftly and silently, as the priestesses poured libations on the stone around him. He stamped his hoofs and his heavy head swung back and forth on his neck. The shadow he cast on the walls and floor seemed even bigger than a real bull.

The stamping was the only sound the bull-prince made until a few moments later when Pasiphae called the boy-prince back. She raised her hands above the animal, and water rained down on his woolly back and tossing head, and he snorted and then roared, as if the water hurt him more than the fire had. When he heaved his human body upright, he whimpered; when Pasiphae put her silver, weeping hands on him, he hissed.

The queen cried, "Thank you, Lord Poseidon, for the mark you placed upon this child—and see how we honour you, by calling it forth."

Chara could see the spaces between Asterion's ribs hollowing and filling and hollowing again. His eyes swivelled and found her beneath the offering table. She stopped biting her lip and smiled at him. She wasn't worried when he didn't smile back; he never did this soon after a change.

Pasiphae kissed his forehead and ran her hands over what remained of his horns. "Anthousa," she said as she turned away from him, toward the youngest priestess, "*please* remember not to pour the wine too quickly, next time; it's a most unpleasant sound and it spatters everywhere—now come, all of you; Asterion needs his quiet. . . ."

Chara held her breath as they left, but none of them looked back. She waited until their footsteps had faded before she crawled out from her hiding place.

Asterion was sitting with his legs crossed, staring at the floor. His shoulders were slumped; when she touched one of them he started, as if he hadn't remembered she was there.

"Freckles." He'd called her this since they were six. His voice leapt from low to high as he spoke, and he cleared his throat roughly.

"Asterion." She had no nickname for him. Just using his real name would get her flogged, if an important palace adult heard her, even though Asterion himself didn't care. "How do you feel?"

The same words every time, like a poem or a prayer— except not, because sometimes they were funny.

"It hurts."

"Baby."

He pinched her ear and she laughed, and he said, "What've you brought me this time?"

She reached into the leather pouch that hung from her belt. (Her mother had tried to make her use an embroidered one, and also to lengthen her loincloth into a skirt, but Chara had refused: things were very comfortable the way they were.) "Something from the sea," she said. "Well, from the kitchens, really, but before *that* from the sea."

He turned his hand up and she dropped a crab shell into it. The shell was purply-blue, but it looked black in the flickering lamplight.

"It's tiny," he said, poking it with a forefinger. "I wonder why they didn't throw it back to grow some more."

"Maybe someone thought it was pretty." She didn't really think this was possible—but the shell *was* pretty. "So," she continued, "now how do you feel?"

"Much better," Asterion said and smiled at her at last.

—— · ——

"Ariadne, please say I can come with you to the summer palace! Please! Remember how much we enjoyed your thirteenth birthday? Well, imagine how much better this year's will be!"

"Princess, come watch Draxos and me wrestle—we always salute you before, and the winner does too—we do all this to honour you, Princess."

"I could carve a better likeness of you now than I did last summer—I've learned much from Master Daedalus since then. If you're going to take Diantha to the summer palace you must take me, too, so that you can sit for the carving."

"Wrestling? No—Princess, you must come listen to my poem. . . ."

They're like a flock of geese, Ariadne thought. *Though of course geese couldn't give me poems and sculptures; nor would they be able to bend metal with their minds or command new leaves to open or float just above the ground, as these ones do. No, my geese are very accomplished.*

They followed her—Diantha, Alkaios, Galenos, and Karpos—along the portico that overlooked the main courtyard. Young people always followed her—sometimes these, sometimes others. So many geese, and she a swan.

She was considering which one of them to address first when she glanced down and saw Asterion. He was folded into the shadows where the grand staircase met the courtyard wall. His head was lowered; she could see the shapes of his horns protruding from his riot of golden curls. Chara was beside him, of course, leaning her head close to his. The dark and the gold, together as always.

Ariadne stopped walking and the geese stumbled into each other as they stopped, too. "Alkaios," she said, smiling into his eyes so that he flushed and floated another foot's breadth above the ground, "I promise to come watch you wrestle tomorrow—tell Draxos this. Diantha,"—who'd begun wearing her hair in the same ringlets and knots as Ariadne did, though it wasn't nearly as thick and shiny as Ariadne's—"I'll speak to the queen about bringing you this summer, too, though I cannot promise anything. Galenos,"—he didn't flush when she smiled at him; he went pale and clutched his hands together in front of his belly— "I look forward to hearing your poem, perhaps after dinner tonight? I'll make sure we have some time alone. And Karpos,"—at last, someone who met her gaze and held his chin high; she deepened her voice to warm honey for him— "Daedalus has already spoken of the most recent likeness you did of me. He says the marble Ariadne breathes just as the real one does. I'll have you show me later. But now there's something I must do alone."

They stared at her. She felt the smile dimming on her lips. "Which means that you should go," she said. "That way." They turned and went back along the sunlit walk, following the scarlet pillars this time, not her. (Karpos looked back once; she spun on her heel before he looked ahead again.)

She approached Asterion and Chara so quietly that they didn't notice her until she was two paces from them. As soon as Asterion saw her, he straightened. Ariadne imagined how his shoulder blades would ache, pressing against the stone. The slave, she noted, didn't move.

"Leave us." She looked away from Chara as she spoke, though the words were meant for her.

"But—" Asterion began, and Ariadne said, "Girl. Leave us."

There was a silence that was slightly too short to indicate insolence, and then Chara said, "As you wish, Princess," in that ridiculously solemn tone of hers, and walked away from them on her irritatingly sun-browned bare feet.

Ariadne drew a deep breath. "Brother." This was her voice of silk (which was quite different from her voice of honey).

"Ariadne." The word was like a question, though not a nervous one. She took another step. In all the years since his first change, they'd almost never been alone together; perhaps he didn't remember it at all, and that was why he wasn't nervous. He blinked at her as she drew closer.

"Where's Androgeus?" she said.

"At the training ground. I'm supposed to meet him there—he promised to teach me to throw a discus. I told him I probably wouldn't be able to throw far. In fact, I'll probably fall over." He smiled a little. He didn't look nervous but he did look tired—she could see this, now that she was an arm's length away. There were bruised circles around his eyes and the streaky scars on his right cheek were a darker purple than usual. She shifted her gaze from these scars to the ones on his arms, which were like purple-brown snakes. They seemed the same—but fresh pink blisters stretched in rows across the backs of his hands, on top of all the old white ones.

"Was there another rite last night?" She tried to make her tone curious but not sharp.

He sighed and rolled his eyes. "Yes." She must have frowned; he said quickly, "But don't worry—it was just Mother and the two youngest priestesses, and they only let me be the Bull for a few minutes."

"Ah," Ariadne said, as if this information didn't interest her. (Though it did, of course—she'd only seen one such rite; why did their mother not include her?) She stepped closer to him. "Well, if you're supposed to be meeting Androgeus, why are you here?"

Asterion lifted one shoulder and held it like that; a shrug, but not really. He closed his eyes and opened them again, so wide that they almost looked like his bull-eyes. Somehow he didn't seem silly, even doing these things. Ariadne clenched her hands into fists.

"I was . . . tired of everyone," he said. "The people who follow me everywhere."

"Like the slave's child? Chara?" Who was even now walking around a pillar at the far end of the courtyard, drawing her hands up and down as if she were tracing the shapes of waves onto the stone. A strange, dim girl; thank the gods she was unmarked.

He shook his head quickly. "Oh, no—she's my friend. It's the others: the ones who make the sign of the Bull and ask me to bend my head so that they can see my horns. I wish they'd go away. I know I'm like a god to them, and I know it's unkind, but I sometimes wish they'd all just go away." He raised both his brows and gave a real shrug. "That's why we were here."

Ariadne unclenched her hands. She took another step.

"Don't," said Asterion. Suddenly he *was* afraid: she saw it in those gold-flecked eyes and in the way his tightening lips made the sides of his neck stand out.

"Don't what?" she whispered.

"Don't get any closer," said Androgeus from behind her.

She shivered with surprise inside but only cocked her head at him and smiled. "I was worried about him. I wanted to see his hands—I think Naucrate has some ointment that—"

"Don't expect to lie to me and be believed." Androgeus was so tall that she had to squint into sunlight to look at him.

"It's all right," Asterion said. "She wasn't—"

"Little brother. Go now—run ahead to the training ground. I'll catch up with you in a little while."

Asterion stared from Androgeus to Ariadne. He opened his mouth as if he'd say something else but instead he bobbed his head and leapt past them. Ariadne watched him go, loping clumsily across the courtyard as if he wasn't sure how to use his legs. Chara sped after him, a blur of limbs and hair. When they'd disappeared between two pillars (leaving a trail of wide eyes and horn signs in their wake), Ariadne swallowed and glanced under her lashes at her brother. His teeth shone from his dark, close-cropped beard. It took her a few moments to realize that he was smiling their father's smile.

"I have news that will make you happy, Sister."

She waited. When he said nothing more, she sighed, said lazily, "Oh? And what is this news?"

"I'm going away. Father's sending me to the Games in Athens."

She couldn't help it; her head snapped around and up.

"Yes—I thought you'd like that. I thought you'd welcome the opportunity to be alone with our little brother, after all these years."

He moved so that the light was beside him, not behind, and she could see his face clearly. Minos's bared teeth glinted at her.

"I'll be far away, but I'll hear news from home." A lizard was walking headfirst down the wall behind him. It was red and black with tiny, clear claws and yellow eyes that rolled just as Asterion's did when he was about to change. Ariadne thought that Androgeus wouldn't notice it, since it was well above his left shoulder—but he put up a hand to it without turning away from her, and it froze, splayed on the warm stone. He tilted his head and murmured. Silver light flowed from his fingertips to the lizard's head, and it skittered down onto his shoulder and lay there, its scaled sides heaving. Androgeus stroked it under its chin.

"I'll be far away," he said again, "but if I hear that Asterion's been hurt—if anything should happen to him, accident or not, I will know. I'll command a bull to toss you on his horns in the dancing ring or send a wild boar to gore you the next time you go to pick flowers near the peak shrine." He scratched the lizard between its eyes and whispered a few more words, and it walked daintily from his shoulder back onto the wall. "I can do these things. I *will* do them, Sister, if Asterion is harmed."

Ariadne wanted to laugh, but she knew that it would sound too shrill. She clasped her hands behind her and thought, *Say something, Ari; there's always* something *to say*—but he was already walking away from her, bright and burnished under the cloudless sky.

———— · ————

Androgeus sailed from the harbour at Amnisos on a hot, still day in late summer. It was so still, in fact, that Minos summoned Deucalion and Glaucus to the cliff's edge and said, "Use your godmarks, my sons, and send your brother out across the water!"

They stood shoulder-to-shoulder—or shoulder-to-ribs, because Glaucus was much shorter than Deucalion. Minos stood next to them, and Pasiphae next to him, and Asterion next to her. Ariadne looked at the row of their backs for a moment before she walked forward and took her place beside Asterion. She moved in so close to him that their elbows brushed against each other, but he didn't flinch as she'd hoped he would. She could feel him trembling, though, as he gazed down at the sea and the ship that was on it.

The sea was like a length of taut blue cloth until Deucalion tipped his head toward the sky and closed his eyes. Ariadne leaned back and watched him. He parted his lips and a thread of godmarked silver slipped out from between them. She knew that if she'd been beside him, and if the crowd behind hadn't been so noisy, she would have heard the low, wavering whistle of his breath. She looked back at the water. It foamed down by the rocks at the cliff's base and ruffled out toward the ship, which lifted and fell gently. She remembered how the lift and fall had felt when Minos had taken her out on the king's ship last year. It was much larger than the others she'd been on—so many more oarsmen to greet her, and a thicker mast, and a deck that seemed as wide as her dancing ground. It had been a windy day, and they hadn't needed Deucalion or Glaucus's help. Not that Glaucus actually helped much at all. He could barely muster a breeze on his own. Whenever he and Deucalion summoned winds together, Deucalion always began so that the weakness of Glaucus's mark would be hidden. (Some said that the queen was the one who made the water move, but that she allowed her sons to be praised for it.)

The sea was full of waves now, all of them climbing and breaking toward the west. The ship angled westward, too, and the enormous wooden fish on its prow sliced through air and water. Ariadne could see the oars and their spray and the straining brown backs of the oarsmen. The dolphins painted on the ship's linen-covered sides seemed to be leaping. She could see the scarlet cloth that covered the king's seat whipping back and forth. And she could see Androgeus when he emerged from beneath the cloth and leaned out over the ship's side. He was tiny, but she recognized the dark brown shine of his hair and the golden trim of his loincloth. He reached an arm down and stretched his hand out and very soon a rounded shape rose from the waves, and another, and a third. Silver light leapt from his hand and touched each of the real dolphins as they surfaced—five, ten; soon an uncountable blur of white and grey and godlight.

He straightened, just before he grew too small to see. He raised both his arms and swept them up into the sign of the Bull. A cheer rose from the people gathered on the cliff path and the rocky beach below. Ariadne heard Asterion suck in his breath and felt the muscles in his arm clench, and when she glanced at him she thought she saw a trail of tears on his scarred cheek—but perhaps it was just spray: there was a lot of it now, borne on the new wind.

"Come, people of Crete!" Pasiphae called to the crowd behind her. "Say that you were there to see Prince Androgeus away before he returned in triumph from Athens!"

"And you, Master Daedalus," called Minos, "come up here beside me, so that you may have the best view of all."

Ariadne watched Daedalus approach. Her heart pounded a bit, for he sometimes flew into rages when Minos spoke ill of his old home—but this time he just did a strange little mincing dance as he approached, and stayed silent. *He's never the same way twice,* she thought; *it's as if he's many people and you can't ever know which will appear.*

"He's so handsome," Diantha said. She was standing just behind Ariadne's right shoulder, her honey-coloured eyes distant.

"Androgeus?" Ariadne shook her head and patted Diantha's hand with mock solicitude. "Perhaps on this small island, Yantha, but not in the wider world. I'm sure of it."

"Well, handsomer than *him,* anyway." Diantha's eyes were sharp again, turned to where the cliffside bent to form the western arm of the harbour. Icarus was there, away from the throng, perched on a boulder that looked as if it would tumble into the sea if he moved.

"An ugly bird *and* an ugly boy," Ariadne said. "And I don't think he'll ever fly."

"Better to have no mark at all than a blighted one."

Now, now, Ariadne told herself as a flush swept up her neck and into her cheeks, *she only meant to reassure you*—but Diantha's words were as relentless and pounding as the waves Deucalion and even Glaucus had made with *their* marks.

"He doesn't care that you don't have a mark," Diantha

said. "Just look—he can't take his eyes off you—I can see it from here."

Ariadne snorted and spun away from the sea and the speck of ship and the bird-boy's unblinking eyes. "Let's go," she said—only there were too many people between her and the way back to the summer palace: people clustering around Minos and Pasiphae, who smiled and talked to them; people smiling at Ariadne, and whispering to each other behind their hands; that insufferable Chara, standing with her hand in Pherenike's, grinning at Asterion when he made a funny, twisted-up face at her. *I wish they'd all just make room*, Ariadne thought. And then they did—but not for her.

Asterion took a step. Right away there was a change: heads turned and eyes widened and hands went up in the sign of the horns. Alkaios, who'd been bobbing about just above the ground, came suddenly and firmly back down. A girl weaving rainbow light between her fingers; a man catching spray and making it into flower shapes: they all stopped showing off their godmarks as soon as Asterion took a step toward them.

He smiled, which made the scar on his cheek pucker even more. Behind him, Pasiphae smiled, too. Diantha murmured, "Those scars should make him ugly like Icarus but they don't. . . ."

"They do!" said Ariadne in a rush. "He's burned and he's a runt and if he didn't have such a wondrous mark he'd be nothing to anyone." The words had begun to tremble, so she stopped speaking—but it was too late: Diantha was staring at her with her mouth wide open.

"Princess! He has been god-favoured more than anyone else—how could you speak like that about him?"

Ariadne said, quickly and coolly, "I am very disappointed that you believed me. Perhaps I won't bring you here next summer."

Diantha said again, "Princess!"—but Ariadne was already

walking away from her, along the path Asterion had made.

I hate my life. I hate my brothers and the people who think they're my friends. I hate this island. I can't sail away from it like Androgeus did, and I hate that too.

Her hatred only grew hotter as the months went on. Androgeus won every competition; Androgeus used his godmark to tame a murderous boar; Androgeus was the toast of Athens. Bull-Asterion presided over a rite and the next day it rained for the first time since Androgeus's departure and there was rejoicing throughout the countryside. Diantha no longer fawned and followed because she had taken Karpos as her lover—her lover, when Ariadne hadn't yet had any opportunity to take one of her own! Hatred, rushing in her veins instead of blood—until one rainy autumn evening, when another message came from Athens.

Oh no, Ariadne thought as the messenger walked around the hearth to stand before her father. *Androgeus can't have won any more competitions. Surely there aren't any more to win.*

But this messenger wasn't smiling, as the others had. "Minos King," he said in a low, breathless voice.

The royal household had been eating when the messenger had come. Now their spoons and knives clanked against metal plates or clattered against wood. (The long trestle tables had been carried into the throne room because the courtyard they usually used for dining was too wet.)

The king rose. "Speak, man! Tell me of my son's latest triumph in Athens!" The king's teeth glinted in his beard. He smiled, while everyone around him went silent and still. He smiled, even as Pasiphae stood and put her hand on his arm and pressed her fingers white.

"My lord king, Prince Androgeus is dead."

Someone gasped—Naucrate, Ariadne guessed, though she didn't look away from her parents. For a moment Minos and Pasiphae were statues, one smiling, the other beautiful. Pasiphae moved first. She turned and put her other hand on his arm and clutched it as if it were the only thing holding her up. Which it was—for when he drew it from her grasp, slowly and carefully, she crumpled. She pulled herself to her knees and raised a hand to him and he wrenched himself around, away from her. He seemed to be gazing at the fresco of the griffins and trees.

"How?" Smoke curled from his mouth. The backs of his hands were webbed with kindling flame.

The messenger swallowed. He was beardless; a man who spent more time in Athens than at home and had taken on Athenian fashion.

"My lord, it was King Aegeus's nephews—the Pallantides— they were jealous of the prince's prowess. They . . . they stabbed him with the tusks of the boar he had tamed. Others were there, too—someone tried to reach the prince, but one of the Pallantides summoned a net made of silver fire and cast it over Androgeus so that no one could touch him. He died slowly. Many watched."

"King Aegeus. What has he done?"

"He has sent a message."

"And what does it say?"

"My King?"

"Say it to me."

"It . . . it says: *Minos, King of Crete, my city mourns your son and begs your mercy.*"

"That is all."

"Yes, Minos King."

"That is *all*."

"It is."

Minos whirled to face the messenger. Flames leapt from his fingertips and seared black lines into the floor.

"Then there will be war."

"Yes, my King. It is . . . expected."

Ariadne looked at all of them in turn: Minos; Pasiphae, her hands buried in her hair, pulling her head down toward her knees; Glaucus and Deucalion, pale and gaping; Daedalus, frozen mid-stride, his own head turned sideways as Icarus's so often was. And Asterion. Asterion, who was crying.

"Leave me." Minos's voice rasped. "Everyone leave me."

The boys almost ran between the pillars and Phaidra followed, tripping over her skirts. Naucrate took Daedalus's hand and drew him out after them. Soon only Pasiphae and Ariadne were left, with the king.

"Husband." Pasiphae looked broken; she sounded broken.

"Go!" Minos thundered. She rose. Her skirts were dark-damp where her legs had been pressing on them. Water ran down her brow and neck but not her cheeks.

"May Lord Zeus abandon you," she said. "May you cry out for him in your solitude and find him gone." She lifted her face to the rain, once she was outside, and then she walked, and it swallowed her.

Ariadne and Minos were alone. He was staring blindly at his hands and the flames that dribbled down from them. She took a step closer. Still he stared.

"Father," she said, very softly.

His eyes leapt to her, saw her, filled with tears. "Ariadne," he whispered. He held out his arms and she ran into them, as if she were still a child—only now *he* was the child. He sobbed and clung and she didn't care that his palms scalded her through her bodice.

"Hush," she said, and smiled.

CHAPTER SIX

Chara fell so hard that all the breath seemed to leave her body. She made a sound like "umf" as the dust from the path rose and settled around her, and then she gasped and flipped onto her back. Glaucus was above her, brandishing the blue-and-scarlet painted stick he carried everywhere. Chara lunged up and grasped the end of it with both hands. She tugged sharply and he stumbled; she hooked her foot around his and he fell even more heavily than she had. As she rolled away from him, she heard Icarus and Asterion laughing.

"That'll teach you to take on a girl who's so much smaller than you," Asterion said.

Glaucus was laughing, too, in a wheezy sort of way. "Peace?" he said as he got to his feet. He extended his hand to her and she took it.

"Peace," she said and snatched the stick out of his other hand. She sprang away from him and he shouted, and their footsteps pounded yet more dust from the sunbaked track. She knew he'd catch her in just a few paces, so she slowed before he did and dropped the stick.

"No peace, next time," he said and ruffled her hair. She swatted at his hand, growling, and he laughed again.

The four of them walked on in silence until Glaucus muttered, "Ariadne's following us."

Icarus appeared to trip over his own feet, and flushed to the tips of his ears. "Really?"

"Shh," Asterion whispered. "Really. Every time I almost look back she tries to hide behind a bush. No, Chara," he said as she shifted to glance back herself, "don't. Let her think we don't know. Just be . . . normal."

Icarus's walk had suddenly gone very stiff. *He looks a bit like a wading bird*, Chara thought.

"So," he said, his tone as stiff as his gait, "where are we going this time?"

Asterion squinted at the path ahead of them, which looked to Chara like a flat, red-brown snake wending its way among the new green of the hills. "Just to the waterfall."

"Good," Icarus said, less awkwardly. "It hurt when I fell out of the tree last time."

Glaucus snorted. "Yes, and the farmer wasn't pleased with us, either."

They left the road when it passed an ancient, lightning-split cypress. Chara drew her hand along its gnarled trunk and one prickly green frond, then hurried to catch up with the others. It was easy to keep pace with Glaucus and Asterion, but Icarus was much faster than all of them—especially when he used his metallic silver string to swing up to the rocky outcroppings that jutted like giant fists from the earth, and leapt off them. Every time he did this, the breath caught in her throat because perhaps this would be it: perhaps he would hang suspended for just a moment longer and then climb into the windy blue of the sky with his arm-wings trailing silver godlight. But his feet carried him back to the ground every time, with a solid, mocking sound that made Chara wince.

"You know, it's heat that makes *me* change," Asterion said to Icarus when they were all sitting above the waterfall. Chara brushed the spray away from her face as if this would help her hear him better. "Maybe there's something like that for you but you just don't know it yet."

"Maybe it's cold," Glaucus said. He was knocking his stick against the boulder he was sitting on—*thwack thwack thwack*, like a drumbeat beneath the water's song.

"Or hunger," Chara said. "Fear, maybe. I don't know," she added in a rush, "of course I don't, because I'm not godmarked . . ." *Not that I mind*, she almost said, only she thought, just in time, that this might hurt someone's feelings.

"Maybe I won't ever find out," Icarus muttered.

She blinked at him through rainbow mist as his head bobbed and his slender toes scritched and dug at the earth. *He looks like a bird. It's not fair that he can't fly.*

———— · ————

Ariadne wondered again why she'd picked a thornflower bush to hide behind. It wasn't just the stubby thorns themselves, which plucked at her skin and clothing whenever she leaned forward—it was also the fragrance of the delicate pink blooms. Such tiny flowers, and yet their scent slid up her nostrils and made her need to sneeze. She squeezed her nose between her fingers. *Be silent*, she thought. *They mustn't hear you.*

They hadn't heard her when she was following them, even though she hadn't been all that far behind, and there was barely any cover once they left the road. They'd been too involved with each other: talking with their heads bent together, wrestling, racing—even the girl Chara, who *still* didn't look like a girl (all that tangled hair and bronzed skin, and the loincloth as short as a boy's). Ariadne heard them laughing. *Glaucus sounds like a sick toad*, she thought. *If only I could skewer him on that stick of his.*

She enjoyed mocking this stick, which he kept by his bed. She'd watched him when he thought he was alone, spinning and stabbing it into the air like a sword. He had no real sword though he was sixteen and Androgeus had had his first before then. Glaucus had wanted the one Daedalus had made, the one that looked like a dagger until you turned a switch in its hilt and a series of bronze segments emerged, but Daedalus had said no: that sword wasn't for boys. So Glaucus had no sword, and no place with the soldiers who'd left last month for Athens.

Now the three boys and Chara were sitting on boulders beside the mouth of a waterfall. Ariadne could see only the tops of their heads: Asterion's jumble of golden curls, Glaucus's finer, darker ones, Chara's mass of black knots, and Icarus's strange, shifting, many-coloured layers. She could hear them very clearly, though, even over the rumble and hiss of the water.

"You know, it's heat that makes *me* change," Asterion was saying. Gods, how she hated his voices—the boy's and the bull's. "Maybe there's something like that for you but you just don't know it yet."

"Maybe it's cold," Glaucus said. He was knocking the stick against his boulder.

"Or hunger," said Chara. "Fear, maybe. I don't know —of course I don't, because I'm not godmarked. . . ."

Icarus's head dipped out of sight for a moment. Ariadne knew he was bobbing it as he always did whenever he was embarrassed or nervous or angry—whenever he was *anything*, really. He muttered something she couldn't hear.

"Don't say that," Asterion said. "Listen: for me it starts like a buzzing—only not one I can hear—a buzzing like something in my belly. Then it spreads until it's even behind my eyes—and after that everything looks wobbly and strange, and all my skin hurts."

Glaucus snorted. "I don't care if it would mean the gods favoured me more—I wouldn't want a gift like that."

"I would." This time Ariadne heard Icarus's words because he stood as he spoke them. "It's all I've ever wanted. I feel the buzzing, too, you know—except it starts on the outside and never moves in. It gives me feathers and a beak and it changes the way things look, but it never goes inside to help me fly."

Ariadne had never heard him say so much at once. She eased herself up so that her head was above the bush, but all she could see was his back. His bony hands were clenching and unclenching at his sides. She imagined his eyes, small and round, fastened on the foaming water below.

"So we'll try this again," Glaucus said as he rose too. "I'll make a wind and you jump and try to let it catch you. It almost worked last time, remember?"

"With Deucalion," Icarus said. "And it didn't almost work."

Chara nudged Icarus's chest with her shoulder. "Come on, Icarus. Just try it. Let Glaucus help."

Yes, Ariadne thought, *give poor Glau a chance. After all, our father didn't, when he sailed for Athens.*

All the children had stood in a row on the cliffside, just as they had when Androgeus's dolphin ship had been below them. Again, people had massed behind them. This time, though, the king didn't speak to the crowd. He hardly spoke at all. He walked slowly along the line of his children. He didn't look at Glaucus or Deucalion or Phaidra, who all gazed at him as if they were waiting for him to. He didn't look at Pasiphae, whose own eyes were fixed on the sky. He stared at nothing—or perhaps at something no one else could see.

"Father?" Asterion's voice was quavery but clear. "Deucalion and Glaucus could make a wind—it's what they did for Androgeus. . . ."

Minos paused mid-step. He squinted at the steel-grey

clouds and cocked his head, as if he'd heard something faint and puzzling. He drummed his fingers on the bronze helmet he was holding under his arm.

"I am glad, Ariadne," he said in the hoarse voice that seemed to be his all the time, now, "that no one has dared speak to me and call me 'Father.' I am glad that no one has been fool enough to do that."

His eyes swivelled to her. They were black and cold. She nodded. She didn't smile but he did, suddenly and swiftly. He reached out and touched her cheek. There was no warmth in his fingertips.

"Bring them to their knees, Husband," Pasiphae said. He spun and walked to the cliff path without even a glance at her.

As the ships—so many, darkening the sea—had turned westward, Ariadne had wrapped her arms around herself. Keeping her joy in, where it would be safe.

Now she hugged herself too, but only to protect her arms from the thorns.

"Very well," Icarus said. "Glaucus can help."

Asterion stood up. Ariadne could just see his head and shoulders. His horn nubs gleamed when he turned to the other three.

Glaucus leaned forward. She couldn't hear anything except the water and a high insect hum from the bushes around her. She knew that he would be whistling notes that would flutter and wander until the god told him which one was right. ("Does he say 'That one!' in your ear?" she'd asked him once. "No," he'd scoffed—but he could never explain what *did* happen.) When he raised his silver-lined hands, she knew it was time.

Icarus's hair rippled. Asterion's and Chara's thicker hair did not, but the ends of their loincloths did. Droplets of spray from the waterfall blew up and away from them in a curtain of mist. A moment later Ariadne felt the wind.

It swirled around her ankles and up her legs, and she had to clutch at her skirts to keep them from billowing. As it grasped at her hair and breath, she thought, *Not bad, Glau,* and immediately after, *Don't let it work—please don't. . . .*

Icarus took a long pace back. He lifted his arms and bent his head low, with his chin parallel to the earth. She saw feathers: they poked out of his skin, more every time she blinked. Soon his arms were trailing streamers of them, and they joined somehow, one to the other, until they were wings. They shone bronze, copper, and gold, and when he moved them quickly they snapped like sails.

His head twisted on his neck. He had no nose or mouth; a long silver beak instead, which opened and shut with a sound of metal-on-metal.

"Well done, Icarus!" Asterion cried. "Glaucus, too—now go, go!"

Icarus took two more steps back, these ones jerky and bobbing. His head lowered even more. He bent forward and ran five uneven steps between two boulders, and out in a sweeping thrust, into open air.

The wind gusted. It howled as it did, so no one heard Ariadne's sneeze. She shoved hair out of her eyes and saw Icarus hovering, his wings catching sun and mist. He hung and then he tilted and banked sharply before his wings crimped and folded . . . and he fell.

The wind died as soon as he disappeared. The splash he made in the pool below was loud. Ariadne bit her knuckles to keep from laughing.

"It's all right," Asterion said to Icarus when he had climbed back up (just a thin, sodden boy). "It is. We'll try again, or we'll try something else."

Icarus said nothing. His narrow shoulders twitched. He was side-on to Ariadne now, and she could see crimson speckles on his arm where the feathers had been. *It hurts him,* she thought, as she often did about Asterion—and again the thought made her weak with envy and hunger.

The children walked back to Knossos even more slowly than they'd walked away from it. Glaucus lagged behind, stopping often to swing his imaginary sword, straining as if it really were bronze, not wood.

Ariadne thought, *Hurry up and leave Asterion alone, all of you, so that I can have him to myself; I haven't been alone with him since Androgeus left* . . . They didn't leave him, and soon the western gate loomed against the darkening sky.

They paused before it. A few people walked past them and made the sign of the horns to Asterion. Icarus and Glaucus made the sign too, before they left him. Ariadne watched them go: together up the steps and between the pillars, then one to the right, one to the left. Chara remained, of course. She and Asterion wandered over to one of the great scarlet entrance pillars and crouched in its shadow (though everything was shadowed, now that dusk had fallen). They stared at the ground, which was good—they wouldn't see Ariadne coming.

The stones of her dancing ground were so familiar; she could feel them even through her calfskin boots. She didn't follow their whorls this time—she walked in a swift, straight line.

"Brother." She could barely keep herself from smiling when he started and fell sideways. Chara looked up slowly, her brows raised a little beneath her mess of hair.

"*Half*-sister," Asterion said, pulling himself back into a crouch. "What do you want?"

His face was tipped up to her. His eyes and voice were steady. *No,* she thought, *this isn't how he should be. This will not do* at all.

"I just want to know what you're doing. Thinking about Androgeus, maybe?"

Asterion's expression didn't change. "I think about him all the time."

"You must miss him terribly. He was your protector, after all."

Asterion smiled a strange little smile. "Oh? What was he protecting me from?"

No. Not right. You can do better than this, Ari.

She shrugged. "You don't *seem* to miss him at all. Look at you—so calm and cold."

"I'm not a baby," Asterion said. "I can hide what I'm feeling."

Ariadne twitched her skirts and brushed imaginary specks off her bodice sleeves. "I remember when you were born, you know. I remember how you squalled, then— and two years later." She crouched, suddenly, and leaned forward so that her forehead was nearly brushing his. "I remember how you screamed when the fire touched you for the first time."

He didn't move, but Chara did. She scrambled upright, her hands clenched at her sides. Her bare, flat, brown chest heaved.

"Girl?" Ariadne spoke carelessly as she straightened, but she felt her own pulse quickening. "What is it?"

"I remember, too," Chara said. Her eyes had no grey in them now—only black. "Just now, suddenly, when you said that . . . I was there. I was on the floor—I saw you put the lamp down. . . ."

Ariadne heard Asterion gasp but she didn't turn to him. "Oh?" She couldn't say more; she thought her words might tremble the same way her insides did.

"Yes," Chara went on, even more quickly, "I remember the heat and how everything changed, all the twisting and the fire. I remember you putting the lamp down. You stood there smiling, even though he was screaming."

He was breathing quickly now, too, and Ariadne thought, *Ah—good*, and a new sort of hunger chased away her fear.

"You were too little to help him then," she said, "and you're too powerless now. It's a shame that he has no one to protect him anymore."

He rose. He was smiling. "I'm not afraid of you," he said. "I can't believe I ever was. And I wish I could tell Androgeus so."

She laughed. "Not afraid? Really? Prove it, little *half-brother*."

He bent his head so that he could see past her. *Yes*, she thought, *look for somewhere to run. I'll only follow.* But he didn't run. He turned and took a few measured paces to a brazier that burned at the courtyard's edge. He gazed into it so intently that he didn't seem to notice the people who passed and made the sign to him. Some of them paused to watch him. Ariadne smiled, in case anyone looked at her, but she also shifted from foot to foot and clicked her tongue against her teeth. Beside her, Chara was motionless.

He stared for so long that Ariadne thought, *Enough*, and took a step forward—but just as she did, he plunged his arms into the brazier. Someone screamed. Someone else cried out, "We see your gifts and bear your marks!" They were the first few words of an ancient prayer to the Great Mother. If the prayer continued, Ariadne couldn't hear it above the hammering of her own heart.

Asterion held his arms still for a moment. When he raised them slowly up, they trailed sparks, as Minos's often did. The sparks settled, some on the ground and some on his clothing and skin—and they caught there and bloomed into flames. Ariadne blinked against the blur of light. The lines of him ran together until he had no body—he was just fire, which swirled and spiralled—and now there *was* a body, but it wasn't a boy's. The new thing rolled itself on the ground until the fire subsided again to sparks.

A bull heaved itself to its four cloven feet and swung its head toward Ariadne.

Her breathing was louder than her heartbeat. *How is the bull so big when the boy's so small?*

She took two steps back and felt the stones of the dancing ground beneath her. Bull-Asterion pawed at the hard earth of the courtyard and moved forward. No one else backed away from him; if anything there were more people, all of them closing silently in behind him. He snorted. Kept moving, each heavy, graceful step bringing him closer to her. His horns swept back and forth, making arcs so bright that she had to look away. She heard him snuffling and pacing—and then she heard him roar.

He was charging. A few more seconds and he would reach her; she whirled and ran out onto the dancing ground. She had no thoughts—where to go or how to get there— but her feet carried her forward and forward and then nowhere because there were people in her way: people in a ring, their numbers increasing as she stood gasping in the centre. She turned to look behind. Bull-Asterion was nearly upon her. Her body led her, once more. Her hands gripped her skirts into two bunches which they tied beneath her, so that her legs would be free. All her muscles bunched and tightened and her knees flexed and she waited for him, as she'd waited for other bulls, in this very place. She launched herself into the air when he was an arm's length away. She felt the metal-smoothness of his horns in her palms, but they weren't cool, as the other bulls' had been: they were scalding, and she cried out as she gripped them. She didn't need to grip them for long, though: she thrust herself upside down and backwards, and finally into a twist that carried her over his flanks and down onto the ground.

She heard cheering, through the pounding in her head. The sound was so familiar that she smiled—but then she heard stamping, too. So many people, all of them stamping and calling out their praise to the Bull.

He swung around and pawed at the ground—at the stones that Daedalus had ordered laid for *her*. He charged again. This time he held his horns lower and her grasp wasn't as firm; she crumpled before she could get into her upside-down position, and slid down off his side. She whimpered as she straightened, but when she turned to watch his retreat she spat his name, over and over, as if it were the vilest curse she knew. He retreated, looped in a thudding arc, came back toward her. Once, twice, a third time—and each time he seemed stronger and swifter, and she a little less graceful.

The fourth time was the last. He tossed his head just before she could touch him and she pitched forward. Any other bull would have gored her then, and thrown her limp body aside. Bull-Asterion swerved, so that she fell on the ground, not on his horns. She lay curled up like a nautilus shell as his hoofbeats receded and stopped. She heard the roar of the crowd. Their stamping shuddered all the way to her bones. *Don't do this*, she thought dimly. *Get up, Princess.*

She rose and stood very tall. As she did, the crowd quieted. Her mother's voice rang out into the new silence.

"Let us offer thanks to the Great God for the spectacle we have just witnessed!" Another cheer. Ariadne stared up at the queen, who was standing on the steps that led to the entrance pillars. The light of the braziers ringed around the courtyard behind her played over her hair and outstretched arms. The strands of golden rings that hung from her ears winked and shimmered.

"Let us offer thanks to my children, who are themselves so blessed!"

Bull-Asterion was standing below Pasiphae. The glow seemed to touch him, too, and to smudge the brown coat, the furred legs, the hoofs and lowered head. All of these things melted and warped until a smaller, brighter form knelt upon the dancing ground.

"All praise to Poseidon's son!" someone cried.

"And all praise to the Princess of Knossos!" cried someone else. One last, scattered cheer went up.

"Now come here to me, children," the queen called.

Ariadne walked slowly to stand beside Asterion. She heard people dispersing around her, murmuring and laughing; she saw them streaming between the pillars, back into the courtyard. (She couldn't see Chara among them.)

Her mother smiled down at them. Her eyes were so dark that Ariadne could only imagine their green. "You have never played together," the queen said in a low voice that did not match her smile. "So I can only assume that what just happened here was no game. Ariadne,"—the word was as hard as a slap—"I do not know what you did to provoke Asterion. I do not truly need to know. But whatever it was, you will not do it again."

"Why do you accuse only me?" Ariadne swallowed to clear the tears from her throat. "How can you be sure he didn't change for his own reasons?"

Pasiphae shook her head. The earrings swung against the long line of her neck. "He promised Poseidon and his priestesses that he would change only in the service of the true gods. He would not break this promise without good cause."

"No, Mother." Asterion's words came out thickly; perhaps his tongue and teeth were still reshaping themselves. "It *was* just a game. I'm sorry. I won't belittle my father's gift again."

Pasiphae looked from him to Ariadne and back. "I am unhappy with you both," she said at last. "Leave me."

They walked together into the courtyard. Ariadne

glanced over her shoulder; Pasiphae was still standing facing the dancing ground.

"So I proved it," Asterion said. He sounded like a normal boy now. "I'm not afraid of you."

Ariadne stopped walking and so did he. She touched a finger to one of his horns and drew it down through his hair and along the line of his jaw. She felt him shiver. She gouged a swift, thin line into his cheek and smiled as he sucked in his breath. "You should be," she said.

CHAPTER SEVEN

A storm blew in from the west, the day Ariadne turned sixteen. That morning, Chara and Asterion sat with their backs against two grain jars—the largest of all the storage jars, which trembled every time the thunder cracked. They laughed when this happened but didn't speak.

"Rats," said a voice from the dimness. "Hiding in the cellar."

"Mother!" Asterion scrabbled to sit up straight. He was tired today, Chara knew; there had been another rite the night before because the fishing in the waters below the summer palace had been sparse so far this season, which meant that Lord Poseidon had to be appeased. (When the rite was done, she'd given him an amber bead she'd found at the foot of the cliff stairs, almost entirely buried in sand. "It's cooler than water," he'd said as he held it to his wrist, where his newest burn was.)

Pasiphae frowned. Chara thought, *She should look funny, so far above us with the lamplight making her nostrils huge and her eyes beady, but she doesn't. She looks beautiful and frightening.*

"Go, Asterion." The queen spoke coldly and clearly, in the spaces between the thunder. "Wait for me in the throne room. Ariadne's well-wishers are gathering there now."

"In that case, *I* shouldn't be there." Asterion smiled and Chara snuffled (which was the sound she made when she was trying not to laugh).

Pasiphae snapped, "*Now.*"

He rose. His eyes glinted as he glanced at Chara; then he walked out of the lamplight and into the darkness.

Chara rose too; she expected that the queen would tell her to, if she didn't.

"Come with me," Pasiphae said, and turned. She strode among the jars so quickly that Chara had to hurry to catch up. She remained a few paces behind, as they went up stairs and along corridors, past altar pools that the rain was turning into tiny stormy oceans.

"In here," the queen said when she finally halted. They were standing before the princess's doorway. Chara had never been inside Ariadne's rooms—not at Knossos and not here at the summer palace either, even when Glaucus tried to persuade her to come with him to rearrange the princess's perfume vials or put fish skeletons in her bed. Now Chara crossed the threshold after Pasiphae, her heart jumping a little in her chest. The room was long and thin and had higher walls than she had ever seen. They were painted bright blue and ochre: the sky and earth of island summer.

The cloth on the bed was yellow and brown.

"A new skirt and bodice," the queen said, gesturing to the cloth.

Chara gazed from it to the woman beside her. "Yes," she said. "They're very nice."

Even Pasiphae's frown was beautiful. "They are for you. Put them on."

"For . . ." Chara knew her own frown wasn't nearly as lovely as the queen's, but she couldn't smooth it away. "I don't understand. My Queen."

Pasiphae bent to brush at something invisible on her skirt pleat. Her gold pendant winked in the pale hollow of her throat. "You are too old to be wrestling with boys, and the way you trail around after Asterion is unseemly.

Your mother apparently had no desire or will to tell you otherwise, when she was alive, and I did not much care when you were small—but now I do. It is time you dressed like a woman of Crete. It is time you acted like one."

"But my Queen—" Chara began.

"Part of being a woman of Crete is knowing when to speak and how. Perhaps you will learn these things when you serve the Lady Ariadne."

Chara couldn't help it: her mouth fell open. "Serve . . . the princess."

"Yes. I am giving you to her—today, for her birthday. She needs a slave and you need a useful position within the household. The arrangement will suit you both. Now dress, girl, before the celebration is over."

——— · ———

Ariadne had been angry in the morning as she gazed out at the lightning-split black of the sky. In the afternoon, when everyone gathered in the Lily Chamber to celebrate, she was happier. The lightning (which flickered in sheets now, not Zeus's bolts) played over Galenos's face as he recited the poem he had written for her. Rainbows streamed from the gnarled fingertips of Phaidra's old nurse and wavered on the floor by the hearth, which shone with its own, real flame. The room smelled of rain and earth, heated oil and poured wine, and the fig pies Naucrate had made. And it seemed as if all the summer palace's inhabitants were there, from youngest to oldest, lowliest to highest, even Minos's priests, who lurked like a line of ravens just inside the outer pillars, where the rain blew in on gusts of wind.

"My elder daughter may be unmarked," the queen said, when the tributes had been made, "but she is still blessed. Anyone with eyes to see knows this."

Ariadne turned slightly in her own chair and smiled at her mother. *Why only "elder daughter,"* she thought as Pasiphae smiled back at her, *when your younger is also unmarked? But no—you never let me forget. You never let anyone forget. I hate you for it, but even you won't ruin this day for me.*

"I, also, have a gift for her," the queen continued. "Step forward, Chara, daughter of Pherenike."

A girl slipped between two of the priests. *That's not her,* thought Ariadne—but then she saw that it was: Chara the scrawny, sun-baked slave girl, draped in clean, dyed cloth, some of her hair wrapped into neat knots at the top of her head and the rest falling reasonably straight behind. She walked closer and Ariadne saw that her wide grey eyes, at least, hadn't changed.

"Well," Ariadne said when Chara stopped before her. "I wouldn't have thought it possible." The princess's gaze flickered to Asterion. He was craning forward from his place in the front row, gaping like a fish on land. His cheek scars writhed into entirely new patterns. Ariadne smiled. "I am pleased to have the most richly attired slave on the whole of Crete. Thank you, Mother. I am sure she will be very useful."

When Chara did nothing but stand, looking at her unblinkingly, Ariadne hissed, "Bow. Immediately."

Chara did, slowly. After she straightened, she plucked at her bodice hem and shuffled her feet, which were smudged with dirt. An awkward little thing—and yet her steady regard made Ariadne want to fidget.

"Now that all the gifts have been given," the queen said, "it is time to—"

"Wait!" Skirts rustled on stone as people drew apart. "Apologies, Princess Minnow, for I am late—but here is something for you. . . ."

Daedalus and Icarus stopped before the throne. Daedalus was panting a bit; Ariadne imagined him running in his ungainly way up all the stairs from his workroom (he had only one, here, and it was much smaller than any he had at Knossos). Icarus's breath whistled a bit, too, but it always did. He was cupping something in his crooked, bony fingers.

"Ooooh!" said Phaidra. She leaned so far forward from her place by Pasiphae's knees that she had to put her little hands on Icarus's arm to steady herself. He flinched, but she didn't. She beamed up at him and his own twisted lips twisted a little more, in what Ariadne imagined might be a smile.

"Phaidra," she said, laying her palm heavily on the girl's back, "let me see; it's *my* present, after all."

Phaidra drew back quickly. "I'm sorry," she said. "It just looks so pretty . . ."

Not pretty, exactly, thought Ariadne as she held out her hands to Icarus. He placed the thing carefully upon them. His dry fingers brushed hers and she flicked at them as if they were small, irritating things: insects perhaps, or specks of dirt. He flinched again and didn't look at her.

It was a large wooden box with eight sides. The top was covered with a web of carvings: lines that angled inward and inward until they met in a tiny spiral that looked like the whorl of a seashell or the mark left by a finger dipped in ink.

"Press the centre to begin," Daedalus said. "After that I'll say no more."

Ariadne pressed the spiral. Nothing happened.

"A little harder, Princess," murmured Karpos over Icarus's shoulder. She scowled at both of them, but she also pressed harder, and this time the box changed. The wood along its edges rose up and outward with a sound of whirring metal. Phaidra gasped and Pasiphae said, "Oh!" but Ariadne stayed silent. She bent closer to the box. In the space beneath where the outer edge had been were tiny tin figures, brightly painted in reds and blues and whites. A boy, a girl, a bird, a dolphin, a boat, a griffin, a snake, and a boar: one for each side. She touched the griffin's crest, which was sharp. It wiggled back and forth but her finger was too big to move it on the track she could see, deep within the box. She tipped it a little and saw eight metal levers where there hadn't been any before; they must have popped out when the box opened. She pushed one and the boy slid to the end of his track. She pushed each of the levers, one by one, until she got to the boar's. When it reached the end of its groove, a second strip of box opened up and out. This one covered the tin figures, but there were others in the new space: the very same figures, except for the dolphin. (A wall of minuscule tin stones had sprung up in its place.) Ariadne used the levers again, in the opposite direction, and a third layer opened, and soon a fourth and a fifth, each of them containing one less figure and one more wall.

The girl was last. Ariadne pushed at her lever and she swivelled in place (her blue skirts nearly brushing the metal track) but wouldn't move forward or back.

"Nothing's happening," Ariadne said. Daedalus's face leaned in from the blur of all the others. A lightning flash turned his skin silver.

"Back and forth will not work anymore," he said.

She frowned. "Lift her!" Phaidra cried.

"Quiet!" snapped Ariadne, but she reached two fingers into the box and plucked the girl out. A compartment whirred open where she'd been. Yet more metal glinted within it: gold, this time.

"A key!" Phaidra said.

"*Quiet*," said Ariadne. She set the key in her lap and turned the box over. Its parts chimed as they fell against each other. She saw no keyhole on the bottom, nor on any of the eight sides. She laid it back down and flipped the key between her fingers. The girl, the walls behind her, the centre spiral rising up above her like a column . . . Ariadne lowered her head toward the spiral and saw a notched hole at its heart, so small she hadn't noticed it before. She smiled, but before she could fit the key to it, Phaidra reached out her own fingers. They touched the spiral, and they glowed with silver that wasn't from lightning. The column clicked open into eight parts like petals, and the silver shone on the tin bull that spun slowly around within it.

"Phaidra!" Pasiphae's voice sounded very far away, to Ariadne. She watched her sister lift her hand and stare at her fingers; watched her thrust all four into her mouth, as if they were burning. Her thumb shone for a moment longer, and then the light dimmed until it came only from the little oblong of her nail.

"She is godmarked!" Naucrate's words rang out above the rain and thunder. The people surged forward: the black-robed priests of Zeus and the white-robed priestesses of Poseidon and everyone who stood between. Ariadne saw Diantha's face and Alkaios's, both open-mouthed. Icarus's head bobbed as he gazed down at Phaidra. Every eye was on the princess with the honey-coloured hair, even though the silver glow had gone.

Of course, Ariadne thought. *It's just I, again, who can never rule. I alone whom the gods despise.*

"Naucrate!" the queen cried, and all the other voices quieted. "You have a locked box, and so do I, on the table by my bed."

"Yes, my Queen," Naucrate said. "I'll fetch them." She smiled at Phaidra before she turned and made her way around the hearth and out into the corridor. Pasiphae was smiling, too, her hand beneath Phaidra's chin, tilting it into the flickering light.

"Daughter," she said, and suddenly Asterion was there, hugging Phaidra, and Glaucus, who tickled her, and Deucalion, who drew them both away from her, laughing as all of them were.

Naucrate's box was round except for one flattened side, where the bronze lock was. Pasiphae's box was small and square, and its lock was gold. Both locks clicked open the moment Phaidra brushed them with her fingertips, which gleamed again with godlight.

"Praise Zeus!" called one of the priests.

The queen stared out across the gathering. "It was not Zeus who marked this child," she said. "He has never opened things that were shut, save for mortal women's legs."

A murmur rippled. *You stupid woman,* Ariadne thought dully. *How did Lord Poseidon sire the bull-brat with you, except by a priest who parted your legs?*

"Athene," Pasiphae said. "She unlocks mysteries with wisdom greater than any her father possesses. My daughter is hers, not his. Now, Amyntor," she said, more loudly so that the second swelling murmur subsided, "take us to your accounting room—for are there not many coffers there that Phaidra could unlock?"

"Yes, my Queen," cried a man at the back of the throng. He moved off into the corridor and everyone else followed (though the priests turned a different way, once they were past the inner pillars).

Nearly everyone else.

"Stop," Ariadne said. Chara, who'd nearly reached the outer pillars, slowed. "You are mine now, remember? You go nowhere unless I say you may."

Chara walked back, her toes curling and dragging just before she lifted her feet. When she reached Ariadne again they stood in silence, looking at each other.

"I'm sorry, Princess," Chara said at last.

Ariadne laughed. "Are you indeed? For what?"

The girl drew a hand over her head, patting at the neat little knots and the hair beneath them (which was beginning to curl and would likely soon tangle). "Well," she said hesitantly, "what just happened with your sister—I know what it is to be unmarked, you see—other children tease me for it, and I know it's even harder for you because—"

"Enough." Ariadne's voice was so low that she could barely hear it leaving her. "If you say any more I shall flog you myself. And stop staring at me"—suddenly the words were shrill—"stop—do you hear me?"

Chara looked at her for a moment longer, then away. "I'm sorry," she said again, quietly, as Ariadne sank onto the throne and put her head in her hands.

———— • ————

On the sixth day after the royal household returned to Knossos, the Priests of the Sky and the Priestesses of the Sea met in the palace courtyard. These two daily processions usually took place at different times; times decreed before dawn by their respective gods. But on this day the two winding lines came together in the great rectangle of the courtyard, where the shadows of the horn carvings lay long and dark.

"Princess!" Diantha gasped. Ariadne stopped walking and looked where Diantha was looking: between two crimson pillars on the highest level of the palace and down into the westering sunlight. She saw the priests' black robes glinting with gold and the priestesses' white ones glinting with silver—two long serpents of cloth and flesh, winding, stopping, holding still.

"The priestesses will fall back," Ariadne said. "Zeus has grown more powerful than Poseidon, these past many years."

"Forgive me, Princess," Diantha said slowly, "but I'm not sure that's true. And look who's there with them . . ."

Asterion's hair and horns shone as they always seemed to; Ariadne was surprised that she hadn't noticed them immediately. He was standing behind the High Priestess, who stepped aside as Ariadne watched, and drew him out to stand before her. From so far up, he was smaller than usual—but all the others were, too, even the High Priest, who usually towered above even Minos.

Diantha leaned forward. Her fingertips whitened as she pressed them into the pillar's grooves. "You see—the priestesses are demanding that the priests make the sign of the horns to your brother—look—you can tell, even without hearing their words."

Diantha was right. The priestesses were fanning out on either side of the prince, all of them holding their hands up in the sign. The priests spread out as well, so that each faced a priestess. The men's hands were at their sides.

"The priestesses won't yield," Diantha said.

Suddenly Ariadne was dizzy with rage—at everyone and at no one; at the beautiful, burnished sky and the gleam of horns, robes, coiled hair, oiled beards. She started running before she could tell herself to. "Ariadne—wait!" she heard Diantha call, but she was already on the staircase.

Three flights and half a courtyard length, and yet she was barely breathing hard when she stopped. (Ariadne the dancer, so swift and tireless that she might have been marked by Artemis or Hermes. Might have been, but had not.) She walked between the two rows until she reached Asterion. The silence was heavy—*Because they were talking until I got here*, she thought. Her anger ebbed and vanished. *Because now they're watching me, not each other.* She felt a smile but didn't show it on her lips.

"Princess." The High Priestess's voice sounded tight.

"Sister of Poseidon," Ariadne said. She made sure her own words were warm and strong, as her father's so often were. "This is a curious gathering. Explain, if you would."

The High Priestess wasn't old, but her frown made unsightly lines in her forehead and beside her eyes. "It seems that the Priests of the Sky will not acknowledge the Sea's son."

The High Priest inclined his head to Ariadne. His brow was smooth, she noted. "Princess, it has been a long time since Zeus's children have made obeisance to Poseidon's. We greet your brother as a prince, as is his due, but that is all."

"This is far less than his due!" the priestess said, and Ariadne said, "You must not speak to the High Priest that way!" and a tide of murmurs rose, with Asterion's voice ringing out above it: "Stop! Please stop!"

They all looked down at him. *Diantha would say he seems older than eleven*, Ariadne thought. *I'm glad she stayed behind and can't see him. And I'm glad I told Chara to tidy my chamber instead of attending to me.*

"I thank you, Sisters," he said, gesturing with one small hand at the line of priestesses. "Your reverence pleases me. But," he went on, raising his other hand toward the priests, "I've never *expected* anyone to make the sign of the Bull. I know that my father has honoured me, and that's enough."

"My Lord," the High Priestess began, but this time it was Ariadne's voice that rose above the rest and made the murmurs stop. "Sweet little brother," she said, smiling her most generous smile, "your faith in a god's regard shouldn't stop you from demanding it from people. You should *want* them to worship you."

Asterion shrugged—a graceful movement that seemed more regretful than careless. "I don't want the same things you do, Sister."

Rage swept through her again. If she had been Minos,

she would have burned him to ash with godfire. "You would not speak to me this way if our father were here."

She saw something flicker in his eyes before they slid away from hers. "He isn't my father—ask him; he will say so."

"Of course," she said, willing him to look back at her so that she would see more of the flickering, and maybe something else, "your father was a man these priestesses chose to rut with our mother. *My* father killed him."

Asterion looked at her. The flicker had gone; there was a dark stillness in its place. "If someone here had a torch," he said, very clearly into the silence, "I'd use it—I'd change into the shape my true father gave me and I'd hurt you so badly you'd never, ever dance again."

For a moment Ariadne, too, was still. Then, because something was beginning to tremble inside her, she laughed. It was shrill, but that was fine: it was louder than all the other noise that had risen around her. "You fools!" she cried at the priestesses before her. "How dare any of you raise your voices when I am here? How dare—"

"Silence! All of you: *silence*."

Ariadne saw Asterion smile, just before she turned toward their mother. Pasiphae was standing at the end of the rows. Phaidra was beside her, her left hand clinging to one of the queen's skirt folds.

"Mother," Ariadne said into this newest quiet. The queen was staring at the High Priest. "Mother—the priests have greeted Asterion as a prince but not a god—the priestesses seek to force them to—I have simply been trying to—"

"*Silence*, I said." Pasiphae walked forward until she was only a pace away from Ariadne. "Hypatos," Pasiphae said to the High Priest. His honey-coloured eyes narrowed. "You will make the sign to Poseidon's child. You and all of Zeus's men will do this. Now."

None of the priests moved.

"You will do this, Hypatos, because if you do not, I shall call upon the Great Mother who bore all the gods. I shall sacrifice to her, deep beneath the earth, and she shall right the wrong you have done to her son's son."

Ariadne drew in her breath and held it as she watched the High Priest. He blinked down at Pasiphae, his lips twisted above his gold-dipped beard. *He won't do it*, Ariadne thought, and breathed out. But then he raised his hands. They came up slowly, and cloth rustled as the other priests' did too. *Stupid old men—such stupid, cowardly men*, Ariadne thought.

"Thank you," Asterion said as they stood there.

Ariadne looked back at the queen and, because she couldn't bear the light in her mother's green eyes, past her at the upper gallery where she and Diantha had been. It was too dim between the pillars to see if Diantha was still there—but the sky above was golden-red, and the shape that crouched upon the roof was very clear. It was moving back and forth, arms tucking and untucking like restless wings. *Bird-boy*, Ariadne thought, with a surge of disgust, *why must you always watch me? And you*—Phaidra, who was craning up over her own shoulder—*why must* you *always watch* him?

"Yes," Pasiphae said, "thank you. And now you must go—all of you. You have already done grave disservice to both your gods." She placed her hand on Asterion's hair as he turned to follow the priestesses. He swung his head up as if it had been the bull's and she ran her fingers over his horns. They smiled at each other.

"Daughter," she said, her voice abruptly hard, "come with me."

No, Ariadne wanted to say, *I won't; I will not obey you.* But she followed Pasiphae and Phaidra, who stumbled a few times because she was still glancing up at the dark blot that was Icarus. Ariadne walked with her head held high; there were people gathered around the courtyard, staring and muttering, and she wouldn't let them see her bend.

Pasiphae led her to the throne room. The last of the sunlight shimmered in the doorway, and lamplight melted the colours on the painted walls: the griffin's scarlet and green, and the white of the mountain irises.

Phaidra skipped over to the throne and pulled herself up onto it. "Mother!" Ariadne said as her sister drummed her heels on the stone. "She shouldn't do that! You've never let me—"

Pasiphae whirled and slapped Ariadne across the face. Her head snapped back and fire coursed over her skin, and tears blurred the griffins even more.

"You meddle," the queen hissed. "You meddle and scheme because this is all you can do, without a mark—and you turn everything around you into chaos."

Ariadne wiped her tears away with the tips of her littlest fingers. She held her hands at her sides then, even though she wanted to put a palm against her burning cheek.

"You weren't out there at the beginning," she said. It was rage that made her words ripple—only rage. "How do you know that I had anything to do with what happened in the courtyard?"

Pasiphae leaned against the throne. Phaidra leaned against her. The girl's eyes and hair looked like spun gold in the lamplight. "I am not speaking only of what happened in the courtyard." The queen sounded weary. "And I know you. That is enough."

Ariadne said, almost exactly as she had to Asterion, "You would not speak to me like that if my father were here. And you would not dare hit me."

The queen raised her brows and smiled a crooked, fleeting smile. "You think? Well, we shall soon find out. I had word only hours ago: the great King Minos has been victorious, on land and on sea. The great King Minos is coming home."

CHAPTER EIGHT

"Father's coming home today," Ariadne said in a voice that sounded very loud, in the pre-dawn stillness. She waited for a reply from Chara, who was likely curled up in the alcove by the doorway, but there was none.

"Girl. Did you hear me? Father's coming home today."

Cloth rustled against stone. "Is that so?" Chara called, her own voice rough and crackly.

"Yes. I feel it." This feeling had come to her as she slept and it hadn't dissipated, now that she was awake. "It's been weeks since Mother told me of his triumph over the Athenians, and yet only this morning am I sure of it: he is coming home today. Help me dress. We're going to wait at the western wall."

As it turned out, Ariadne waited *atop* the western wall. She clambered onto Chara's shoulders and hauled herself up to stand between the two massive stone horns that loomed above the gate pillars. Chara stayed beneath, except when Ariadne commanded her to fetch food and water. She heard laughter, a few times, and knew that Asterion was beneath too, but this time his and the slave girl's unseemly association didn't bother her.

The first she saw of the returning army was the flash of the heralds' horns, far out along the road. She stood, even though she knew it would be ages until she would be able to see the men who held them. But soon she heard the horns

too—waves of sound rising and receding like tidewater—
and she strained forward into the cooling wind, bracing
herself on the two curving stones that rose on either side
of her. "Princess!" Chara called out from below. "Take care!"
Ariadne thought, *Ignore her; just look for them—o gods, let me
make out their forms before the darkness falls . . .*

But the darkness fell swiftly. The people of Knossos
gathered in thick rows on either side of the road; she
watched the bending and craning of their shadow-heads and
heard the distant murmur of their voices, and she blinked
at the bobbing of their lamps or godfire—but she noticed
these things only in passing. They were unimportant. Even
Pasiphae and her other children, standing at the foot of the
outer staircase, were unimportant.

The line of soldiers was speckled with light as well:
orange and pink and blue sparks that dipped and wove
like godmarked fireflies. One light was much larger. It
pulsed dark orange to crimson and back again, curves and
splotches that coalesced, as the soldiers grew closer, into
the shape of a body.

Father. Ariadne backed out between the stone horns
and slithered over the roof's edge. Chara was no longer
waiting, beneath. Ariadne wished that Karpos were there
to catch her—his hands would wrap around her waist and
tighten but she would wrest herself away from him and
leave without looking back. Now, without him, she landed
hard and ran.

"Where've *you* been?" Glaucus muttered when she
slipped between him and Deucalion. She was silent. He
jabbed her in the ribs with his elbow; she didn't move at all.
Unimportant, she thought as he growled and Phaidra craned
to look. *All of them.*

The soldiers came into view—lines of ten that stretched
across the width of the road. Some bore horns (silent, so

close to the palace); others held torches. The torchlight seemed feeble, lost in the glow that shone behind. It flowed over the bronze of horns, spearheads and short swords, the wood of bows, the hide of quivers. It lit sweat-slick brown skin and oiled beards and all the pairs of eyes that gazed ahead, at home. The light's source was six lines from the front. *Father*, Ariadne thought again, even as Deucalion murmured the same thing.

Minos was made of godfire. He had limbs but they were indistinct, lying like wood at the heart of the blaze. His face warped and smoothed in heat shimmer. The soldiers left a wide space around him; the ones who walked behind stepped in the black, smoldering holes his feet left.

"He's gone mark-mad," Deucalion muttered, and Glaucus hissed, "He hasn't; he's just excited. . . ."

The front rows fanned out on either side of the palace steps. The king walked between them. He crackled. The cloth wrapped around his waist and thighs spat gouts of golden sparks (though it burned only a little, itself, because it was touching Minos's godmarked skin). He stopped before Pasiphae, whose fingers dripped water onto the flagstones.

"Husband," she said over the sounds of the other soldiers who were approaching. "Knossos hails her triumphant king. Your people welcome you home."

The flames were dimming—the ones outside him, anyway. Rivulets of light still ran beneath his skin. He didn't speak.

Pasiphae shifted. "Husband," she said again. Ariadne heard the anger in the word, and she clenched her fists. *He won't say anything to her; he'll turn and look at us—at me. . . .*

He turned. Embers spiraled from his hair and beard. He looked at Phaidra, at Deucalion; his orange-lit eyes leapt past Ariadne, to Glaucus and Asterion. *Now*, Ariadne thought, already smiling. *Only now—because he's saving me for last.*

"Now, Husband!" Pasiphae said, wrapping her hand around his arm. Steam rose in ribbons between her fingers. "Enough talk of vengeance! You have won a great victory, and there are those here who wish to do you honour for it."

She gestured with her free arm and a little girl approached the thrones, holding two figs in her upturned palms. Squeezing her eyes shut, she raised them into the air without touching them. They spun in wide, silver-blurred circles, even when she added a ball of thread, a little round box, and an oatcake from Glaucus's plate (he reddened and grinned as the crowd cheered). The king stared, hardly blinking, as an old man skirted the hearth and lifted his hands. Wisps of colour bloomed between them: orange, pink and green streamers that twisted as if in a wind. They lengthened and drifted over the hearth's glow, and twined among the objects the girl was juggling.

"My King," the old man said, a bit haltingly, "see the breath of the gods, who watched your victory over the Athenians and rejoiced with all of us."

Minos stared. Chara thought briefly that the smoke curling from his skin might join with the colours, but it didn't; it wended up, and vanished.

"Lord Minos!" Daedalus emerged from between two pillars at the end of the chamber. He walked a few paces and bowed.

Asterion's hand clenched around his piece of bread. "What is it?" Chara whispered.

"Daedalus never bows to my father," Asterion whispered back. "Something's not right. Maybe all that talk of punishing Athens . . . ?"

Daedalus straightened. "Your son could command all beasts. He spoke to them, and they to him." He smiled, but something in it—beneath it—made Chara draw back on her bench.

He looked at her. A moment passed. His mouth didn't move. His gaze was steady, but it didn't change. "Father?" she whispered, and he turned once more, and walked past all of them, up into his palace.

—— · ——

"Ariadne," Deucalion said, "calm down."

Ariadne whirled to face him and Chara thought, *Oh, Prince, why did you have to speak?* The princess's face was mottled, as if she'd been crying, but Chara was fairly sure she hadn't been. What she *had* been doing was pacing—the length of her room and the corridor outside it.

"How can I?" she said in a low, rich voice that sounded very much like her mother's. (*And Ariadne would have me flogged, if I told her so.*) "How can I be calm when he has not come to me? It has been two days!"

Deucalion took a deep breath, as if he were about to summon a wind, but all that came out was a sigh. "Sister. He's been fighting a war. Allow him a few days of peace, now that he's home. And in any case," he went on as she opened her mouth to reply, "you'll see him at the feast tonight. Perhaps he'll even put you at his right hand, as he does so often."

But he didn't. The royal children sat at a long trestle table that had been set up by one of the throne room's walls. Chara sat at the end of the bench, beside Asterion—because he'd said that she should, "since you're my sister's special slave—but really because you're my friend."

The king and queen were on their thrones. Pasiphae looked at ease except for her hands, which clutched at the carved armrests. Minos's skin still glowed faintly orange, and smoke wreathed his head—*Like a crown of cloud over his real gold one*, Chara thought. He gazed into the glowing embers in the hearth, smiling a thin, hungry smile, and didn't speak. He did eat, at least; Chara heard grease hiss in his beard when he wiped it with the back of his hand.

When the last of the food had been cleared away, and the folding table removed from its place in front of his throne, he stood. His people's murmuring stopped abruptly.

"People of Knossos!" The king's voice cracked on the first word, then steadied and rolled like his god's thunder over the crowd. "I have returned to you a conqueror—victor and master, mightier than I have ever been. And yet," he went on, more quietly, "in the days following my triumph, I was wretched. My son, who should have ruled this island, was dead. My victory had not brought him back to me. And it seemed, in my grief, that my god was lost to me as well—for while his fire burned even more hotly beneath my flesh than it had before, I received neither comfort nor counsel from him."

Minos cast his eyes over his family and the ranks of onlookers, to the dark sky beyond the columns. "I pleaded with Zeus, in my battle tent, and at an altar in the city I had laid low. I begged him to show me his favour again. I sacrificed to him: a sheep, every day for the seven days, and then a calf for seven more. And on the fourteenth day, the Great Father came to me."

Pasiphae's green eyes were wide, as she gazed up at Minos. Her knuckles were whiter than they had been. *She hasn't heard this before,* Chara thought. She glanced at Ariadne, who was frowning. *He hasn't told his family anything. . . .*

Minos raised his hands and clasped them in front of his heart. "Zeus told me what I must do to show my devotion and earn my ease. I ravaged Athens' water and land with my fire, but it was not enough. He told me what more I must take from them: their young."

Chara's throat went dry. She glanced sidelong Asterion, who shrugged both shoulders at her. Peop stirred and milled at the pillars and beyond, as the wor was passed to those who couldn't hear the king.

"At first I thought to demand the life of Theseus, tl son who not long ago returned to Aegeus, after years concealment. I have seen him: he is a fine, strong youth, golden as Androgeus was dark. But I could not, for I wish the Athenian king to see that Zeus the Father marked r with compassion, as well as flame.

"And so," Minos said, holding his hands out so th everyone would see his fire-limned palms, "I had h brought to me, in his own audience chamber. I sat up his throne and he knelt before me—just him, without l counsellors or the remnants of his guard. I command him to send seven young men and seven young women h to us—fine Athenian calves and sheep, fourteen of the to be offered up as sacrifices to the Great Goddess. Ev two years, I said, as his shoulders shook."

Minos smiled. "He raged against me. He refused accede. I set the chamber on fire and said I would do same to what remained of his city. I said that if he still not relent, I would set his golden son alight, too. He wept. grovelled and begged me to be kind. He promised fourt Athenian young, every two years, for the Goddess. I h simply to tell him when to begin. And I *shall* tell him, moment my god speaks to me again. For I know now t he has not forsaken me."

The noise outside had stopped. The noise inside Cha head hadn't; it was like a roar of distant water. She blin but Minos's face swam. Asterion's hand on hers was c though. She put her own hand over it and pressed down h

The king was swaying—and not just in Chara's stra blurred vision.

"Androgeus did this, my King—and so, now, do I."

There was a noise—a hundred skittering feet, a hundred swishing tails. "Gods and winds!" Glaucus gasped—and other people muttered too, and some cried out. Creatures flooded across the floor. Snakes, except they had legs—and fish, except they wriggled through air and over stone.

"Come to me!" Daedalus cried, leaping from foot to foot, beckoning with open hands. "Come and show the Great King that his beloved son's godmark lives on in you!"

Pasiphae stood up so quickly that one of her shoes tangled in her skirts. "Daedalus!" she called as people murmured and the metal beasts whirred and scampered toward the throne. *"Master Daedalus—"*

Minos rose. Sparks showered and settled and died.

"You mock me." He sounded as if his mouth were full of rocks. He sounded half-asleep, or drunk. "Though you were exiled, you will always be Athenian. My triumph angers you, and now you seek to wound me."

The last words were clearer than the first, but they were difficult to hear over the creatures' noise. Two of the snakes—scarlet with green spots—bent around the angle of the hearth and clattered up to the throne. Minos brought his foot down on one, then the other. They flattened and stilled with a singing sigh of metal.

"Do I?" Daedalus was very still, now. "If Androgeus were here, I believe he would delight in these creations."

"Do not speak his name."

Minos's right arm burst into flame. He took a step toward Daedalus, who didn't move.

"Prince Androgeus," Daedalus said, over all the skittering and ringing. "Prince Androgeus, who went to Athens for sport, not slaughter."

Minos sprang forward. The fire leapt out before him. Someone screamed, and the bench lurched beneath Chara.

Asterion hunched forward; Glaucus scrambled back; Deucalion stood, his fists on the tabletop, with Ariadne beside him. Phaidra sat motionless, big-eyed.

"Asterion." Chara couldn't hear her own voice over the noise, but she was certain she'd spoken. "*Asterion* . . ."

He slipped beneath the table and ran.

Chara was up and didn't remember rising. She watched Asterion throw himself between Minos and Daedalus. It was all so slow: the boy's flailing advance, Daedalus's surprised stumble backward, Minos's bright, smoky recoil.

"Stop! Just stop! Father—*please* . . ."

A mechanical crab tipped onto its back. Its pincers screeched open and closed in the silence. The other machine animals had stopped in their tracks.

"What?" Minos's voice seemed to ripple as the lines of his face did, beneath the fire's glow. "What did you call me?"

Asterion stood facing Minos. The boy's hands were up, palms out, as if they'd be enough to combat the flames. His legs were planted wide. But his lips trembled, even as he spoke.

"Father?"

Minos's eyes widened. The whites of them were orange; the pupils were silver-blue. "You." The word was a rumble. "*You* should have died." And he lunged, reaching and flaming.

Asterion stepped to meet him.

No no no no! This time Chara didn't say the words: she thought them, only, as fire licked along Asterion's fingers and arms and kindled in his hair. *Turn around*—run. Her heart hammered as he knelt, arms spread wide, head thrown back. Smiling up into Minos's face.

The king fell back a pace. "Lysander!" he called. "You and your men—take this *thing* from my sight."

The soldiers clustered together between the pillars stepped forward, but too late: the change had already begun. Asterion fell to his side, writhing, his bones cracking and popping like the fire. Within moments his broadening head and stretching limbs were covered in pelt. He heaved himself up—*When did he start changing this fast?* Chara thought. He snorted, sweeping his head back and forth so that his horns scraped across the floor and tossed mechanical beetles and snakes and snails up into the air. When they fell, onto plates and into the laps of those few people who were still sitting, no one even looked at them. Everyone was gazing at the bull-boy.

He huffed and turned away from Minos. Picked his way almost delicately around the hearth, his round brown eyes rolling. Daedalus put out his hand, as Asterion passed, but didn't touch him.

"Seize him!" Minos bellowed, spewing smoke. The soldiers put their hands on their bows, but when Pasiphae cried, "No! Do not dare harm the god's son!" they glanced at each other and didn't stir again.

The bull-boy swung around when he reached the end of the room. He pawed at the ground twice.

"My King," said the High Priest in his voice that was soft and ringing at the same time, "move back, behind me . . ." He walked from the throne to where Minos stood, but the king held up at hand.

"No, Hypatos. I will not hide from this creature."

Pasiphae made a strangled sound and raised a hand with fingers hooked like claws. Before she could move, though, the bull did. He roared and charged, and his hoofs struck sparks from the floor. Minos laughed a great plume of fire and held his burning arms up. The bull ran faster, around the curve of hearth. He shifted his head sideways and down. Minos laughed again, and a wall of flames sprang up in the air before him—but the bull broke through it without slowing and wrenched a horn up and into the king's belly.

Chara heard Minos's flesh tear. Even though Glaucus was screaming, and Phaidra too, and many others besides, Chara heard it: a wet, ripping sound that ended very quickly but went on and on inside her head. The wall of flames dissolved. The light in Minos's body went out. He sagged to one knee, holding a hand against his stomach. Hand and cloth were instantly wet and black. He laughed— breathlessly this time—and sat down, hard.

The three soldiers sprinted from the pillars to the king, as did Ariadne. Three more soldiers appeared from somewhere, short swords in their hands. They edged toward the bull, who was tossing his head, his feet firmly planted. "No!" Pasiphae cried, and pushed her way past them. She put her arm across the bull's neck and murmured something into one twitching ear. He sagged almost as Minos had and lay down, pelt melting to skin and tousled golden hair.

"Take it." The king's voice was thin and slurred. A priest was kneeling behind him; Chara saw the gold-dipped beard shudder as he tried to hold him upright. Ariadne was crouched in front, clinging to her father's hands. "Take it away . . . from here. Do not . . . kill. I will not have a god. Angry. But take it from me. Quickly. And take it . . . from her."

"No. No no no no." Chara thought these words, too, were hers, but they weren't. Each sound rose until it wasn't a word—just a meaningless, gurgling shriek—and water coursed down Pasiphae's arms as she scrabbled at the soldiers who were trying to wrest her away from Asterion. She raked their cheeks and arms with one dripping hand while she clung to Asterion with the other. The boy was lying on his side. He was facing Chara, staring—too far away for her to see the gold flecks in his eyes, though she could imagine them. There were fresh pink ribbons of burn on his arms. *Run, slave girl,* she thought. *Go to him.* She couldn't move.

The soldiers turned to Minos, their swords hanging limp

in their hands. As they waited, priestesses drew forward—a line of white, encircling the men who encircled the queen.

"God Brother." The king's voice was just a whisper, now. The High Priest bent close to him. "Call upon your . . . mark. Upon our Father. Send all these . . . fools away."

Hypatos rose to his full height. He tucked his chin in against his chest. Already people were scrambling to leave the chamber. Glaucus was among the first to flee; Deucalion followed more slowly, glancing over his shoulder. Phaidra stayed at the table where she'd been all night. She was nibbling on her thumb.

Chara stepped closer to the hearth. One step—and then lightning flashed: not in the courtyard, but in the throne room. For a breath, everything was flat and stark and white. As the light died, thunder cracked. The palace's stones shuddered. A brazier fell onto its side with a clang, and plates and cups slid off the table. Daedalus's mechanical beasts juddered and leapt as if he'd just wound them. Daedalus himself was standing with his eyes closed, smiling.

The High Priest turned in small, swaying circles. He stood straight, even when the earth shook again, though everyone else—Pasiphae, Chara, Ariadne, the soldiers— lurched or stumbled. He turned and he chanted, and there was more lightning, more thunder. A crack zigzagged across the floor, from throne to hearth. The stones parted right where Pasiphae was kneeling; Asterion's hand flopped into the dark space between them.

"Stop!" A priestess's cry, which echoed in the silence after the thunder. "Call off your brute of a god, Hypatos!"

Four priests converged on the five priestesses. The soldiers in the room raised their swords; the ones by the pillars nocked their bows. The High Priest didn't stop his turning. He lifted his arms as if he were trying to touch the lightning that forked above them. Thunder shook the chamber once more. This time, when it growled into nothing, it was a child's voice that called, "Stop!"

Asterion was standing. Pasiphae put her hand on his shoulder and he shook it free. He craned up at her, then looked at the priestesses, the priests, the soldier, Minos. Minos last and longest, though the king's head was slumped against his shoulder and his eyes were closed. "No more," Asterion said thickly. "I'll go—take me—I don't care where. I started this; let me end it, too."

"Asterion!" Pasiphae's wet curls were clinging to the corners of her mouth but she didn't wipe them free. "Don't say such things! You'll go nowhere—you'll stay here with—"

"*I'll go.*" His voice trembled a bit, and his hands clenched and unclenched at his sides, but he stood very tall.

"The king must go, too," said the priest who was holding him up. "To his chamber, immediately. His wound is grave—see, he has just fainted. . . ."

Two priests carried Minos out of the throne room. His hands dragged on the floor; each one left a dark, snaking trail. The other two priests led Asterion away. He turned back, when Pasiphae cried out his name, but he didn't look at her; he looked at Chara, who started toward him with a cry that hurt her throat.

"No!" he called to her. "Stay there or it'll go badly for you, too. . . ." And then he was gone, and she stayed, her eyes leaping blindly for a bit, until they settled on the queen.

Pasiphae stood staring down at the crack that had opened in the floor. Water dripped from her fingers into the crack, which looked deep. *I've seen her summon waves from a calm sea.* The words in Chara's head were strangely clear, almost bright. *I've seen her call water up from beneath the earth. Now look at her.*

Phaidra walked slowly over to her mother. She laid her head against Pasiphae's skirts. The queen didn't seem to notice her at all. Ariadne didn't seem to notice either of them: her eyes were fixed on someone just behind Chara, and they didn't waver as she drew closer.

"Minnow." Chara started and turned. Daedalus was right there, shifting from foot to foot, his eyes darting. "Princess—come away. To my workshop, if you like, or to Naucrate; she'll have some sweets, I'm sure. . . ."

Ariadne took one last step and tipped her head up so that she was staring past his close-cropped beard, at the eyes that wouldn't be still. "This was your fault," she said. "Yours, just as much as my brother's. Did you *intend* to anger the king? Or are you simply stupid?"

Finally Daedalus's gaze fastened on the princess. "Ariadne," he said in a hard, strange voice, "you are exceedingly clever, but you will never be wise." He barked out a laugh that made Chara start again. Behind them, Phaidra was saying, "Mother? Mother, are you all right?" A cup was rolling on its side; perhaps the ground was moving yet, somewhere far below.

Ariadne turned away from Daedalus. "You," she said to Chara, in a strained, high voice Chara hadn't heard before. "You. Slave. Come away with me, now."

Chara wanted to look at Daedalus, but instead she fixed her gaze on the sweat that was beading above Ariadne's lip. "I will come to you later, Princess," she said quietly.

"Then you shall be flogged later."

"Very well," Chara said. She lowered her eyes to the floor. There were Ariadne's embroidered scarlet slippers, stitched with golden thread in patterns of sea fern and shells. Daedalus's boots, plain leather, scuffed and caked with marble dust. Chara's own, also plain, but clean. Chara watched Daedalus's twitch and scuff at the ground, then move away. She watched Ariadne's move away, too, lightly; she always seemed to be dancing.

105

When Chara raised her eyes at last, she was alone.

Go, she thought. *Even though he commanded you not to—go and find him.* But she couldn't make her legs obey her. They wouldn't stride; they would only crumple. She sat on the floor. *Help me. If any gods can hear me: please help all of us.*

——— . ———

Ariadne couldn't sleep, of course.

Father will live—he has to—and he'll do away with Asterion. He's already said he won't kill him, but there's always exile. Asterion, banished—gone, invisible, powerless . . . Our mother and her priestesses cowed, and poor, sweet, newly-godmarked Phaidra, too . . .

Her thoughts seemed very loud, and the sheets rustled as she twisted about in them, but even so, she heard the scritching. It was above her—on the roof? She slid her legs over the side of her bed and sat very still, barely breathing.

Call for your slave, she thought, but then she remembered that the slave had disobeyed her, and likely wouldn't be in her usual place. *I won't have her flogged, after all. Even though I have no godmark, people will think me generous and merciful.* The scritching continued for a moment, then stopped. Ariadne stood up slowly and walked to the doorway, supporting herself on the balls of her feet as she did when she danced. She put her head out into the corridor—and something fell from the darkness, so close to her that she felt a prickly warmth against her skin before she stumbled backwards.

Icarus folded his arms across his chest. His arms, his wings—whatever they were. She ran her hands over her own arms, where his feathers had touched her. "*You.*" Her heart was pounding up into her throat, but her voice was steady. "How dare you?"

His pointy, elongated toes twitched on the stone. It must have been them making the scritchy noise, up on the roof. His lips were even more purple and twisted than usual; she imagined his beak retracting, grasping at flesh.

"I wanted to see you—I heard about what happened. . . ." He swallowed and gulped and coughed a moist, trailing cough. "I'm sorry. I thought I would ask you if you needed anything."

"By lurking about on the roof above my bedroom in the middle of the night," she said, as evenly as she could, "and then jumping down into my doorway?" She blinked at his strange little roll of metal string, which was glinting copper and silver from its usual place at his belt.

He uncrossed his arms. They hung at his sides, patchy with feathers and the little red holes where other feathers had been. "I . . ." He shrugged and looked down at his bare, twitching feet. "I'm sorry."

"You've already said that, you idiot thing." She giggled. She hadn't expected to; the surprise of it made her giggle more. She bent over, her hands on her knees, and gasped around the tears that were rising with the laughter. When she finally straightened, Icarus was gone.

CHAPTER NINE

Ariadne stared at the screen in front of Minos's quarters. It hadn't slid aside in four hours, since the priest-physician had gone in. She was supposed to dance in another hour—a thanks to Zeus for sending such gentle autumn rains; a plea to Zeus for the Great King's recovery. She wouldn't leave, though. Not until she'd seen her father.

He'd been shut in his rooms for a week, attended only by the priest-physician and his apprentice-boy. "No one may enter"—Ariadne had heard the boy say this to a kitchen girl who'd come, two days ago. The boy was short and officious, and Ariadne almost wished that her mother would come and strike him across the mouth as she passed him. But she didn't. Pasiphae had spent the week in her chair beside the empty throne. She'd heard petitions and signed them, and dealt with tradesmen and ships' captains. She'd spoken to them, calmly and clearly, but to no one else.

Asterion was being held in the eastern arm of the palace, in a tiny room between storage chambers. Men with swords guarded him. Priests paced the length of the corridor, ten at a time, in pairs. Glaucus had told Ariadne this; she'd snorted and said, "There'd be no room! They'd bumble into each other like night beetles!"—but later, Deucalion had told her that it was true.

She sighed and leaned her cheek against the wall. She was well along the hallway, away from her father's doorway; the priest-physician always turned to go in the opposite direction when he emerged. She could still see enough of the screen, though, to focus on. She held its scarlet-painted linen in her vision until it blurred.

The sun was casting low, pink light—dancing light, almost—when the screen slid open. Ariadne heard the scraping of its wooden frame on the stone, and the slapping of the priest-physician's sandals, and then he was there, turning back to the room, calling, "I'll be back before sundown, Ampelios. Close the screen behind me."

He walked away from her. He didn't glance back.

The screen scraped again, of course, when she started to move it. "No one may enter," cried the boy, and he appeared in the opening, scowling and breathless.

She shook her head so that her dark curls tangled briefly over her breasts, which were bare and oiled, because of the dance. "Now, now, boy—don't be a fool."

He gulped. "No one may—"

"I am the Princess Ariadne," she snapped. "Open this screen. All the way."

He nudged it, his fingers white-knuckled on the frame.

"*All the way,*" she said very sweetly, to his right eye (which was level with her left nipple).

The screen edged wider. She thrust it aside with both hands and strode into the antechamber. The boy scuttled backward, his hand to his cheekbone, where the screen's edge had grazed it.

"My Lady!" he cried, and looked back over his shoulder at the entrance to the inner chamber. The pink sunlight was falling through the tall windows there; she could see its glow on the floor, in the air.

"I must see my father." She spoke slowly, in a reasonable tone she imagined the scrawny, big-eyed boy would understand.

"I . . . I cannot, my Lady! No visitors—no one at all—the king himself has ordered it!"

"Boy," she began—and then the king's voice called, "Who's there, Ampelios? Who? I said no one—I'll have you flogged . . ."

He sounded strong and weak at the same time. Ariadne closed her eyes for a moment. When she opened them, Ampelios was standing in the open doorway, his mouth working soundlessly.

"Leave," she said. "He says he'll give you trouble, but I'll give you more. Go. Now."

He stayed motionless for another breath, his eyes fastened on her breasts. She thrust them out just a little more. "*Now*," she said, and he went, with a whimper and a scuffing of sandals.

"Ampelios!" Minos bellowed—but breathily, somehow.

Ariadne took two paces. She was nearly at the entrance to the inner chamber.

"Not Ampelios." Her voice trembled, though she'd been sure it wouldn't. "Ariadne."

Silence. She drew a deep breath; felt it filling her and leaving her again, sweet and fleeting. She took five more steps, these ones quick. She was inside, bathed in pink light, squinting at the low, broad bed beneath the columned windows. She was by the bed, kneeling, bending her head.

"My King, I should not have come—but I could not bear it any longer. I had to see you for myself."

His hand was dangling by her forehead. It was bronzed, beneath its dusting of short black hairs. It was limp and knobby-knuckled, and it didn't dribble smoke or sparks.

She waited. She held her straining body still. She bit her lip so that she wouldn't say anything else.

"Look at me, then, child."

She could hear that he was smiling. *Thank you, gods and goddesses*, she thought, and lifted her head and shoulders up above the side of his bed.

His own head was turned toward her. His teeth glinted in his beard, but his eyes were so sad that she had to look away from them for a bit.

"Father," she said, looking back at him, "I miss him, too."

It wasn't what she'd planned to say, but the king looked so helpless—the words had rushed out before she could check them.

Minos gazed at her. *Too much*, she thought; *too fast*—but then his hand came up. He raised it, held it flat, just touching her face. She lowered her head until her cheek was resting on his palm.

A tear ran from his right eye, across the bridge of his nose. It fell onto the sheet and left a perfectly round mark.

"Ariadne," he said. "Love," and he shut his eyes tight against all the other tears.

———— • ————

Three days later the palace rang with shouts and stamping feet, and it glowed with torches and godfire.

Ariadne sat at the little desk in her room, pressing seals into wax. A boar, a honeycomb, a stag's branching horns—all crafted by Karpos. Under Daedalus's supervision, it was true, but they bore Karpos's mark: they moved when she held them, circling and warming her skin as she imagined his hands might. She'd pressed six stamps already, and intended to press eight more. One for every Athenian youth who would die: two straight rows, hunkering on Egyptian paper.

Slow, halting footsteps sounded in the corridor outside. "Glau!" she called. "Go and make a little wind somewhere, why don't you?"

The footsteps stopped outside her doorway.

"*Glau.*"

"Princess."

She spun on her stool, so quickly that she nearly tipped off. Minos was leaning against the doorframe, smiling—or grimacing, maybe; she couldn't tell. His left hand was pressed against his belly. No blood oozed there now.

"I've taken worse wounds in battle," he said. "I do not understand this weakness." He was watching her eyes.

Ariadne stood. There was wax drying on her fingers; she rubbed them against her skirts.

"This wound was godmarked," she said. "I am surprised you are not weaker." She paused. "Girl!" she called, and the slave emerged from the inner chamber. "Leave us. Immediately."

"Very well, my Lady," the girl said. "My Lord King," she added as she passed Minos. He didn't even glance at her, and so didn't see her impertinently raised eyes.

He was still for a moment, after the slave had gone. Then he cocked his head toward the corridor. "I came the back way," he said. "To avoid the . . . unrest."

Ariadne cleared her throat. "Yes, well, the people are upset. The Sea God's people."

"Upset." She heard a ringing of metal—a sword tip meeting the stone floor, perhaps. Soldiers outside her door. "A riot, I heard." Minos's thick brows climbed. "No?"

She nodded. "Yes. Yes—I saw, yesterday"—all the priestesses, and the others—people of Knossos, crowded down the stairs to the storeroom corridor. Shouting, "Asterion, Asterion! Sea God's blessed godmarked son!" Priests and guards had pressed them back up to the courtyard. There were fewer of them today, but the courtyard was still filled with lamps and globes of godfire, and people were still chanting his name, brandishing bronze daggers and fashioning flaming nets out of air. She'd seen a bull's head made of fire, as she went along the pillared walk above them. A bull that roared and burned as Asterion did, only even brighter.

Minos took a step toward her. She said, "Sit, Father, please!" but he waved a hand at her.

"Those people." He bent over, pressing his belly even more firmly. "My wife—that bitch and her priest-gotten spawn. And Daedalus—that *Athenian*, daring to tell me what my own son would have wanted." Smoke puffed out of his mouth as he panted. Ariadne pressed her own lips together, waiting.

"I will not be able to keep him here," he said at last. "Asterion." He looked at her. *He's waiting for me to speak*, she thought. Her blood sang with hunger and hope.

"You will not," she said.

"And yet I cannot kill him. My wife and her priestesses would overrun the palace."

Ariadne laughed—she couldn't help herself. "I'd kill him for you, if you asked it. But you're right: it would be unwise. No—he needs to go away." She could feel wax beneath her nails; she chipped at it with her thumbs, part of her thinking of stag's horns splintering and honeycombs cracking.

"He needs to disappear. If his people know he's alive but can't see him, they'll stop causing trouble." She paused and ran her tongue over her lower lip. "You could make it seem like he's too divine to live among mortals. You could say that you will do him honour by sending him away."

He laughed. This made him gasp and take two heavy steps back. His shoulder thumped against the wall; the force of it dislodged Daedalus's box from its place on the shelf by the doorway. The box fell. Its outer layer sprang open with a jangling of metal.

"What," Minos said through gritted teeth, "is that?"

Ariadne picked the box up. The tin griffin had bent

double, and its beak was curled like a pig's tail. "Daedalus made it for me," she said. "It was locked and Phaidra opened it with her godmark. At first I thought I'd throw it into the sea, the next time we went to the summer palace—but then I thought I'd keep it. Because I hate her"—she glanced at him under her eyelashes, almost certain that he wouldn't care she'd said this, because Phaidra was Pasiphae's pet and she, Ariadne, was his—"and I want to remember this all the time."

"And what of Daedalus? Do you hate him, too?" The king was leaning again, but he looked relaxed now, not pained. His bushy brows were raised. "He has been more your father than I, these many years."

Ariadne shook her head. "He amused me when I was a child. He doesn't realize that I've grown up, and he still gives me children's toys."

She let the box fall. A little tin wall leapt up behind the griffin. The dolphin tinkled free onto the stone, followed by another wall.

"Walls," she said, staring, seeing nothing for a moment. Nothing, and then an image, wobbly around the edges and dark within, but quite clear.

"We need to put Asterion in a box," she continued slowly. Her father's face swam into focus. His bushy brows had drawn together. "A big one, with lots of walls and turnings—beautiful walls, but ones he can never escape from."

"A prison," Minos said, "yes, of course—but there is no place here that would satisfy his followers, and in any case, I want him far away, beyond—"

"The Great Mother's sanctuary. The mountain that's hollow and hot inside." The words spilled out as if she had been planning them, but she hadn't—they were just there, filling her mouth. She thought, even as she spoke, *They should be silver—godwords glowing when I part my lips.* "We could put him there because there are already tunnels—except that we would have to carve out new areas and close off the old ones—build walls that will lie within the ones the mountain built, to make sure there were no ways out. A sacred space, we'll tell his people—and it will look like one; even his god will be well pleased. But it will be a prison, too, where he'll roam and suffer and someday die, forgotten."

Her father stared at her. "By Zeus, you *are* my daughter." His smile was slow. She thought she saw smoke coiling behind it.

She walked to the doorway. Three soldiers were standing in the hallway: one on either side of the door and one across from it, looking out over the courtyard where the crowd seethed, with its fire and shouting. The voices sounded like waves from here. "A hot place," she said slowly. "A place where he would always be the bull, wild and hungry . . . Father." She turned to look at the desk—at the paper where she'd pressed a stamp for each Athenian youth. "The gods will want to see the Athenians die well. A simple altar stone would not be good enough. So we will send them into the mountain, too. We will send them into the hot earth, and the hungry bull-god will be waiting for them."

Minos gave another broken-off bark of a laugh that ended in a gasp. "Oh, Daughter," he wheezed. "You are as wise as Athene and as fierce as Artemis. Now be wiser yet and tell me how I will have this thing done. For the queen would never permit anything like it."

Ariadne felt the words crowding her throat. "Daedalus. He's the only one who can build it; he's so good at mazes and working with stone."

"Daedalus." Minos shook his head. "He built many things for me, when he was newly exiled from Athens and had promised to serve only me—but that was years ago. Why would he make this wondrous prison?"

Sweat was crawling down her spine. Her heartbeat was so loud that she thought she wouldn't be able to hear her own words—the ones that wended their smooth, silvery way from some nameless god to her tongue. "Because you will promise him his freedom." She turned back to her father. "You'll say your need of him is done. You'll tell him that there will be no more watches placed on the ships in our harbours, once he's finished this last, great work. His exile here will be at an end. *That* is why he'll make it for you."

Minos crossed the floor to her. He put his hands on the back of her head, only lightly, but she felt the warmth coming from them. "But he should be punished, too," he said softly. "For his impudence. For the lack of respect he and his accursed family have always shown me, in the home I gave them. All of them deserve to die."

Maybe his wound has made him feverish, Ariadne thought as she reached up to cover his hands with her own. *Maybe he's as wounded in his mind as he was in his body.* "There must be no reason for the gods to demand your blood for his," she said. "Send them away forever. Be rid of them—but do not kill them. There will be plenty of killing as it is."

The king dug his fingers into her hair so hard that her eyes filled with tears. She didn't blink them away. They gathered on her lashes and blurred his face to something strange and looming. "And what shall I do with Poseidon's son in the meantime, daughter of mine?"

She wanted to laugh as he had, but instead she swallowed hard and set her jaw so that it wouldn't tremble. "Honour him. Install him in the Great Goddess's altar-room for a time, then let my mother choose a secret place far away from our palaces where, we will say, he will be safe. Let her think he is still hers." She licked her lips and swallowed again. "Placate her now so that you can hurt her later. Do not tell her that you intend to put him in the mountain box.

Surprise her with this, when she thinks she is safest. She will have to pretend to rejoice, but she will die in secret, without him."

Minos's teeth glinted. "Yes. She will wonder at my lenience, when I offer her this choice. And she will hate me, when I take him away forever." His fingers grasped and groped, loosening the curls in Ariadne's hair.

"The gods have not marked you," he said, as her head thrummed with fire and pain, "but they speak through you. You are their instrument; their gift to me. You are a queen."

He stepped even closer to her, and his left foot sent Daedalus's box spinning across the floor. He held her to his heart, and as she listened to its pounding, she watched the tiny, broken bull rock and still against the stone.

CHAPTER TEN

"What do you think they're going to say?" Glaucus muttered to Icarus. The royal household had assembled, at the king's command, along with as many people of Knossos as could fit into the courtyard: thousands, it seemed, chattering, crushed up together in the wide space below and lined row upon row in the narrow ones above. Minos and Pasiphae stood upon a tall dais that Daedalus had made: it looked like stone, but was actually painted wood, mounted on wheels so that it could be rolled about. The king was leaning on an ornately carved crutch, resting his hand on the bandage wrapped tightly above his loincloth. He was gazing at the queen, who was gazing at the line of storm clouds advancing in the sky above the highest horns. Deucalion, Phaidra and Ariadne craned up at them from one side of the dais; Icarus, Glaucus and Chara from the other.

Icarus shrugged one bony shoulder. "Why would I know? It's not as if either of them ever speaks to *me*."

Glaucus sighed and turned to Chara. "What about you? Heard anything?"

Ariadne's eyes were wide, fixed on her father. Chara said, "They're planning something—the princess and the king. I followed her to his sick room without her knowing it, and I saw her go in. She stayed a long time. And yesterday, he came to *her* rooms. She dismissed me, which is strange; she usually doesn't care when I'm around. Doesn't notice me at all, unless she needs to be angry about something."

"Huh," Glaucus said. "Why didn't you try and listen, from the outside? Isn't that what slaves *do*?"

"There were guards!" Chara said, loudly enough that Deucalion frowned at all three of them. "Several guards," she went on, more quietly, "and they heard her tell me to go. . . ."

"What about Asterion?" Icarus whispered. "He's still being held in a storeroom cell; will he—"

His voice faltered as Minos raised his free hand. The crowd quieted. Chara saw Ariadne smile, and thought, *She knows everything the rest of us don't. He's told her, of course. Let's see what he tells the rest of us. . . .*

But Minos didn't speak; Pasiphae did.

"Asterion," she began, and fell silent. She closed her eyes. The High Priestess, standing on the second storey of the palace, directly above the dais, raised her hands in the sign of the horns. Hundreds of pairs of hands did the same.

I can't make the sign to him, Chara thought. *Gods and goddesses forgive me, but I've never been able to. He's my friend.* She blinked at the gold and scarlet ribbons that had been threaded through the spokes of the dais's wheels for a moment before she looked back up.

Pasiphae's lovely eyes opened. Chara expected to see tears in them, but they were dry. "My child," the queen continued, "my beloved Asterion, son of Lord Poseidon, is now too powerful for life among men. Many of you saw the proof of this when he struck out at the king." She gestured at Minos but didn't look at him. Minos bent his head, for a moment. There was a splotch of blood on his bandage, easing slowly into a new shape.

"For now," Pasiphae said, "we have sent him back to the place in which he was born: the Great Mother's sanctuary within this palace. He is being tended and protected by guards: two soldiers of my husband's company, two priests of Zeus, and three priestesses of Poseidon. No one troubles him, and he troubles no one. But the boy is more and more the bull. And as he grows, his godmark will only become more unpredictable. So, in consultation with the king, I have decided that he must leave us all. He must be put somewhere secret and sacred, where only I and a few others will go."

The crowd murmured. Someone shouted Asterion's name; someone else sobbed. But Ariadne's voice was loudest; it startled Chara, who hadn't noticed her crossing the stones before the dais. "You've gone so white that your freckles look like stains," the princess murmured. Chara swallowed and turned her face away from Ariadne's gaze and her sweet, warm breath.

"So surprising, is it not? That our dear Asterion won't be able to live among us anymore."

You're not surprised. You knew exactly what would happen, and you know what's yet to come. You, and your mark-mad father. Chara tried to keep still, but her hands trembled. She twisted them in her ridiculous skirts but the trembling didn't stop; it spread inward, to her belly and chest.

The queen took a step back. One of the priestesses behind the dais lifted her arm to keep Pasiphae from falling.

"Silence!" Minos shouted, and the crowd's murmuring subsided. "My thanks, Wife," he went on. He ran his tongue across his upper teeth. Its tip was blue, flicking fire. "Your devotion to your gods and your son and your people warms my heart. And it puts me in mind of a different kind of devotion. It puts me in mind of the fourteen Athenian youths who will be delivered to us and sacrificed to the ancient gods of this island."

Pasiphae's eyes were closed again. Their lids were tinted violet and silver.

Like the inside of a mussel shell, Chara thought.

"I have decided that we will not make these sacrifices at

Knossos or even at Amnisos. No: we shall give them to the Mother in her mountain sanctuary, where she bore Zeus, her mightiest son."

The crowd's voices surged again. There was a roar in Chara's head too, like a distant waterfall.

The king nodded, as if his people were children who'd pleased him. He held up both hands. "But the mountain sanctuary is too crude—sufficient for a stag or boar, but for noble Athenian youths? No. They require more. Zeus and the Mother demand more. And so I, Minos of Crete, shall build all of them an altar unlike any other." He paused, then swept his orange-veined arm out toward the crowd. "Master Daedalus: step forward."

Robes hissed on stone as the crowd parted. *He looks like he's just drunk one of the cook's bitter coughing draughts*, Chara thought. Daedalus's cheeks were sucked in and his eyes squeezed almost shut. Even when he reached the foot of the dais, he didn't open them to look at Minos. She glanced at Icarus, who was even paler than usual, and motionless.

The king's teeth flashed in his beard. "Our renowned craftsman will build a palace beneath the Mother's mountain. He and his workmen will fashion corridors and chambers, and an altar as large as Ariadne's dancing ground. The fourteen Athenians will be sent in alive, and locked in, and the Goddess will decide how best to claim them. And while she decides, they will be surrounded by beauty the likes of which they will never have known before. Daedalus will see to this."

"And then I will leave this island." Daedalus's first word was quiet. Every one after that was louder; the last one was nearly a shout. He threw his head back and the silver in his close-cropped hair glinted in the light that was coming from the sky, and from Minos's hands. Chara wanted to glance at Icarus again but couldn't.

CAITLIN SWEET

The king continued to smile. His fingers twitched smoking paths into the air. "Yes," he said. "And then, after all your years of service to this royal house, you will be free to go." He lifted his own face up, as if he were straining to see all his subjects. "A year. The great sanctuary will be finished in a year—a little less, even, for King Aegeus will send the first tribute at the end of the summer, in time for the Mother's celebration. She will bless us all. Praise the Mother!" he cried, lifting his arms. "Praise Zeus!"

"Praise the Mother!" the people called back. "Praise Zeus!"

The king banged the end of his crutch on the dais. Four slaves bent to lift a handle that might have been made from a tree trunk; they drew the dais slowly toward the staircase that led to the royal apartments, as the crowd parted and thinned. Chara watched for a moment, then turned to Icarus—but he was already steps away, his arm around his father's waist, clinging or supporting; she couldn't tell which.

"Well, well," Glaucus muttered, as Icarus and Daedalus moved off into the dispersing crowd, and Pasiphae climbed the staircase with Minos limping behind her, "imagine that: Master Daedalus to earn his freedom so that fourteen other Athenians can lose theirs to the gods."

"Indeed," said Ariadne, and drew a deep, satisfied breath. "Such news we've had today! How shall we come to terms with it all? Especially the bit about our brother no longer living among us."

No, Freckles, Chara told herself. *Don't.* She unclenched her fists. She tried to hold Asterion's imagined, vanishing voice in her ears and failed.

"Well, girl," Ariadne said, smiling down at Chara, "shall we pay a visit to my dear brother, before he is taken away for good?"

Chara didn't answer. The princess didn't expect her to,

122

after all—and in any case, she wasn't sure she would have been able to speak.

"Yes!" Glaucus said. "Let's go see him!" but Ariadne waved her hand in a long, languid arc in front of his face. "No, no—not you. No one except me. And my slave." She dug her fingers into Chara's shoulder and turned her around.

The rain began to fall again, as they threaded their way across the courtyard. By the time they reached the threshold of the Great Mother's altar-room, water had darkened the stone. The antechamber was dark too, though the painted anemones glowed as Chara had seen real anemones do, when she'd gone out with Asterion on the royal ship once, at night. The soldiers stationed at the outer columns bowed their heads to the princess. The priestess sitting on the long stone bench didn't.

"Princess Ariadne," the priestess said. "What is your business here?"

Ariadne smiled her dazzling, false smile. "I will see my brother."

The priestess rose. "That would not be wise."

Ariadne took a step toward the tall wooden screen that stood in front of the inner columns. As she did, two other priestesses appeared around either end of it. They didn't bow their heads to her, either.

They're her mother's servants, Chara thought as she watched Ariadne straighten her shoulders. *Her mother's and Asterion's, not hers.*

"I will see him," Ariadne said evenly. "Now."

One of the priestesses looked very young. She held a small lamp in her left hand; her right was on the wood of the screen, digging at the double axe shapes carved in it. "Princess," she said, a little haltingly, "he's too much marked now, since that night when he wounded the king—turns into the bull for no reason—he's strong and full of anger, and then he's just a boy again, silent and strange. . . ."

"Myrrine!" The other priestesses snapped the word at the same time and the girl drew back against a pillar.

Ariadne frowned, as if she pitied Myrrine. "I thank you for this warning, but I assure you that he will do me no harm. And my mother will be pleased to hear that I have visited him in this place."

For a moment the pattering of the rain was the only sound in the antechamber. "Very well," the one by the bench said at last. "We will allow this—but only for you, Princess."

The screen scraped along the floor as Myrrine tugged at it. "Thank you," Ariadne said to her, and swept into the chamber beyond. Chara stared at her feet so that she wouldn't have to meet the priestesses' eyes, but the moment she was down the steps, she looked up.

Two priests were standing by the central pillar. They bowed their heads to their breasts and Ariadne nodded. Chara's gaze leapt away from all of them. At first all she saw was lamplight and shadow swimming over the statuettes and walls and floor. *Where . . . ?* she thought—and then she saw him.

He was crouched in one of the deep offering pools, swaying slightly; his horns caught the light and scattered it up against the ceiling, where it wavered like water. Horns— not the nubs he usually had, when he was only a boy. And yet he *was* only a boy: shoulder blades and ribs protruded from his pale skin, and his hair was a tangle of gold.

He lifted his arm. Water cascaded from his hand, which was holding a votive pitcher.

No, Chara thought, *not water*—for she smelled something sour. *Milk*. Asterion poured and poured, soaking his curls and back with the milk that was meant for the Great Mother.

"Brother."

His head swung slowly up. He stared at Ariadne with round, black eyes that didn't seem to be seeing her. She was about to speak again when his eyes rolled past her and found Chara. "Freckles?" His voice was rough and uncertain—a man's, a beast's. Chara hardly recognized it. His other hand came out of the pool, dripping and groping at air.

She ran past Ariadne and fell to her knees beside him. His slick fingers trembled in her dry ones. "Asterion," she said quietly, "it's all right; hush, now. . . ." For a moment she watched the milk branching like tiny rivers over the scars on his chest—and then Ariadne was wrapping her own hands around Chara's upper arms and wrenching her away.

"You forget yourself," the princess hissed. "You are a *slave*. How dare you presume to touch the Great Bull?"

"I don't presume," Chara said, so dizzy with anger that she could hardly hear herself. "He's my *friend*."

Ariadne slapped her across the face and Chara stumbled backward. Her cheeks and ears flamed. A strand of hair came loose from its knot and stuck between her lips.

"Out," Ariadne said as the priests stepped away from the pillar and advanced on Chara. "You stupid, stupid girl: leave this sacred place."

"No!" Asterion rasped. He lunged forward; milk and water sloshed over the pool's side. "No, no, no—you mustn't hurt her like that. . . ."

Chara managed to take three paces toward him before the priests put their hands around her arms. Ariadne walked back and forth in front of them for a moment, then stood still, blocking Chara's view of the pool.

"Very well. Look at him once more, girl. Just this once more."

She moved aside. Asterion was slumped over the pool's edge with his head on the floor. Chara tried to smile at him.

"Chara." He stretched a wet, shaking arm toward her.

"Help me—I'm so lonely. . . ."

"Lonely?" As the priests took her elbows and turned her around and led her up and out, Chara heard Ariadne's voice, fading but still too clear. "Oh, no you're not, little brother. Not yet."

———— · ————

Daedalus and his workmen left Knossos for the Goddess's mountain a week after Pasiphae and Minos's speeches. Asterion left, too, by a different road.

The riots had ended. A few people still hung about the courtyard, but their torches were fireflies, not molten streamers.

"I miss the shouting," Ariadne said to Chara as they stood on the roof, far above the two processions that were forming at the eastern and southern gates.

Chara didn't speak, afraid that if she did, Ariadne would send her away. The princess had invited her here merely to gloat, after all—and this was the only (the last?) place she would be able to see him.

"The shouting," Ariadne said with a slow smile. "The excitement. And all of that will leave with Asterion today. Now. But you already know this, my dear, do you not?"

Chara stayed silent. She watched Daedalus's long line of men wind away along the eastern road; men with axes and shovels and strange, rolling machines that sounded like thunder. She followed Ariadne's eyes, when they strayed down to the king and queen, standing so close to each other that their shoulders touched, and then back up to Icarus, who was perched two sets of horns over, staring at his father's shrinking figure. But these were fleeting images to Chara. It was the southern road that mattered.

They'd put Asterion in a palanquin: a great, lurching,

wooden thing with a latched door and no windows. Two burly slaves held the cross-bars. Two priestesses walked ahead and two behind, each of them holding scarlet and gold banners—but that was all.

Why not just have him taken away at night, if he's to leave for his secret place with so little ceremony? Chara thought—but then she saw the queen's head turning to watch this second, smaller procession. *This is for her.* Her heart began to pound. *And, though she doesn't know it, for me.*

"Mistress," she said. Ariadne didn't look at her. "Lady," Chara said, more loudly, and the princess grunted. "I do not feel well. It is the height, perhaps. . . ."

"Get down, then," Ariadne said. Her eyes were on her father, whose blazing made the sunset pale. "I do not need you here, anyway. But girl," she added, "if you are not ready to help me prepare for dinner, I will have you flogged. Do not take it into your head to go . . . wandering."

She knows, Chara thought as she slid to the ground, scraping her palms and elbows in her haste. *She wants me to go after him. And I will, even so.*

She waited in the shadow of the great cypress that grew by the south gate's pillars until the palanquin was out of sight and the crowd's eyes had all turned to Daedalus's procession. It was still coiling eastward; she could hear the creaking of the machines and the tramping of feet. The sun was slanting sharply now, turning the ground to bronze. The marks of the palanquin bearers' and priestesses' feet made a long, clear, burnished trail along this road which, Chara knew, branched into three just beyond her sight.

Go, she told herself. *Even if the princess isn't watching, she'll find a reason to punish you. Just go, so you'll be sure which way they're taking him. And don't think at all about what'll happen after that.*

The calfskin boots Ariadne insisted that she wear were

too tight and too hot, so she left them under the cypress and walked barefoot onto the southern road. At first her back and neck prickled, as if the entire palace were staring at her—but after a few moments she heard a great, distant cheer go up: no doubt the crowd watching the endless line of workmen dwindle, at last. She walked faster, through the bronze light that had begun, suddenly, to dim. *No*, she thought, *it can't already be night.* She glanced back and up and saw a mass of cloud boiling across the western sky. Pink-gold drowned in black.

She looped her skirts up around her girdle and ran.

By the time she reached the crossroads, the rain was so thick that she could barely make out any of the three branches, let alone the one that had once been dry and marked. She let her skirts fall and the cloth clung immediately to her legs. Her toes dug into mud.

"You!" she cried to the teeming air. "All you gods and goddesses who saw fit not to mark me when I was a child— please, *please* favour me now, just a little, and show me which way they took him. Please!" She spat out a sodden strand of hair and yelled something else that was just a high, broken sound, not words.

"Chara?"

She whirled, nearly tripping on the tangled skirt. Icarus was standing behind her. Rain was plastering his hair to his cheeks and neck. "I saw you from the roof," he said, his voice loud and crackly. "Which way did they take him?"

She shook her head. Cupped her elbows with her palms, as water trickled between her shoulder blades. "I don't know—but I'll find out. No matter how secret it is, I will."

He nodded and wiped the back of his hand across his forehead. They went back to Knossos together, slowly, bent against the warm, dark rain.

CHAPTER ELEVEN

"Taller," Minos said.

Ariadne smiled as Karpos's eyes narrowed. He'd been working so hard, these past few months, carving a statue of Androgeus even as Daedalus carved out the Goddess's mountain. Yet every time Karpos came close to finishing something (a torso, a leg and foot, a lock of hair, the crease of an eyelid), Minos stopped him. "There is a flaw, just there, where the middle knuckle rises," he said once, and, weeks later, "His chest is not broad enough. He is not *good* enough—start again."

This was Karpos's third attempt at a likeness of the prince, and it was finished, except for the painting. It was pale and perfect, and Ariadne knew that if she touched it, it would feel as warm and yielding as flesh.

"Yes," the king said again, more loudly, "he must be taller."

Ariadne saw Karpos's chisel shake in his lowered hand. The statue was exactly as tall as Androgeus had been.

Minos stared intently at the marble. "Also," he said, gesturing with one orange-lined hand at the walls of Daedalus's outdoor workshop, "this is the wrong place for the crafting of his likeness. He must be seen by all Knossians as he takes shape. You will move your marble blocks to the flat place just beyond Ariadne's dancing ground. Perhaps the people's gaze will inspire you to be more rigorous about your art."

Karpos opened his mouth. Ariadne wanted to clap like a delighted child at his anger and helplessness. When he glanced at her she nodded at him serenely. "My father speaks wisely," she said. His mouth snapped shut. "And I look forward to watching with my people as you honour my beloved brother."

She followed the slaves as they pulled a new, unworked block of marble over her dancing ground. Her chest felt tight, but it wasn't an unpleasant feeling—just a vast, spreading one that made her breathing shallow. "He *was* beloved, you know," she murmured to her own slave, who was walking beside her, scuffing her already dirty feet in the dust. "Especially by Asterion."

Chara didn't look up, but Ariadne was certain she saw the girl's shoulders stiffen. "Yes, Princess," she said. Her voice was so even that Ariadne's lovely, vast feeling shrank a bit.

"I imagine," the princess continued, "that Asterion would have been the most excited of all of us, to watch Androgeus's likeness taking shape. Poor Asterion. If only he were not hidden away in some deep and secret place. If only we could simply walk beneath his doorway and take his hand and lead him out with us, to see this."

Chara did look up, now. Her strange grey eyes were unblinking. "Yes, Princess," she said quietly. "If only."

Say something else, Ariadne commanded herself. *Say something that will make her cringe.* But she didn't. She leaned down a little and set her fingers to the wall, as the slaves hauled on their ropes, and the marble that would perhaps, finally, become Androgeus lurched forward. Daedalus's tiny bulls— some warm, some cool—moved beneath her fingertips.

———— · ————

"Some what?"

Chara sighed and scraped hair away from her sweat-slick

130

face. "'Some deep and secret place.' That's what she said."

Icarus scratched his knees. He and Chara were crouching between the great stone horns that faced the western entrance and the dancing ground. The moment they'd climbed up (Icarus using his ball of humming metal string, of course, and Chara following more slowly, with hands and feet and nothing else), feathers had begun to sprout all over his arms and legs.

His body wants to fly so badly, Chara had thought, as she so often did. *Why does his god taunt him like this?*

"How can we be sure the princess even knows where he is?" Chara nudged him with her bony left shoulder. His feathers had nearly disappeared beneath his skin; only their soft tops brushed her. "Don't pretend to be stupid. I'm sure her mother told her father, who told her. The entire family probably knows."

"Glaucus doesn't. I asked, and he said so. He's a terrible liar, so it's true."

Chara blew out her breath so gustily that the curls pressed against her forehead nearly stirred. "Godmarked oysters, Icarus: you're talking, but you can't stop staring at *her*!"

He set his chin on his knees and rocked from side to side. A flush seeped up his neck to his cheeks but he didn't look away from Ariadne, who was standing on the palace steps. Her arms were crossed; even from so far above, Chara could see the princess's fingers drumming as she watched Karpos shouting and motioning to the slaves who were positioning the marble. A single strand of hair stirred on the bare, bronzed swell of her breasts.

"I can't," Icarus said. "But I can talk to you while I'm doing it. So. Somewhere deep and secret."

Karpos waved the slaves away and picked up his hammer and chisel. Icarus blinked with every blow. Chara forced her own eyes to stay open. Showers of marble dust blurred in the sunlight.

"Yes," she said. "Like . . ."

"Caves."

Icarus shuffled his feet on the stone until he was facing her. His thin, pale brows arched.

"Yes." Chara stood up so quickly that her head spun and she had to lean against the carved horn beside her. "Why didn't I think of this the moment they took him away? Artemis's cave-shrine isn't far; Lysippa told me she went there once and it took her barely an hour!"

Icarus's twisted lips curled even more. "If I could actually fly, I'd be there and back in less—and I've walked there often enough, myself."

"So you know your way around, inside?"

He shrugged. "A bit. It's not a very big cave. So—when will we leave?"

"Ariadne always notices if I'm not nearby—so, tonight. She sleeps like the dead. If we're back by dawn, she'll have no idea I ever left."

"Tonight." He stood up beside her, hunched over, as always. His gaze was on the princess again.

"Icarus," Chara said, "if you're so besotted with her that you'd rather not help me, I'll—"

He held up a bony hand. "No. I want to know where they're keeping Asterion. What they're doing to him." He blinked as he turned to her. "I'm coming with you."

"Good." She touched one of his talon-tipped fingers. He flinched but didn't pull away. "Bring a lamp."

——— · ———

The cave seemed much farther away, in the dark. Chara's lamp cast a shivering, circular glow on the ground by her feet, but lit nothing beyond that. Icarus had brought another light: a cylinder that seemed to be made of shell, which shone a soft, pulsing blue. "Your father's invention, of course," she'd said to him when they met by the eastern gate, and he'd bobbed his head in a nod.

They spoke a little, at first—"It's so strange, being outside the palace at night"; "Oh? I go out at night all the time. I don't know why. Maybe I think the darkness will help me change"—but soon fell silent. Their breathing, and the scuffing of their bare feet, sounded painfully loud.

I should sing, Chara thought, *just quietly—or hum, at least. "Anemone of mine/I've left you far behind . . ."*

"We're nearly there," Icarus said at last. The moon had moved in the sky above them, but she had no idea how long they'd been walking. She recognized nothing until he held up his blue light and she saw a jagged edge of hillside. "The priestesses come just after dawn. There'll be no one to get past now—lucky for us."

"You know so much," she said, and he shrugged.

"I told you: I come out here all the time. Mostly to try to fly, by jumping off that." He gestured at the lip of the outcrop above them.

The entrance to the cave was a tall, thin cleft in the rock. In front of it was a row of three-legged bowls. Chara bent down and brushed her fingers across them. Ash and blossoms, ghostly in the blue glow, floated and settled on her skin and on the ground.

"If you come here all the time," she said, as softly as she could because her own voice felt coarse in her throat, "and you've been inside before, you *should* go first."

She saw the quick glint of his smile. "Follow me, my Lady."

The air inside was cool. Chara took a deep breath and tasted this air, and her pulse quickened. She ducked but still felt the rock plucking at her curls. It pressed against her shoulders, too—prickly, pitted, slippery with damp.

The lamp shook in her hand and orange light rippled over the lumpy earth. Somewhere far and deep, something screeched.

She stepped on Icarus's heel and they stumbled, then righted themselves. His blue glow and her orange leapt and twined around them.

"Sorry," she gasped. Her voice returned to her, over and over, as if it had plunged into the passage ahead and found a much larger space. *Asterion*, she thought, as she straightened and steadied her hand, *you're here. If it weren't for the echoes and the bat squeaks I'd be able to hear you calling me.*

She ran forward, around Icarus, into the much larger space. The ground was smooth, the ceiling invisible, the walls just shadows curving at the edges of the light. Wings blurred into a black, twisting, disappearing column above her, but she barely glanced up. She ran for the sunken altar pool. He had to be there, crouching in fresh water, ringed by tall, flat-topped stones; he had to be there, perhaps bound, waiting for a priestess to come, with food—but it was Chara instead, and he would tip his golden head back when he saw her, and his horns would throw beautiful weaving reflections onto the rock. . . .

The pool was empty. She stared down at its unruffled water and felt tears thickening in her throat.

"Chara?"

She turned to Icarus with a smile that felt mostly steady. "Let's keep looking," she said, and he nodded and blinked.

The passageway that snaked out of the chamber soon split into two. "Which way?" she said, and watched his eyes flit from one entrance to the other.

"I've n-never been this far," he said, and swallowed. "I've only ever been to the pool, never past it."

"But you told me . . . Oh, never mind. We better not get lost." She pointed at the entrance on the right. "This way. I guess."

They walked for what felt like a very long time, until his blue light washed over a writhing mass of snakes. They both fell back—but after a moment she laughed breathlessly and slipped past him to put her hand on the stone. Flat, smooth heads, motionless ribbon tongues, notched scales.

Have you eaten the Great Goddess? she thought, then frowned as her hand traced their shapes up and up and still didn't feel the end of them.

"It seems to be a wall," he said.

"It does indeed. Ah well." She drummed her fingers on a tapered point of tail and sighed. "Back we go."

This time they took the other passage, which in turn split into three. They encountered a second wall, this one a single, enormous carving of an octopus, and Chara thought, *You poor, trapped ocean thing.* As they retraced their steps yet again, she muttered to Icarus, "'Not a very big cave,' you said. Not very big." He cleared his throat but said nothing.

They found two chambers, off different corridors. One held only dripping moss and mud; the other, a row of unlit braziers and clay figurines of double axes and bulls' horns, set into natural ledges in the rock. She caught her breath, when she saw the figurines; Poseidon's objects, and so Asterion's, too. But there was no sign of him.

After another hour, or possibly more, Icarus called Chara's name, from many paces behind her. She held up her lamp. Its light was flickering wildly now, dying.

"What is it?" Her voice was pinched and small.

His chin jabbed at his chest. His own light, as strong and lovely as ever, trembled. "We're lost."

She opened her mouth to say something annoyed or cheerful, but instead she said, "I know." She sagged against the wall and listened to the words echoing in a horrible new silence. "I had no idea it would be so complicated in here! Neither did *you*—and you made me think you'd been

in here before!" More words, to fill the silence. "I thought
there'd be one passageway leading to an altar chamber. We
should have brought some thread! Tied it to the entrance—I
even heard a priest's acolyte talking about this once, when
he was telling another one not to get lost . . ." She pushed
away Icarus's hand, which he was waving about near her
shoulder, perhaps attempting to pat it. "And why are we
even *here*? Ariadne mentioned somewhere deep, but there
are other caves. Why did I think it would be this one? How
can I be sure he's even *in* a cave?"

Icarus's hand found her shoulder and squeezed it. "He's
somewhere," he said as she drew one shuddering breath
after another. "He's alive. Protected—after all, he's pretty
much a god."

The bitterness in his voice, and the sudden, convulsive
flexing of his fingers on her shoulder made Chara gasp and
thrust him away. "Icarus!" she said. "Are you *jealous* of him?"

His small, unblinking eyes glinted with a sheen of blue.
"Of course I am," he said at last, very quietly. For a moment
he stood, hunched and still. Then he moved away from her,
into the darkness.

They didn't talk any more, as they walked. Chara's lamp
went out; she shuffled just within the circle of Icarus's light,
trailing her hands along the walls as if this would steady her.
What time is it? Where are we—o gods of dirt and rock, where
are we? Dead ends and low doors; steps forward and back;
silence, until Icarus mumbled, "Finally," and Chara stepped
up beside him and felt stone snakes beneath her palms.

They moved quickly, after that—through the corridors
they'd walked before, and back into the chamber with the
altar pool, and the passageway that led gently and unerringly
back to the sky. *Grey sky, not black*, Chara thought as she
squinted at it, her hand shadowing her eyes. *Oh no.*

There was a beaten track across the hills; she saw it now,

in almost-daylight. Two priestesses passed them, as she and Icarus were running along it. She felt their eyes on her, and knew that if she turned she'd see them turning too, staring, the sheaves of wheat in their arms maybe dipping a bit.

Icarus slowed and stopped when the highest of Knossos's horns came into view. He leaned over, his fists on his knees, and spat repeatedly into the dust.

Chara saw that feathers had started to sprout on his arms and legs. *His body wants him to fly, not run*, she thought. *Of course he's jealous of Asterion.*

The horns looked black against the sky, which had lightened to blue. "She'll be furious with me," Chara gasped, angling her head so that she could see Icarus. He straightened and wiped his mouth with the back of one stubbly hand.

"She will." He smiled crookedly. "With you. She won't have noticed I was gone at all."

"Icarus," Chara began. That was all. Just his name, and her hand, briefly, on his shoulder, and the two of them walking back to the palace as the sun flooded everything with gold.

———— • ————

Phaidra was waiting for Chara and Icarus at the eastern gate. When they reached her, she tipped her pale, pretty face up to Chara and said, "You're in trouble. My sister's been looking for you since she woke up. The whole palace knows it."

Chara turned to Icarus. "Go, before she sees you. You could still—"

"Oh, she's seen you." Phaidra gestured behind her at the steps. She was gazing at Icarus. "She's been up on the third storey, watching for you. I ran, to reach you first. To warn you."

Chara heard Icarus sigh. "Another time when wings would be very useful," he said in his pebbly voice, and then Ariadne was above them, framed between the shadows of the gate's horns. She paused. Chara couldn't see her eyes.

When she reached them, she didn't speak. Her hair was full of pins whose ends jutted out at odd angles. *Because I wasn't there to put them in for her.* Chara felt a stab of something made of both pity and amusement, and her stomach twisted.

Icarus bobbed on the balls of his feet. Phaidra looked from him to Ariadne, her mouth a little open. Chara wanted to lift a hand and pat at her own hair, which she knew was even more matted than usual, and probably smelled of damp moss, but she kept her arms at her side.

"Come," the princess said at last. The word was flat and quiet.

They followed her into the palace, as people glanced and whispered, and down to a small storeroom that held only a low table, a chest and a glowing brazier. The room seemed even smaller when they were all standing in it.

Ariadne leaned against one of the doorway's columns. "Where have you been?"

I could lie, Chara thought, and felt even more sick. *I should.* "Looking for Asterion," she said. Beside her, Icarus stiffened.

Ariadne's mouth sagged open for a moment before she snapped it shut. She pushed away from the column as gracefully as if she had been dancing.

"Looking for Asterion," the princess said. The spaces between her words seemed to echo more loudly than the words did.

"Indeed, yes," said Chara, as Icarus hunched forward and pressed his pointy chin to his chest. "I could repeat myself, if you wish."

She could no longer feel the sickness in her belly because her chest was burning. She imagined her breath emerging as hot and bright as Minos's; imagined it falling on her skin and searing bright pink welts like Asterion's into it. Then she thought, *No, Freckles: you're not godmarked—just foolish.*

Ariadne paced to the doorway. "Icarus—" she began, turning.

Chara said, "I made him come with me. He said no at first, but I begged him to." She glanced at him. He cocked his head and met her gaze. His thin lips parted and pressed together again.

"Well, then, girl: only you will be punished." Ariadne walked back to them. She ran a finger along Icarus's cheekbone and down to his jaw. Even though she wasn't touching him, Chara felt his shiver; it stirred the air between them like a wave beneath water.

"Only you," the princess repeated. She withdrew her hand from Icarus's chin and leaned down a bit to set it lightly on Chara's tangle of hair. "Shall I shall throw you out of the palace? Is that what I should do?"

"No, Daughter." Pasiphae drifted in from the corridor.

Like smoke, Chara thought, clenching her fists. *Like a dolphin skimming just under the surface of the sea. How does she do it?*

Ariadne's hand lifted from Chara's hair. The princess smiled, and her face looked as beautiful and cold and still as the funeral mask from the mainland that Chara had seen once, among Daedalus's things.

"She is Pherenike's daughter," the queen continued. "I valued Pherenike. And I promised her, as she lay dying, that I would see to the wellbeing of her child."

Chara stared up into Pasiphae's face; watched her lips forming Pherenike's name. *Mother*, Chara thought, as she hadn't in so long—and that last image returned to her:

Pherenike tossing fitfully on a dirty blanket, pouring sweat and blood as Chara tried to hold her.

Pasiphae took Chara's chin in her hand, so gently that Chara almost didn't feel it. "And she is young. You, Ariadne, will teach her the obedience she will require, if she is to continue to live among us." She gazed down at Chara. "Do you wish this, child? To continue living among us?"

Chara swallowed. She nodded and couldn't look away from the queen's green eyes, though the fire in her had gone and she wanted to. "Yes," she whispered. "It's just . . . it is that I miss the prince. That is the only reason I was disobedient."

Pasiphae's smile was as warm as her daughter's was cold. "Your affection for my son does you credit. But he is beyond you now—beyond all of us. And you belong to the Princess Ariadne. You neglected to serve her, in your pursuit of a god who must not be found." She let go of Chara's chin and her smile vanished. She said sharply, to Ariadne, "Very well, then. Punish her as you see fit—only do not hurt her too badly."

"But," Chara began—and that was all, because Pasiphae was already drifting away, and Ariadne was opening the chest and leaning over to lift something out of it. A slender branch, Chara saw when Ariadne turned to face her.

"I shall enjoy this," she said, and stepped toward Chara.

Her voice is trembling, Chara thought, but she knew better than to hope.

Icarus made a gasping noise. "No," he whispered. "Ari, do not—"

The princess snapped the switch. The sound of it leapt from wall to floor to ceiling to the chattering space in Chara's head.

"Bird-boy." No trembling, now. "If you protest—if you try to go or stop me—I will have the captain of the king's guard beat you. In front of the statue of Androgeus." She

140

waved the switch in lazy arcs and it whined.

Chara watched Icarus press his chin into his shoulder. *He'd put his face under a wing if he could*, she thought, and longed not to care about this.

Ariadne pulled Chara's bodice up and off with one hand (it was too loose, as all her bodices were). "Over there." The princess jerked her badly coiffed head at the low table in the corner.

A three-legged bowl stood on the table. Chara looked at it, imagined it falling, as the princess thrust her onto the cool, smooth stone. She imagined herself twisting away, running from Ariadne and Knossos.

No, she thought as the princess did thrust her onto the cool, smooth stone. The bowl didn't fall. *I can't. I'll lose him, too, if I do.*

For what seemed like a very long time, nothing happened. Chara squinted up, saw Ariadne's raised hand, and her face. Her eyes were wide, as if she were afraid or trying not to cry—but just as Chara was thinking how impossible either of those would be, the princess blinked and scowled. The switch came down on Chara's back. The sting was so deep that the numbness that came after it did nothing to take away the pain.

"Promise me"—*lash*—"that you will serve me truly. That you"—*lash*—"will not try to leave me, for whatever reason."

Chara moved her head and felt the dampness of her own saliva against her cheek. *Ariadne is the way to Asterion. Ariadne is the way.*

"I promise."

Another lash. Chara squeezed her eyes on tears.

"What did you say?"

Chara drew a shuddering breath. "I promise," she said again, louder. She tensed her shoulders and back, waiting for the next blow. She strained to hear the whistle of the descending switch.

All she heard was Icarus. He keened and keened; through a blur of tears and sweat, she saw him rocking back and forth, his hands waving as if he were trying to swim.

He came to her later, as she was lying face down on her pallet. She knew he was there because he was sniffling, and his talons scratched her when he laid them on her shoulder. "Chara," he whispered. She rolled her head so that she could see him. Otherwise she was motionless. Her bare back throbbed whenever she breathed, wherever the cool night air touched it.

"I'm sorry. . . ."

She shrugged one shoulder and felt her skin crack. "No need for both of us to suffer."

"But," he said in a rush, "I will, a bit: she's sending me away. To the Goddess's mountain."

Chara stared at him with one eye. His edges were wavering. *Maybe he's a fish, not a bird*, she thought. *Maybe that's been the problem all along.*

"That's not so bad," she said. "You'll get to see the labyrinth. And your father."

"But I'll miss it here. I'll miss . . ." He twitched and bit his lip. Chara gave a low, raspy laugh and he leaned down, so close that she could feel his breath on her cheek.

"Be good with her," he said. "If she imagines she controls you, she won't think to distrust you."

Chara was so tired that she didn't have the strength to say, "I know." She only thought it, as he rolled his shoulders back and rose and slipped away.

Later still, the princess bent down beside Chara's pallet. Her teeth glinted as she smiled. "One more time," she murmured. "Will you serve me truly, from now on?"

Chara licked her lips, which were cracked and tasted of

blood. *I'll be the most biddable slave ever known to sky, earth or sea. Until you lead me back to Asterion, I will.*

"Yes," she said, and closed her eyes.

— BOOK —

TWO

CHAPTER TWELVE

Ariadne loved to watch Karpos work. Sometimes others watched with her, and other times, especially rainy ones, she was almost alone. He hardly ever looked at her, but she was certain he knew she was there. She watched the sweat run in gleaming rivulets down his back and belly; she watched him walk around the great block of marble, staring at it as if it were a door to the Underworld, with Androgeus waiting on its threshold. And Androgeus appeared, chisel-stroke by chisel-stroke. Minos said nothing more about mistakes when he visited the site, and so his son grew steadily clearer and brighter.

"Gods, how beautiful he is," Diantha said one day in spring.

"Karpos or my dead brother?" Ariadne laughed as Diantha scowled.

"Your brother," she grumbled. "You know perfectly well that Karpos and I aren't lovers anymore."

Ariadne squinted at Karpos, who was squatting on a scaffold, brushing his hands over the stone that was becoming Androgeus's shoulder. "I don't remember: why is that?" she said.

Diantha flushed. "He found me appealing but not alluring." She cleared her throat. "That's what he told me, anyway. I don't think he enjoys girls at all."

"Well, that doesn't mean he's not beautiful," Ariadne said. "You have to admit, Yantha—he's the handsomest man at the palace. You were a lucky girl, while you had him."

Diantha spun on her heel and walked up the stairs into the courtyard. Ariadne stretched her arms above her head, her fingers clasped and straining into the warm, sweet wind.

One day when she arrived at the dancing ground, there was such a crowd that she could see only Androgeus's chest and head. She picked her way along one of the spiral pathways, and people stepped back to make room for her. One of Daedalus's workmen was standing with Karpos at the foot of the scaffolding.

"What is this?" she said, loudly enough that most of the crowd would be able to hear her.

They both turned to her. "My Lady," the workman said, a little breathlessly. He was sweating, but not nearly as prettily as Karpos was. "I've come from the Goddess's mountain. I'm here for two weeks or so—I injured my back digging, and Daedalus sent me back to heal. I'm just telling Karpos here—well, everyone here, I suppose—about our work."

"And what, precisely, are you telling him?"

The man wiped his hand across his brow. His eyes leapt and darted, lighting on everything but her. "Well, Princess, about how it's . . . well, it's amazing, is what it is. The caverns inside, and the carvings—the staircases that go down into the belly of the earth and up to where the sky would be, if the mountain opened up . . ." He cleared his throat. "But that's about all I can say. Daedalus made us swear we'd not give too many details to anyone outside."

Ariadne smiled—at Karpos, not at the shifty-eyed workman. "That is as it should be. It is a sacred place, and its mysteries should be secret." *And this sacred place was my idea*, she thought, turning her eyes back to the man. I *should be seeing the carvings and staircases, not you.*

"Yes, Princess," he said. "That's just what Daedalus says—and it's why he won't let any of us see how all the parts fit together. We each have our own place to work in, and he leads us in blindfolded. No one knows the whole plan except the Master and his son." He cleared his throat again. Ariadne wriggled her fingers to keep from scrabbling at his throat. *His son. Marksblood, why did I send Icarus there, to see these things I can't?*

"And now," the workman went on, almost stuttering in his haste, "if you'll excuse me, I'd like to speak to Karpos and his apprentices about this likeness of your royal brother—for we've all heard of it, at our camp, and my fellows wanted me to bring back reports of it."

"But of course." She laid her hand lightly on a fold of the statue's loincloth and felt it crinkle—soft, cool cloth that looked like stone. "We're so very proud of our Karpos, and grateful for the honour his godmark does our family."

"I see what you've done," she heard the workman say to Karpos, as she turned away. "Just here, and here, where the veins run deep within the block—gods, this must be rough going! You're nearly done now, though. . . ."

But Karpos wasn't. It was Androgeus's face that slowed him. He knelt on the scaffold, his hands held up and dribbling silver godlight onto the marble. Ariadne began to watch him at night because the light was so beautiful then, turning the dark shapes around it to water. Karpos's skin, the statue's skin, the space between—all bathed in rippling silver. Sometimes she danced while he worked, or tried to. She spun slowly, lifting her arms into air that was now heavy with early-summer rain. She looked up at him and rejoiced in his stillness. He hardly ever raised his chisel, during those days and nights. He stared and stared, lifted his hands and lowered them again; once he slammed his fist against the scaffold's wood with a crack that made Ariadne's heart race.

He'll never be done, she thought. *My father will punish him*—and her heart raced even faster.

"You enjoy watching me, Princess," he called one night. She was bent over, weaving her arms so that their shadows looked like seaweed caught in a current. His voice startled her upright.

"I do." She tossed coils of hair over her shoulder and stepped into the circle of light that was spilling down from his fingers.

"Somewhat as Icarus enjoyed watching *you*, when he was here at Knossos."

She laughed. The sound seemed to echo in the darkness. "I'd have you flogged, if you didn't amuse me so much."

"If you had me flogged, who would finish *this*?"

"Perhaps my father should find someone else, anyway. You don't seem up to the task, for all the godfire that's leaking out of you."

He leaned on the scaffold's railing. His clasped hands still dribbled silver. "Oh, I'll finish it," he said evenly. "My god will show me how."

"You'd best hope so," she said, and walked away from him before he could say some other calm, infuriating thing.

The next morning he was still on the platform. "His apprentice-boys say he never went to bed," whispered Phaidra as Ariadne joined her on the usual step. Ariadne said nothing. She watched Karpos's hands slide over Androgeus's jawline and up to his brows; she watched Karpos bend for the chisel and hammer and set them to the marble. Dust fell in waves. Every time the hammer hit the chisel's haft, she flinched.

"Mistress," Chara murmured once, from the step below Ariadne, "shall I fetch you some water?"

The princess didn't look at her slave. The girl had been extremely attentive since she'd been beaten nearly a year ago. This attentiveness unsettled Ariadne, though it should have pleased her. She waved a hand dismissively in Chara's direction and said nothing.

An hour later, Androgeus's eyes stared at her through a shimmer of dust and heat.

King Minos was summoned. He strode past Ariadne—as he always seemed to do, now, though she had no idea why—and stood at Androgeus's feet. Karpos swung himself to the ground. For a time no one spoke or moved. At last Minos lifted a fire-veined hand to Androgeus's, which was cupped and empty, and touched its fingertips. As he did, a bird fluttered down toward him. It hovered, its iridescent green and blue wings flashing, and then it landed in Androgeus's palm. One of the fingers twitched. Androgeus's eyes blinked once, slowly. Ariadne heard Minos's gasp, even though the whole of her dancing place lay between them.

"Master Karpos." The king's deep voice trembled. He stroked the bird's tiny scarlet head and it puffed out its chest. "The god has sent this creature to show us: this likeness *is* my son. He is complete."

Karpos shifted his bare feet and marble dust turned them white. "My King," he said, "there is still the paint to apply—I was hoping you would advise me as to—"

"No. He is complete; he himself has stirred and shown us so."

"My King," Karpos said, "forgive me, but it was my godmark that made him stir."

Minos's head swivelled around to face him.

Ariadne saw a spark float from between his lips; she thought, with a shiver that might have been dread or excitement, *His fire never seems to leave him anymore. Perhaps he is going mark-mad, just as Deucalion said.*

"Master Karpos. The gods have spoken, as have I. Your work is done."

Karpos nodded. "Very well, sire. I shall just . . ." He stopped speaking and turned toward the road, and a sound of swift, running footsteps. The rest of them turned, too: the king, and Ariadne and Phaidra, and the knots of people who had begun to gather. The runner crested the rise that hid much of the road from view. He was little more than a boy, lanky and smooth-cheeked.

"Minos King!" he gasped, doubling over and straightening quickly with a hand to his side. "I bear . . . tidings . . . Master Daedalus has completed . . . the Great Goddess's sanctuary!"

The bird shook its wings, in the sudden stillness. It sang four pure, climbing notes and then it climbed too, up into the wide blue of the sky. Minos watched it until it was gone.

"A year," he said, running his finger around the knob of Androgeus's knee. "A year to remake my son; a year to remake a mountain." He smiled an orange-tinted smile. The young messenger swallowed and took a step backward. "And the first young Athenians will be on their way to us before this week is out." The king tipped his head back and closed his eyes. He gave a guttural roar, and the messenger fell back even farther to escape the sparks that cascaded from the king's mouth.

"Excellent," Minos said as the sparks faded to cinders on the earth. He turned and looked steadily at Ariadne, and suddenly she felt as light and lovely as the bird. "We leave for the summer palace tomorrow."

———— · ————

Ariadne imagined the Athenians' arrival, as the palanquins jolted toward Amnisos. *Rain*, she thought. *It will rain, and the ship will be hidden by fog and the young people's dull clothing will make them invisible: grey against grey. In any case, their audience will be inside. It will be a damp, dark, unremarkable arrival.*

But it wasn't.

"Look at what the gods have given us!" said Minos that day, sweeping his arm out toward the sea, the sky, the perfect horizon between that curved away forever. Even in the brilliant sunshine Ariadne could see the light that pulsed from his fingertips to his shoulders. "They have made the way clear for their sacrifices. And look—look there!"

"A ship!" cried Phaidra. She took three steps toward the cliff's edge and Pasiphae pulled her gently back.

Oh, gods, thought Ariadne, *you gave her your mark. There's no justice at all.* She dug her linen boot's heel into the grass and flower scent wafted up to her. When she raised her head, her slave was gazing at her—inquiringly, perhaps, but maybe also a little impudently? Cleverly? Ariadne scowled and looked back at the water.

The harbour was far below, but the cheering reached them in waves that grew louder as the ship drew closer. It was very different from a Cretan ship: it was much longer and sat lower in the water, and its wood was all black with a single scarlet line painted on it in from bow to stern. Its square white sail was full of wind—precisely the right wind, it seemed, for the oars didn't come out until the ship was nearly at the harbour mouth. Ariadne watched it slip into Amnisos's mirror-water, and then she stared at her feet. Even though the cheering was like thunder now, she heard the captain's shout and the heavy splash of the anchor.

"Silence!" cried Pasiphae—and silence did fall somehow, along the cliffside, down the snaking staircase, over the crescent of beach. Ariadne lifted her gaze and saw the priestesses' altar-boat sliding toward the Athenian ship. The boat was much smaller, and yet so bright that it looked immense. The seahorse prow reared and twisted—the work of a man with a godmark like Karpos's, who'd lived a hundred years ago. The seahorse glowed as well, staining the altar behind and the water beneath to a green like firelit emerald. The priestess had one hand on its ridged neck and the other on an altar-horn; she stood straight and still, even though both creature and sea were moving.

"I see them!" Glaucus murmured. His breath was warm on Ariadne's cheek and she bent her head to escape it. "Coming to the ship's side: six—no, seven—all youths. . . . Where are the maidens?"

Ariadne snorted. "Don't be too hopeful, Glau: I doubt you'll have any more luck with a sacrificial Athenian maid than you've had with that olive farmer's daughter— or indeed with any of those palace slaves you're always pursuing."

"Ari." She didn't shy away from Deucalion's breath on her other cheek. "Be nice. Just for once."

She glanced at him. His beard was nearly as thick and dark as Minos's, and his smile was nearly as gleaming, though it was much, much kinder.

"Why must you always defend me before I can defend myself?" Glaucus hissed. "Oh," he continued, in a very different voice, "*there* they are."

They'll be ugly, Ariadne had also thought, when she imagined the Athenians' arrival. *The girls, especially. King Aegeus will choose the plainest, plumpest ones he can find, so that he can give silent insult to our land and goddess.* But even from this distance she could see that these were girls with long, straight hair in shades of honey-gold and ebony and even red; girls whose white shifts clung to their slender limbs and the gentle curves of their breasts and hips.

"You're right," Glaucus said. "I'll have no luck with them, even if they *are* about to die."

And the youths are fine, themselves, Ariadne thought, squinting beneath her hand at the seven young men. Such crisp, clean tunics (for Athenians, it was said, considered loincloths immodest), and all of them were tall except one, whose shoulders, at least, were broad.

It took a long time for the priestess to ferry them all to shore. Their wrists were bound with silver cord, so they had to be lifted over the side of the Athenian ship and into the waiting altar-boat. Four of them crossed at a time. Ariadne expected that some of the observers would drift away, but they didn't: they remained, murmuring as the Athenians were set on the black pebbles of the beach, and quiet in between, when the only sound was the seahorse's snuffling and the surging of water as it drew the boat forward.

When all of them were across, the priestess led them through the crowd and up the cliff stairs. A child screeched, and then a gull. Ariadne stepped to the cliff's edge and peered down. She saw heads, bent in concentration, and feet lifting and falling—and a girl with long, straight, red hair, spinning on her narrow step and lunging toward the open air. Even as the people below stirred and gasped, the priestess leapt, too. She landed on the girl's step just as her bare feet were about to leave the stone. The priestess grasped the girl's shift in both hands and pulled her sharply back. They fell together, their shoulders knocking hard against the cliff.

"She's got spirit," Glaucus said.

Ariadne snorted again. "Anyone who's afraid of dying should."

The cheering began again and didn't stop, not even when all fourteen were standing before the king and queen. This time Pasiphae didn't call for silence. She smiled at the priestess, and she smiled at the Athenians. (The red-headed girl was crying two perfect, soundless rivulets of tears.) Ariadne couldn't remember the last time she'd seen her mother so happy.

"I bid you welcome," the queen said in a voice so low it cut through all the other noise. "I and the Great Goddess who is mother to us all. We honour the journey you have just made and the one that awaits you."

One of the young men was very handsome. He lifted his head, as Ariadne looked at him, and he looked back at her from beneath his tousled brown hair. His eyes were a blue she'd never seen anywhere but the sky. She took her lower lip gently between her teeth and smiled at him. His own full lips were slightly parted; she imagined him breathless from the climb, and his nearness to her.

"Come," Minos said. Ariadne saw some of Athenians gazing at the smoke that came from his mouth and the flame that coursed beneath his skin and fingernails. She saw their sweat and snot, their clenched fists, their shoulders, either rounded or thrust pitifully back. *Thank you, Androgeus*, she thought.

She managed to slip up beside the king, when he turned to lead them all back to the summer palace. He gestured to the soldiers who lined the road, and held up his arms to watch the coursing of his own fiery blood. He didn't notice her.

"Father."

He blinked. "Ariadne." He spoke the word thickly, as if it belonged to another language.

She laughed lightly. "What—no longer 'Little Queen', am I?"

He blinked again and frowned at her. Red light ran along the furrows in his brow like incandescent threads. "Little Queen?" he repeated. "Little Queen . . . ?"

A long, cold shiver slid up Ariadne's back. *Father*, she thought, *what is* wrong *with you?* "So," she said lightly, "when will we be taking these Athenian wretches to the mountain?"

He smiled into the air above her head. "The gods know," he said. She waited, but he said nothing more.

"And Daedalus and Icarus. Asterion—when will you

move him from Apollo's cave to the other?"

Minos tipped his head back. He closed his eyes and swerved into Ariadne and laughed as he stumbled and righted himself. She pressed her arm, which ached where his own hot skin had touched it.

"The gods know all," he said, his eyes open again and fixed on the gauze of cloud that hung above the palace walls. "They speak to me, and I to them."

"Speak to *me*!" Ariadne cried. "Please, Father: you haven't even looked at me in days!"—but he was striding ahead, so quickly that she faltered.

"Not doing your bidding any more, is he?" Glaucus said—and then he was past her; they all were, Cretans and Athenians alike, and Ariadne stood alone, breathing smoke and strange, hot tears.

CHAPTER THIRTEEN

For three days the palace rang with the sounds of flutes and laughter and the singing of amphorae and goblets as they met, with wine between. It seemed like one feast that went on and on because every time Chara followed Ariadne past the courtyard, she thought she saw the same people: Pasiphae and Phaidra, Minos, the Athenians with their bound hands being fed from gold plates by novice priestesses. Ariadne didn't join them.

"They are too taken up in their own affairs to miss me," she said on the third morning, as Chara was twisting her curls into rows of tiny, delicate knots. "So I will not go to them."

She paced her chamber instead, once the knots were done. It made Chara dizzy to watch her; these quarters were much smaller than the royal rooms at Knossos.

"Why has even Icarus not sought me out, now that we are closer to him?"

"Because he and the great Daedalus are probably doing very important things, at the Goddess's mountain. Where you sent him."

"Yes, of course. And tell me,"—turning, smiling coldly—"have you managed to guess where the great Asterion has been hidden? Go ahead: speak. I won't beat you just for *guessing.*"

Chara slid her gaze to the fresco on the wall behind Ariadne. It was made of different shades of green: green for sea grass and water, dragonflies, fish with great fans for wings. Chara thought these walls were even more beautiful than the ones in Ariadne's chamber at Knossos, though Ariadne claimed that they bored her.

"No, Princess. Please do not tease me."

"You poor thing. I am sorry. And I will tell you something, so that you will not think me too unkind." She smiled and touched Chara's cheek with a fingernail. "Asterion will join us for the procession to the mountain."

The fresco blurred, for a moment—the many greens, running and spinning—and then was so abruptly clear and bright that Chara had to close her eyes.

"He will be contained, of course," Ariadne's voice said, from a distance. "In a litter. You will not be able to tussle with him in the dirt, as you used to."

"Of course." Chara's ears hummed; she could hardly hear her own words.

"It will be tantalizing to all, for no one except his guards and the queen have seen him in nearly a year."

Chara watched her own hands arranging combs and vials on the table. Straight lines; metal and glass. When she spoke again, the words were as clear as all the fresco greens.

"Even you have not seen him this year?"

The princess snorted. "Why would I have wished to? Only my mother is weak enough to miss him. My mother and you."

Chara had crept to the queen's chamber door at night, after the palanquin had borne Asterion away. One night, two, three—knowing the mother would seek out the son; hoping to follow. And yet the queen never emerged from between the two scarlet pillars of her doorway while Chara watched. *Enough*, she'd thought on the last night, as she scuttled toward deeper shadows as priestesses or guards approached. *This isn't how you'll find him.*

"Wherever he is," she said now, her eyes cast down but wide, all the same, "the gods will keep him safe."

Ariadne laughed, and Chara raised her head. The princess fanned one of her skirt's pleats before her. It looked like a small blue sail filling with wind. "They say my brother *is* a god—and he did a very poor job of keeping himself safe, not long ago."

Chara imagined retorting, *And how was he to keep himself safe when he was barely more than a baby and you set him alight?* She felt these sounds filling her mouth, but before she could blurt them or bite them back, a slave appeared in the doorway.

"Princess," he said, his hands up in the sign of the Bull. "The king summons you."

Chara saw Ariadne's eyes go bright and her hands tighten—but just for a moment. She blinked, loosened her fingers, lifted her chin.

"And why does he summon me, after all these days?"

The slave lowered his eyes. "He wishes you to dance, my Lady. For the Athenian sacrifices."

Ariadne whirled so that her back was to him. Chara watched her smile.

"Very well," she said. "After all, my royal father commands it, and my people will be expecting it. Chara— find me my dancing dress."

———— · ————

The red-haired Athenian girl cried again as Ariadne danced. The others looked quiet and composed, sitting on the benches on either side of the thrones—no more snot or clenched fists. In fact, the blue-eyed boy Chara knew had caught Ariadne's fancy smiled as a novice leaned over his bound wrists and set a piece of honeycomb on his tongue. But the red-haired girl cried and shook her head, and her piece of honeycomb flew from her mouth and stuck to the wall.

He's nearby, Chara thought later that night, twisting from her back to her side on the low bed. *I'll see him tomorrow. Tomorrow. May Poseidon's oldest fishes send me patience—or sleep, at least. . . .* But they didn't.

The morning sun was so strong that it hurt her dry, aching eyes. Ariadne insisted that she redo her hair knots several times, and Chara did, her hands steady and sure, as if they had no connection at all to her heart. By the time the knots were done and breakfast eaten (by the princess, at least), the courtyard was full of voices and music.

"Oh, child," Ariadne sighed, leaning out beyond two pillars that overlooked the crowd, "is it not a perfect day for a sacrifice?"

The Athenians were standing in two rows just inside the main gate. Chara saw them immediately—not because of the girl's red hair, but because there *was* no hair. One of the other slaves had told Chara that all of their heads would be shaved by the priestesses' razors during the night, in the privacy of a chamber far below the earth. Now all she saw of them was dark leather masks, covering them from crowns to just beneath noses. The masks were topped with bronze bull horns. Though they shone in the sunlight, they looked nothing like Asterion's.

The princess descended the steps to the courtyard so lightly that she seemed already to be dancing. Chara followed almost as quickly, but far less gracefully. Colours blurred by her: the dark blue and scarlet of the columns; the white and gold of the friezes with their black shell patterns; Ariadne's layered skirts, which were all of these colours and green, too (for it matched her eyes so well). Chara's vision swam even more once they reached the courtyard, which was awash in embroidered banners and girdles and drums with metal rims that caught the light.

Minos and Pasiphae went out onto the road first. The Athenians, in their rows, were next, flanked by priests on one side and priestesses on the other.

When Chara fell back to walk behind Ariadne, the princess said, "No, no: walk *beside* me, today." Her smile was sly and sparkling.

She smiles at me that way because she knows everything that's going to happen, Chara thought, and dread chilled her, even as her skin throbbed with heat.

The procession made its way along the eastern road, which curved slowly north and up. Chara had loved this walk the other times she'd accompanied the royal family to the Goddess's mountain shrine. Clumps of cypresses covered the slopes to the left of the road. Olive groves fell away sharply to the right in rows that were silver, then green, then silver again as the wind touched them. Beyond the olives and the parched, red ground was the flat and endless gleam of the sea.

She hardly noticed these things today. *No Asterion yet,* Chara thought. *Where is he? When will he . . . oh, stop. Stop, and see if you can guess who the red-haired girl is, now that she has no hair. . . .*

Despite the masks, the girl was easy to find. Some of the Athenians were standing straight, taking measured steps. She was weaving, stumbling sideways and back. As Chara watched, she pitched forward and fell to her knees, and a priest hauled her up by her wrist bonds.

"Wretched thing," Ariadne said. "She discredits her country and her gods." She chuckled.

Chara felt a wave of heat and nausea. "She's afraid."

The princess didn't so much as glance at her. "The others may also be afraid, but they, at least, are being dignified about it. This is a great and wonderful destiny. She is obviously not worthy of it."

She had a home, Chara thought, as dancers spun by. *She had red hair. She has a name. I wish I knew her name.*

Someone far behind them cried, "All praise to the Goddess!" and someone else with a deeper voice answered, "And the Bull-god who guides us to her mountain home!" Ariadne laughed as people cheered. Flutes and horns played a flourish of notes that echoed as another cheer went up.

"Princess," Chara said, "you have never enjoyed the people's worship of your brother. Why has this changed today?" Her tone was polite, as it always was now, but Chara felt a twinge of fear: *Too bold?*

Ariadne turned her green eyes to Chara. She arched her brows, considering. "Servant of mine," she said at last, "I have never enjoyed it when you speak to me, yet this has also changed today. Who knows when I may regain my senses? Take care."

"Mistress," Chara said, and turned her head away. The road was winding its way into a cleft between two peaks; she saw cool, shadowed walls dotted with bushes and twisted trees and bright pink spills of flowers. Even though there was already music around her, she hummed: a tune she and Asterion had made up, crouching on a beach not so far from here, watching anemones and snails in a tidal pool.

The procession left the canyon at midday, when there were no more shadows. "Halt!" the queen cried then, in a voice that soared above all the other sounds. Music and voices fell silent. The crowd fanned out past the edges of the road. Beside Chara, Ariadne gave a low laugh.

"See what is waiting here for us!" Pasiphae went on, and swept her bronze-ringed arm at the road ahead—but Chara had already seen.

The palanquin that had borne Asterion away from Knossos was standing there, on its blue-and-gold legs. No priestesses or priests stood beside it: it was alone and still, though the bull's head painted on its side was so lifelike that it might have been nodding.

"Marked blood of Zeus," Glaucus murmured, but Chara hardly heard him. Her own blood was rising, pressing against her ears and forehead from the inside.

The queen went to the palanquin and laid both hands and her brow against it before she faced her people. "My son is here." She wasn't shouting now, but her words rang. "He will journey with us. Poseidon's son will bless the Great Goddess's sacrifices."

Two of the Athenians dropped to their knees. The girl who'd had red hair swayed—but Chara was swaying too, just enough to blur the palanquin's lines and colours.

"Come, Wife!" Minos called, and held out his hand to her. "The Goddess waits for us all."

Pasiphae returned to the front of the procession. Slaves passed her—four of them, brawny and sweat-slicked. They each seized a long wooden handle. One of them grunted, and all four heaved upward. The wooden box listed, straightened, swivelled so that its front was facing the road. Palanquin and slaves lurched forward. Minos and Pasiphae followed it.

"Ah, girl." Ariadne whispered the words into Chara's ear, and Chara shrank away from them—the triumph in them, and their heat on her neck. "Is that not better? There he is. Your beloved Asterion: there he is."

Don't look at her. Don't even look at the box. Not now, when there's nothing to be done.

"Ah, girl . . . you poor, poor girl: he's so close, but you cannot get to him. . . ."

Hours passed. Chara's bare feet were red with dust and her hair clung to her neck. She tried not to look up, but had to, when people jostled her from behind. She saw priestesses tipping waterskins to the Athenians' mouths as they walked; the formerly red-haired girl choked and wrenched her head away and water spattered the dust. Pasiphae put her hand on the palanquin's side and kept it there.

She's holding his hand, Chara thought, and shook her head. So dizzy—so hot and sticky with sweat that she wished she, too, could shave all her hair off. Leave her curls in the dust, like footprints.

The sun was slanting west when the procession halted. "Gods," Ariadne said, "look at that." Chara stumbled a little as she lifted her gaze from her feet. She looked up and up some more, to where the peak met the sky. Golden clouds wreathed its sides and ragged top—but no: not clouds. Smoke. The Goddess's breath, curling lazily up as she slept, inside the mountain.

"No tree anymore," the princess whispered. "No owl . . ."

There was a double door in the stone, covering the place where the opening to the cave had been. The door was taller than all three storeys of the palace at Knossos. It was made of black metal, and its halves were closed with a gigantic lock—surely far too big for any key. But this was Daedalus's work, after all—and he stood before it, bouncing on his heels like an eager child as everyone else pointed and gasped. Icarus was beside him, hunched, poking at the ground with his boot toe.

"Bird-boy," Ariadne said. She was still many paces away from him, but Icarus's head came up anyway, as if he'd heard her. His eyes lingered on her for a moment, then darted to Chara. She smiled at him, and he at her. His eyes leapt again, this time to the palanquin. She saw him swallow and blink.

As soon as the palanquin bearers set it down, two priests and four priestesses arranged themselves around it, facing out. "I'm sorry," Ariadne said to Chara. "You were probably intending to steal over there in the middle of the night. Maybe you and he had a secret whistle, when you were children? Ah, well. That was long ago. He's probably forgotten—and in any case, you obviously won't get close."

Chara imagined herself whirling and clawing at Ariadne's cheeks and breasts and perfect, pinned-up hair. She'd never imagined anything quite so vividly—and the vividness of it was what made her squeeze her eyes shut and wrap her fists up in the folds of her infernal skirt, sucking in air like an oyster diver returned to land.

She smiled as she opened her eyes on the princess's sneer. "He hasn't forgotten," she said quietly.

"Now," Minos cried, "here, outside the Great Goddess's temple, hewn in her name by our own Master Daedalus, we shall eat!" Servants were setting braziers around the gathering; the king walked from one to the next, lighting them with his fingertips. Chara thought she could already smell the fat of the hares that were being spitted above them. "Yes, we shall eat and dance and sing, all in praise of our Mother—and tomorrow, just after dawn, we shall give her our greatest gifts: these fourteen youths of Athens, as strong and lovely as Androgeus's majestic stags."

Pasiphae stepped past her husband, into the sudden silence. "Yes," she said, in a rich, ringing voice that reminded Chara of the way she'd sounded years ago, "we praise the Mother and her sons—*our* sons, absent and present. Now dance and eat. Rejoice!" Minos blinked sparks at her, brushing them absently away from his beard.

Night fell slowly in ribbons of crimson and pink. Chara slipped away from Ariadne and her brothers and hunkered down in the shadows beyond the braziers' glow. Icarus found her there. "Chara," he said as he crouched awkwardly beside her.

"Icarus." She set her palm lightly on his finger talons, which seemed sharper than they had before. "It's good to see you."

He waved his other hand at the palanquin. "That's the same palanquin they took him away from Knossos in. He's in there again, isn't he?"

A dancer spun past them. His feet weren't touching the ground. They made silver trails in the air that lingered, thinned, vanished.

Chara said, "Yes."

"Where was he?"

"I don't know. The litter was just there on the path, when we came out of a mountain pass. But it doesn't matter anymore where he *was*."

"Have you seen him yet?"

She shook her head. They watched the priestesses arrange the sacrifices in two rows before the door—short ones at the ends, tallest ones in the middle—and then ease them to the ground, where they sat still. The girl who'd had red hair was in the middle, at the front. Her chin was touching her chest; her bull mask rose and fell a little with her breath.

"How was it here, all this time?" Chara asked, still watching the girl. She felt him shrug.

"Strange. Dusty. Amazing. But I missed home."

They were silent, as the sky deepened to starry black. At last Icarus gave a ragged sigh and murmured, "The princess..."

Chara turned, about to say, "Where?"—but Ariadne was already above them, hands on hips.

"What are you *doing*, girl?" she demanded. "Come with me. I have a tent all to myself, thank the gods—Deucalion and Glaucus are sharing one, and Phaidra's in Mother and Father's—won't that be charming for everyone. . . ." She paused and eyed Icarus, who'd lurched to his feet and was standing, swaying a little. Chara watched feathers sprout from his ankles to his knees, unfurling like tiny, downy blossoms.

"Bird-boy," Ariadne said.

"Ari," he said, and quickly, when she frowned, "Princess Ariadne." His voice was as scratchy as ever but also deeper.

She waved her hand in the space between them as if she were dispersing smoke, or an unpleasant smell. "Girl. Come with me, now."

Chara rose. Her knees and ankles ached. She rolled her eyes at Icarus, who grimaced and bobbed his head.

She undid all of the tiny knots in Ariadne's hair as firelight swam over the dark blue cloth of the tent. After she finished this, she unfolded the princess's quilted pallet. Ariadne lay down on it and rolled onto her side, away from Chara.

"Sing to me," she said.

"Princess?"

"Sing, I said. I heard you and Asterion singing together once. You have a passable voice. I wish you to use it now."

Sometimes he'd asked her to sing after a rite, when he was quiet and far away, nursing fresh burns. Chara would hold a damp sponge to the burns and croon something that was also quiet—and after a few moments he'd stir and smile at her and she'd sing nonsense verses they'd made up together.

The hermit crab's got pretty clothes
Alas, he hasn't got a nose . . .

Once, Asterion had laughed so hard that he'd made no noise at all. Once, after they'd sung a chorus about a man trying to wrestle a giant clam, the prince had fallen off the edge of the basin they were sitting on and lain on his back, squinting into the sunlight, grinning up at her.

She sat down by the tent opening and stared past the guttering braziers at the palanquin. *I'd go to you right now,* she thought, *but they'd stop me and I'd never get close again. No. I've been patient for an entire year; I can wait one more day.*

She sang, softly, gently, until she and the mountain were the only things awake.

CHAPTER FOURTEEN

The red-haired girl was lying on her side when Chara emerged from the tent in the morning. The air was thick with steam and mist, except for a clear, bright, silver path that wound from the girl's upturned mouth. Chara drew closer—past the palanquin that was still flanked by priests and priestesses—and heard what was making the path: singing, godmarked and pure. Her own voice in the darkness, the night before, had been nothing.

She picked her way around the other Athenians and stood above the red-haired girl. Her voice spun a coil of silver around Chara. She felt it against her skin, beneath it, tugging like longing or loss.

The melody stopped. "Who are you?" said the girl in her mortal voice, which was thin and trembling.

Chara shook her head to clear it of godmarked mist. "I'm . . ."

The girl rolled her head. She was looking up, though Chara couldn't see eyes: just two blank, dark holes in the bull mask.

"I'm Chara. Your godmark is beautiful. Is it Apollo's?"

"Yes." The girl's lips curved. "And it will save me, won't it, when I'm inside this mountain prison."

Her voice was stronger now, though the words sounded strange—Chara's language but not quite; edges rounded or bitten off.

"And who are you?" Chara said.

The girl hummed. Two wisps of silver puffed from her

mouth and disappeared. "The Great Goddess's breakfast, I expect." Her laugh turned into a sob.

"No," Chara said—whispering, because other Athenians were stirring, and priestesses too, "please tell me your real name—I've wanted to know ever since you tried to run away, at the cliff—I don't know why, but it seems important. Please: please tell—"

"Polymnia," the girl sang, in four gleaming, descending notes. Then she said, "I've told you. Now leave. Unless you intend to rescue me, leave."

She rolled her cheek back against the ground. Chara stared down at the smooth glint of her head, and at the livid red line where the mask had dug into it.

"Goddess protect you, Polymnia," she said at last, and whirled away so quickly that she nearly tripped on the Athenian lying beside her.

A few hours later, sunlight had burned most of the mist away—though the smoke remained, clinging to the mountain's slopes and smudging the sky. Chara was squinting at the crowd, looking for Icarus, when the king strode to the double doors.

"It is time!" he cried, and his people—rested, fed, eager— pressed in toward him. "Time to offer up the first of our gifts to the Goddess!"

Glaucus, Deucalion, and Ariadne were standing in front of Chara. She saw Glaucus lean in toward Deucalion and heard him mutter something. Deucalion growled a response. Ariadne elbowed Glaucus in the ribs and smiled at him.

Chara thought, as she had on the road, *She smiles that way because she knows everything that's going to happen*—and again she felt clammy with dread.

"Come to my side, Wife. Ariadne, Deucalion, Glaucus, Phaidra . . ."

Ariadne and her brothers and sister walked over to

Minos. Pasiphae followed them slowly, holding the long pleats of her skirt above the fuzz of grass and tiny, opening flowers. Chara was alone, now, at the front of the gathering. She glanced over her shoulder at the palanquin, then at Polymnia, who was standing with the others, her head hanging limply. No one was looking at Chara. She edged her way back and sidled over to the palanquin. Not even the priests and priestesses around it paid her any attention.

The return of Chara the invisible slave, she thought, which made her remember a verse she and Asterion had made up, about a lobster with invisible claws. She slipped even closer to the palanquin, as she was remembering this. She was an arm's length away. She could see the gleam of the paint and the grain of the naked wood, as whorled and wispy as the mist that parted before Polymnia's godmarked voice.

"Daedalus!" the king called. "Great Daedalus, come here by me!"

Chara had to watch Daedalus walk to the door. He frightened her, as he had the one time he'd spoken to her, after she'd reeled into him, trying to escape Asterion. "Careful," he'd said, "the world is hot and spinning." He'd smiled down at her and placed his large, cool hand briefly on her head, but his eyes hadn't truly seen her. His eyes were seeing things she couldn't: she knew this, as his hand dropped away.

Now he was standing utterly still beside Minos. Chara didn't think she'd ever seen him be so still before. His dark gaze was fixed and so were his feet—he didn't bob or weave or pace. His hands dangled by his sides and didn't seek out the close-cropped black and white of his hair. Something caught at Chara's vision; she turned and saw Icarus perched on a jagged boulder halfway up the mountainside. Even from so far below, she could see that *he* was looking only at Ariadne.

"The Great Daedalus made the wondrous, sacred place that lies beyond these doors," the king said. "The place that will soon welcome sacrifices and gods." Pasiphae frowned. She was holding her chin high—haughty, but also, perhaps, unsure. Ariadne's hands twitched, at her sides.

Chara inched closer to the palanquin. She'd be able to touch it soon.

"Because we who must live outside it will never see its riches, I have asked one who helped to build it to show them to us. Step forward, Amon."

Amon was just a youth—maybe fifteen, bulge-eyed, tripping his way to the king. He inclined his head awkwardly to Daedalus, who didn't seem to notice him. He inclined his head to the king, who beamed and set an orange-veined hand on his shoulder. Amon flinched. His smile trembled like water.

"Guide us with your godmark, boy. Show us the altar of the Goddess, blessed Mother of Zeus."

Amon nodded and swallowed. Chara saw Ariadne smile that thin-lipped smile that was actually a sneer. The princess's gaze was fastened on Amon, though. Everyone was gazing at him now, except for Chara and Icarus.

Just as she was reaching her hand past one of the priests to the palanquin door's handle, the air went black and silver.

Her gasp was lost in the wave of sighs and shouts that rose around her. Silver images were stitching themselves into an impossible night sky: images of corridors and staircases; pillars and friezes and urns; bridges over empty spaces of deeper darkness—and, finally, above and beneath everything else, an enormous altar stone engraved with writhing, lashing lines: snakes, carved and living.

Blessed Mother, Chara cried inside her own head, while others cried it aloud.

"Look at what Daedalus has wrought!" Minos called. The king was invisible except for his rippling, firelit outline, which seemed very far away. "See what *we* have made for these fine Athenian youths, and all those who will follow them! The most beautiful, most majestic temple in the world—and only its designer knows all its turnings and corners, all its steps and pits and scalding, steaming fissures!"

For a moment more the silver shimmered against the black. Then it died, bit by bit, from its altar heart to its furthest, curving edges. The daylight returned, and people cried out again. Chara blinked and rubbed at her eyes, as others were. She smiled a little because Ariadne was glaring at Amon—poor, godmarked boy, kneeling pale and spent on the yellow grass. Pasiphae bent and laid a hand on his neck. Chara thought that the neck was probably hot, and the hand cool and moist.

Minos was staring at Daedalus. Chara felt her insides twist with fear, looking at the king's face. He was a starving man; a starving, angry, exultant man, panting smoke and sparks.

Daedalus's right shoulder jerked convulsively and he raised his hands to his ears. His face was as twisted as Chara's insides were. His eyes swivelled toward the Athenians, but hers didn't, even though she was curious. All she wanted to do was hunker down beside Asterion in the dark.

She shuffled even closer to the palanquin and set her hand on the door.

"Amon!" Pasiphae's voice was so commanding that Chara had to glance at her. The queen's hand trailed up through Amon's black hair, as if it were a smooth, black fall of water. The youth lifted his head and Chara saw silver licking around his mouth and eyes. "My thanks to you for revealing the wonders of your godmark. There is perhaps only one other here whose gift rivals yours: my son, Prince Asterion."

Everyone turned to gaze at Chara—or so she imagined, in the endless instant before one of the priestesses hissed, "Slave! Off with you!" and thrust her away from the palanquin. She stumbled backward, keeping her balance only because Glaucus and Icarus and Asterion had so often tried to trip her up when they were children, and she'd taught herself to dance around them. She straightened, ready to glare defiantly back at anyone who glared at her— but all were looking again at Pasiphae.

"My husband the King, in his wisdom, has agreed that Asterion, Bull Prince of Poseidon, shall watch this first sacrifice—and that the Athenians shall, in seeing *him*, witness the might of the gods of this land."

The priestess who'd shooed Chara off was at the palanquin's door. She set a tiny key to a lock Chara hadn't seen, and turned it. A priest wrapped his fingers around the handle and pulled. The door swung silently open.

Legs and backs closed in front of Chara as people drew nearer each other, watching. She craned between two of them—old women, gnarled as olive trees—and saw him. He was crouching in the doorway, because there wasn't enough room for him to stand. One of his hands was in front of his eyes. Even from this far away, Chara could see the ribbons of scars, old white and new pink, on his palm and the inside of his arm. His horns seemed to be as long and curving as the ones that lined the highest roof at Knossos. He was wearing a white loincloth trimmed with gold. His chest heaved with breath.

"My son!" Pasiphae's voice broke on the words.

His hand dropped. He blinked down into the crowd, though his eyes didn't seem to be focusing on any of them. A priestess held up her hand; he didn't seem to notice it, either. But he jumped. Everyone gasped again as he landed, on all fours. He stayed that way. He raised his head, but his shoulders were rounded, his back arched, his fingers and toes digging into the earth, white-knuckled.

"Asterion, son of Poseidon!" cried Pasiphae. "Stand! Stand and see these youths from the land that murdered your brother!"

Two priestesses put their hands on him: on his back and underneath, against his chest. He straightened slowly.

Gods, Chara thought, *he's so tall!*—but of course he was; it had been a whole year. Taller, and stronger, too: the scars on his chest wound over muscle.

His eyes—bull-round, very dark—rolled a bit, then settled, not on the two rows of bald, masked Athenians, but on the king.

"Phaidra," Minos said, so quietly Chara almost couldn't hear him. "Daughter. Come and open the Goddess's door." A gout of cinders fell from his waggling fingers. His gaze didn't waver from Asterion's.

Phaidra walked to the door and set her palms against its metal. She looked tiny. Her golden hair gleamed as she leaned her forehead between her hands. Chara looked quickly at Ariadne, whose lips were pressed tightly together. The princess seemed to be studying an unremarkable piece of sky.

Phaidra's hands began to pulse with silver. She strained up onto her tiptoes and touched the enormous black lock. The godlight washed over it like Pasiphae's water, licked it like Minos's flame. Chara sucked in her breath, waiting for the massive halves to screech open—but instead, when the lock parted with a crack and a clang, a very small door sprang open beneath it. A door within the door; a door that looked like it had been made for a child to pass through.

Minos laughed. "Ah, Daedalus! Greatest and cleverest of builders! Of course our noble sacrifices must enter their place of sacrifice as supplicants. Of course." Daedalus sucked in his cheeks and said nothing, looked nowhere.

A movement caught Chara's eye: Polymnia's head, bobbing down toward the ground. She was grinding her bound wrists together savagely in her lap. Chara thought she saw blood on them, and on the golden rope. She swallowed and looked back at Asterion, who was smiling a little, as he stared at the king. She didn't recognize this smile.

"My lady wife," Minos said, "it is time. Speak of this sacrifice. Send them within."

Priestesses were walking among the Athenians—ten priestesses, twelve; where had they all come from?—and Asterion was twisting toward them, his nostrils flaring. Chara paid no attention to the queen. She watched Asterion's eyes, and Polymnia's slender shoulder jerking as a priestess put her hand on it. Chara listened to the murmuring that thrummed beneath Pasiphae's droning: prayers, whispered in Athenian ears. She saw silver threads winding their way out of Polymnia's mouth, though she couldn't hear the girl's song.

The air feels like storm. Chara shivered, deep in her belly.

Even though she wasn't listening to Pasiphae, Chara knew when the queen's voice stopped. Silence settled, just for a breath.

Then the High Priestess cried, in a clear, ringing voice that Chara *did* listen to, "Accept our gifts, Great Mother!"

A boy—the handsome one, and the closest to the open door—was first. An old priestess pulled his bull mask off while a young one cut the bonds at his ankles and wrists with a long, glinting knife. He rolled back on his heels, reeling as the light struck his eyes. He flailed his just-freed arms and his white robe flared.

Minos laughed and strode toward Asterion. People fell back, leaving room for the flames that leapt from his heels and swinging hands.

"O son of Poseidon," the king said, still laughing. "Bull-boy. It is time."

"Time?" one of the old women in front of Chara muttered. "What can our Lord King mean?"

The king was reaching his hands out, now. The Athenian youth was gaping, his narrowed eyes shifting from Minos to Asterion.

Minos stopped walking and lifted his arm. Fire spat from his fingertips and dribbled from his palms.

"You, Athenian," he said, turning his smile on the handsome one, "you, whose eyes can see now: look on this, as your fellows will after you. Look on the might and horror of this land's ocean god."

He reached toward the cloth at Asterion's waist.

No, Chara thought, as Pasiphae drew herself up, and Ariadne too—both of them smiling as Minos was, while the crowd went still. *No—not now; not again, already . . .*

Asterion stepped forward to meet the flame. Chara heard a pop and flare and hiss as the cloth kindled. She watched Asterion bow his head.

"Asterion," she said. She spoke softly, but he looked up. His eyes rolled and found her. His lips parted—on his own smile, perhaps, or her name—but the flames had him, and he was changing. He dropped to his hands and knees again. His back arched and darkened with hair, and his legs bowed and bent. "Asterion," Chara whispered. He didn't look up, this time. He snuffled and pawed at the earth with his great, gleaming hooves.

A cry rent the quiet. The Athenian youth sprang free of the hands that held him—but other hands were waiting. They seized him, pushed him toward the small, dark door.

The High Priestess raised her snake staff. The gold trim on her bodice arms flashed. "Go to the Great Goddess," she called. "Assuage her hunger." The priestesses who grasped the youth's arms shook him until he was mostly straight. They walked him to the yawning black emptiness of the doorway. His heels bobbed and scuffed, raising puffs of dirt and clots of grass that seemed to Chara to hang in the air forever.

Asterion roared. An Athenian girl screamed. (Not Polymnia, Chara saw; she was turning her masked face toward the sounds, her lips pale and pressed together.) Two dragging steps, and the youth was at the door; two more and he was stooping inside; one more and he was gone. His second cry was loud, then soft, softer, nothing.

He fell, Chara thought. *They dug a hole or a trench— something so that the Athenians couldn't turn and force their way back out, even for a moment.*

The bull snorted and snuffled as the next masks came off. Five boys, six, seven—all of whom were silent as they walked and bent and then disappeared.

The first girl cried, "I die for all our gods!" and the observers shouted with approval or protest—Chara couldn't tell and didn't care.

Beast-Asterion huffed his way closer to the girls after that first one had gone. His tail swished back and forth. Many of the onlookers raised their hands in the sign of the horns.

Polymnia was the fourth girl. When the priestesses whisked her mask off and cut her bonds, she squeezed her eyes shut and then opened them wide. She fastened them on the bull, who was close enough for her to touch, and didn't blink. Chara could see a shadow on her skull; the red of her hair, waiting just beneath her skin.

The priestesses took her arms and she didn't try to shake them away. She let them point her toward the darkness. She took a step before they urged her to. Just as she was about to pass beyond the daylight she craned over her shoulder. She smiled a broad, beautiful smile at the bull and at everyone beyond him, and her lips parted. Four notes: the ones she had sung the night before, when Chara had asked her name—except that this time they were just melody, silver and sweet. She wrenched her arms away from the priestesses and bent and took a long, last step.

Chara's eyes stung but she didn't blink or rub them. She gazed at the door until it blurred, then turned to the bull. She watched the tufty hair along his spine quiver in the hot mountain wind.

Asterion, she thought. *Look at me?*

——— . ———

Ariadne hated the heat. It lapped at her in waves, from the sun and from her father's skin. Even when the dark-haired boy had plunged them all into godmarked shadow and shown them the vision of the labyrinth, she hadn't felt cooler—maybe because her heart had been pounding blood up into her head with such force. Those images: the corridors and chasms, the bridges, the filigree sprays of crystal—more beautiful even than the whorls of her dancing ground—that seemed to burst from the earth and walls like water.

And they'll see all of it, she thought as she watched the Athenians from beneath sweat-slick eyelids. *I almost envy them.*

She turned to order her slave to fetch her some water, but Chara wasn't beside or behind her.

When one of the Athenian girls cried "I die for all our gods!" Ariadne couldn't summon the strength to laugh. When another of the girls sang four lovely, silver notes, the princess could barely curl her lips in scorn. Phaidra's demure posturing beneath the lock she'd opened made Ariadne feel mere ripples of annoyance.

Only when her mother began to walk slowly toward the bull-thing, after the last of the Athenians had disappeared into the Goddess's mountain, did she draw herself up and thrust heat and nausea away. *It's time*, she thought. *At last.*

The bull's head swivelled toward the queen when she was still a few paces away. Ariadne saw one of his brown eyes widen and roll. He huffed and nodded his huge wedge of a head and she touched it with her dripping hands. The water soaked into his hair, turning it silver-black from neck to haunches. As it traced its path down over his sides, the hair shrank back into his skin, just as Icarus's spiny feathers did when he was changing. Moments later the bull's body wrenched and thinned and fell back into the boy's.

He looks more like a man than a boy, Ariadne thought, as she had when he'd stepped out of the palanquin. *And he's handsomer than Glaucus and Deucalion, both. The gods still favour him.* She tore her eyes away as he rose, naked and scarred, and stood panting before them all: priests and priestesses, royal family and adoring crowd and . . . Chara. Ariadne narrowed her eyes at the slave, who was standing behind two wizened old women. Standing stiller than one of Karpos's statues, her face so starkly pale that her freckles stood out like fever blotches.

Pasiphae laid her hand on Asterion's heaving shoulder. "Husband," she said, "let us return my son to his secret home. Let us return, ourselves, to the summer palace, and celebrate in comfort."

"No." Minos's teeth shone. "We do not return, yet. There is one more thing that must be done." Murmurs; shiftings of feet and cloth.

At last . . . Ariadne thought again, as the queen's lips tightened.

"One more thing?" She spoke evenly, but Ariadne saw Asterion flinch as her fingers dug into his skin.

Minos waved an ash-caked hand at her, and at the low, gaping doorway. He waved his other hand and watched its arc in the air and laughed.

Daedalus was beside Ariadne. "What is he up to now, do you think?" she said innocently, and he sucked in his breath as if she'd struck him in the gut.

"Who knows?" he said in a thin, tremulous voice. "Oh, Minnow—who ever, ever knows?"

I do, Ariadne thought. She said—she was so excited that she had to say *something*—"Why do you call me that?"

Daedalus's upturned hands clutched at nothing. "You were a silver child," he said. His voice was steady now. Deeper than she'd heard it in a long, long time. "Silver and small and graceful, slipping through the heavy corridors of Knossos as if they were nothing but water. My Minnow. Ours. Then."

Ariadne wanted to look at him, but just then Pasiphae stepped toward Minos with both her hands extended. As if she knew what would come—though of course she didn't.

The king stepped around his wife and cried, "It is not enough!" Silence fell and settled. The queen twisted her green-gold skirts sharply in her hands. "Not enough that the fourteen youths of our enemies wander the great Daedalus's halls and chambers until they give themselves to the Goddess. No—they must be hunted, as all sacred prey is hunted."

Ariadne could barely breathe.

Asterion stood behind his mother, gazing at Minos with round, bull-boy eyes, his arms swinging a bit.

"Husband. What do you intend to do?"

Minos didn't even look at her. "Son of Poseidon," he said. He held out his hand to Asterion, who'd begun to walk slowly past the queen. "*You* are the hunter."

Asterion blinked and frowned like a half-wit, but he

kept walking. As he did, a voice from deep within the crowd called his name—just once, but it was enough. Asterion turned quickly and made a sound: "Fraxle" or "Freck"—something meaningless.

Chara broke through the ranks of people like a dolphin-prowed ship. She ran toward Asterion, who was smiling now, stumbling to meet her.

Poor, pining slave, Ariadne thought.

Minos took two long strides and set Asterion's hair alight.

Chara fell against the bull-boy, flailing her arms at the fire. Pasiphae was behind her, fanning with her skirts—but it was too late. He was changing. God-taken. Gone.

"For Androgeus!" Minos shouted, fastening a hand onto Asterion's lengthening, bending forearm. "For Crete and her gods!" He wrenched the bull-boy to the door. He shoved, hard.

Asterion rocked on the threshold for what seemed like forever. Long enough for Chara and Pasiphae to cry out, as one, in their separate voices. Long enough for Ariadne to raise her hands in the sign of the Bull, and laugh.

"Father!" Asterion cried, very clearly—and then the cry turned into the bellow of a beast, and he fell.

CHAPTER FIFTEEN

The mountainside sucked at Chara's knees. Her fingers sank up to their knuckles in mud, even as her eyes and throat stung; smoke still rose from patches of smouldering grass around her. She could see the grass and mud, now that a thin, smoky dawn was breaking.

Minos had sent blasts of flame from his hands and mouth and even his eyes, after Asterion had vanished into the darkness—because Pasiphae had thrown herself at him with a shriek, and all her priestesses had run toward her, followed by Minos's priests, and the crowd had surged forward and back, gabbling with wonder and fear. The fire seared hissing trails into the earth and up against the mountainside. Chara was close to the doors, but for a moment she couldn't see them: too many people, and too much pain, blazing along her palms, which had touched Asterion's hair and skin. When she'd finally reached the small door-within-the-door, it was closed, the lock back in place. She couldn't see Phaidra—and if she had, what would she have done? Grasped the princess by her slender shoulders and shaken her until a guard slit her throat?

Hours later, crawling up into the stillness of the upper slopes, Chara tasted wet ashes. The queen, thrust back by her husband's fire, had brought down rain. Chara had watched her turn her arms and face up toward it. Chara had heard her, above all the other sounds, crying out Poseidon's name and other ancient, terrifying words. The rain hadn't started gently: it had hammered and pierced, sheet after sheet of it. People had fled down the road, which was already more of a river. Chara had seen Ariadne turning her own face to the water, her mouth open and smiling, her curls flattening to long snakes that clung to her neck. She'd seen Glaucus and Deucalion leaning on each other as they stumbled down the river-path. Everyone had gone down—even, at last, Minos and Pasiphae, though they didn't go the same way as their subjects. Chara watched Minos's flames arcing and sputtering and blooming again, turning the cascades of water to orange-tinted silver. She watched king and queen wend their own path away and, after a long time, down.

Chara went up.

Go back, some part of her thought, as she fell to her knees in the muck. *Find the others. There's nothing you can do except go back.*

But she climbed. Crawled, because it was so dark and the earth was so wet. She learned quickly to pat the way ahead with her hands; while some patches of grass burned a sullen orange, many of the other hot bits were invisible. She tried to keep the horrible burning smell out of her lungs, but it was hard; she was breathless and weak.

What do you hope to find, on this mountain?

She panted and slid.

Another way in. There must *be another way in.*

Not long after that she started up from the ground, gasping, shuddering with cold. *I was asleep. Gods and goddesses and soft-shelled crabs: what is wrong with me? He's down there and I sleep?*

She stood up slowly. The air was lightening, though it was still thick with smoke—Minos's, or the mountain's, or both. She blinked at the slope above. She saw the earth and where it ended, in a long, bumpy edge that looked like Asterion's bull-spine.

"Goddess," she said aloud, "I'm nearly at the top!"

"Yes," said another voice, out of the smoke, "you are."

She turned slowly, though her heart was racing. A shadow loomed on the slope to her left—distended and warped, but she knew it, just as she knew its voice.

"Icarus," she said, and walked up to him.

He was standing with his left foot tucked behind his right knee. A wading bird, waiting for fish. She waved her hand so that the smoke between them drifted away.

"Well," she said, staring at the matted, layered mess of his hair, "at least you didn't run after the princess." She wasn't sure why these words had come out. Why she sounded angry instead of cold and lost and sad.

Icarus flexed his hands. The bird talons on the ends of his boy fingers glinted. "Asterion's my friend, too. You know that." His voice was high and quavery; he'd just changed. She glanced at his arms and saw clusters of livid red marks and two stray, tufty feathers.

She hadn't understood her anger, and now it was gone. "I know," she said. "I'm sorry. You've been looking for him, just like I have."

"No." He moved his foot from behind his knee and set it very slowly on the ground. His knobbly toes sank into mud. "I'm sorry, but I haven't been looking for him. Just thinking about him. He can't be found now."

"No." She was whispering because otherwise she'd be shouting. "He can. There has to be another way in or out—and you know this! You know what it's like in there! You were there when your father built it—so you *must* know this other way!" She cleared her throat, trying to retrieve the whisper, or at least the steadiness. "Take me to it."

"There *is* no other way, Chara. I'm sorry. I know I said that before, but I really am."

She shook her head. "There must be another way—a

fissure, a cleft—some place where the mountain's rock is thin. . . . Daedalus says that anywhere hidden must have two doors—I heard him say this once, to Ariadne!"

Icarus opened his mouth. His lips were so swollen that she couldn't see his teeth or tongue.

His beak, she thought, *his change, his godmark; the torture of it.*

"Well," he said slowly, "there *are* shafts. Made long ago, my father said. By the mountain, when it still ran with living flame."

She stepped closer to him and put her hands on his bony chest. She felt him shudder. "Take me to these things," she said quietly. "Now."

"It's no use."

"*Take me.*"

He blinked at her. His eyes were beady silver. "Very well," he said at last. "But you're not allowed to be cruel to me when you see that I'm right."

He picked his way delicately over the slanting earth as she stumbled behind him. He led her up, over and down a slope that wasn't muddy or pocked with dying fire. "As you can see," he said over his shoulder, "the king and queen didn't come this way." She snuffled out a laugh. A few moments later he stopped, and she stopped too, and raised her eyes.

The sky was so blue and bright that she had to stare back at her feet. Blue and sun—but blurred by smoke, she saw when she looked again. Up and up and up some more—because the ridge was not the top of the mountain: *this* was. This jutting, crumbling, endless cliff face, which was studded with black, gleaming necks.

"They're like pipes," Icarus said from beside her. "Made of cooled fire."

"Lava." Daedalus had used this word once, in his

courtyard workshop at Knossos. Ariadne had wanted to pretend to disdain Karpos, and Chara had trailed behind her—willingly this time, as Daedalus's workshop was so full of wonders. Lava. Daedalus had said this to Ariadne, pointing to a shard of shiny black on the ivy-thick ground.

"They're big enough for a person," Chara said now. She walked down a little dip and up again, to where the cliff bowed out above her. She knew, many paces before she got there, that the angle was impossible. She knew that the cliff would crumble into pebbles and clots of earth beneath her gouging, slipping fingers; that she'd get nowhere.

"Chara."

She could barely hear him over the roaring in her head. Two of her fingernails had broken. She watched blood seep onto the cliff she couldn't climb and then hit her head against it, hard.

"He's in there." She thought she'd whispered the words, but Icarus said, "Yes." He was beside her—suddenly, silently. He flexed his talons on the stone beside her head.

"He's in there, but you can't reach him. You must see this."

"But if I could! If I could, I could drop down . . ." Her voice cracked. She ground her forehead into the rock. *I'm here, Asterion. I'm right here.*

She lifted her head quickly. "That string you carry!" His hand went to his belt, where the metal ball hung. "You could weight one end of it, throw it up into the mouth of one of those pipes, and I could climb it—it's strong; I've seen you climb it often enough. . . ."

Icarus rolled his shoulders and stretched his arms like featherless wings. "I've thrown it to the tops of columns, yes—but those pipes are far too high."

"Try. Please, Icarus."

He took a few paces back, to where the mountain's flank

sloped sharply down. He dug his heels into the ground and pulled the string out and out until it was looped around his feet in a slippery, shining pile. He swung it above his head in widening circles as Chara slithered down behind him, out of the string's range. With a grunt he let it go, and for a moment it soared. Then it fell.

"Again," she said.

He glanced at her over his shoulder. The circles seemed wider, this time, and her breath caught in her throat—but again the string hissed back to the ground.

"Again." Her voice was quieter.

He tried, over and over. He tried until he could barely raise his arm, and the circles were small and low.

Chara swallowed a lump of tears as she walked back to the mountainside. She set her shoulder blades against the cliff and slid slowly down until she was sitting. "We could build a ladder," she said, as Icarus bowed his head. "Your father could. Before you leave."

Icarus didn't answer. She hadn't expected him to.

"If only Prince Androgeus were here," she went on after a while. "I've heard the stories. He could have whispered in a bird's ear; it could have flown with the string's end in its beak and fastened it to a pipe."

"Yes," Icarus said. "If only we had a bird that could do that." He yelled and smacked his fist against the stone. Chara watched the rock dust settle on her bare legs.

"Gods, but I envy him." He raised his small round eyes to the sky. He didn't blink, even though the sun was blinding gold. His purple, misshapen lips were cracked and dry: not human, not bird. "I said something like this before, that night when we tried to find him in Artemis's cave. It's still true. Even now, it's true."

"You . . ." Chara licked her lips and tasted ash.

"You know how it's been for me!" he cried, thrusting

himself away from the cliff. He paced—a heron, she thought again. A leggy, awkward wading bird whose wings weren't quite ready.

"I've been sprouting feathers since I was two, but Asterion—yes, Asterion gets to be a bull at four, and now he's a god. He used to try to help me—he told me I just had to find the thing that would change me forever—he was quiet and calm while I thrashed about trying to be a bird— and now he's in the mountain. He's six years younger than I am! He's got an altar. I've seen it: it's amazing. He's a bull and a boy and he's a god's son and yes, I envy him. Because look at me. I can't help. I'm useless."

Chara gave a laugh that hurt her throat. "Please, Icarus. He gets to eat some Athenians. He gets to wander around beautifully carved corridors and lounge around on a beautifully carved altar—but he's *trapped*. He's never coming out until I find a way to let him out. And that may not be for a while."

She tipped her head back and squinted up the curve of the cliff at the lava tubes. Even so, she knew he was shaking his own head in slow, jerky arcs. "For a while. Oh, Chara. I wish I could be here for this rescue attempt of yours. I do."

"Stay, then. Your father's always longed to leave, but surely you get to make your own choice."

Icarus shrugged one thin, crooked shoulder. "There is no choice. When he and my mother sail, so shall I."

"I wish you wouldn't," Chara said. "I wish . . ." *That Glaucus was walking along thwacking his stupid stick against rocks, and you were scattering rainbows from your wings. That Asterion was here with us. That we were still children.*

Icarus was craning up, too, though not at the lava tubes—at the speck of a bird, drifting in and out of cloud. "Where will you go?" she said. Speaking felt strange— echoing, vanishing, solid as the cliff.

He looked back at her and shrugged his other shoulder. "Anatolia, maybe. Or Egypt. Anywhere that isn't an island."

"Well, please tell me you won't miss *her*."

He smiled. His lips were less swollen now. "She's never been anything but cruel to me. You and Asterion always told me so, and of course I knew it myself. But I'll miss her. And you," he added.

"Though I've always been kind."

They both laughed, but only for a moment. The wind sighed across the lava pipes—four descending notes, like something red-haired Polymnia would have sung. "Chara?" Icarus said at last, and she rose, before she could think or feel, and said, "Yes. Let's go."

———— • ————

It rained for two days after the procession returned, raggedly, from the mountain. Ariadne listened to it drumming against her bedchamber's roof and watched it turning the little courtyard's earth to mud, and yet she was in neither of these places: she was in Asterion's mountain box, drifting its corridors like a restless shade, sniffing out helpless Athenians. She smiled and didn't care who saw it.

"The Queen is mad." She heard people say these words, or ones like them. "She is mark-mad and we will all drown— but the king is mad too, so maybe we will burn, when he returns to us! Gods protect us. . . ."

Ariadne smiled.

On the third day she woke to her slave's hand on her shoulder. "Princess," the slave said, in her flat, quiet voice, "your mother is standing on the gallery above the courtyard. She has ordered everyone to attend her there."

"Ordered, has she?" Ariadne said as she sat and stretched away sleep-knots. "Perhaps none of us should obey." But everyone did—even Ariadne, though she didn't stand with the rest; she stood above them, at the end of the gallery in which the queen also stood, in shadow.

"Mother," Ariadne said. When Pasiphae didn't move, Ariadne thought, *She didn't hear me because of the rain.* But the rain was slackening—sheets thinning to mist; mist scattering in a gust of wind that stirred Ariadne's hair. The people who'd been wraiths, below, were clear now. They craned up at the shadows as silence fell.

"Mother," Ariadne said again, and stepped forward. The queen still didn't turn to her. Instead she too took a step, out of the gallery's shade and into a wash of bright new sunlight. Ariadne watched arms go up to shade eyes. She heard cries of wonder. *Please,* she thought, *be crazed. Soak them again, so that I can come out behind you and reassure them as a queen should.*

Pasiphae smiled a steady, loving smile. She lifted her arms, and the jewelled snakes wrapped around them flashed gold.

"I am sorry if I frightened you," she said, in the voice she hadn't used with Ariadne since she was small and trembling, just woken from a nightmare. In the voice she'd almost always used with Asterion. "I was a mother at that mountain. A mother whose child had been taken from her forever. All of you who are mothers will understand this pain. Some of you may have felt pain like it—but mine was godmarked and fierce, and I am sorry." Her arms came down. Her hands hung, palms out, in front of her. "I was a mother, then. Now I am a daughter. Poseidon's . . . the Mother's. I am theirs, and wiser for it. They have given me peace—as has the great Daedalus."

Heads bobbed and turned, but the great Daedalus was nowhere to be seen.

And where is Icarus? Ariadne wondered. *He should be*

lurking on the roof somewhere. . . . She looked up and saw only sky and rain-darkened stone, and was briefly, stupidly sorry.

"He has told me much of the place that he made, beneath the mountain. Of the food that shall be delivered to the temple—for that is what it is. My son's temple. Men will provide for him, and so will the goddess. The flesh and blood of the sacrifices will make him even stronger. I thank Daedalus for this knowledge and for every one of his many gifts to us. We will all lament his leaving."

"So we will."

Ariadne gasped along with everyone else as Minos appeared between the pillars of the opposite gallery. No godfire rippled beneath his skin; no ashes fluttered down from his fingertips. He looked dimmer but more solid. For a moment Ariadne imagined taking his hands and burrowing in against his chest as she had when she was a child. Then she thought, *Stop remembering: think only of what is now and what's to come.*

Minos and his wife gazed at each other across the sunlit air of the courtyard. A bird trilled, somewhere very close. Water dripped. Ariadne waited for clouds to mass and flames to kindle, but there was none of that—just a man nodding slowly at a woman, who nodded slowly back.

"His ship is ready, then," Pasiphae said, as if Minos hadn't been gone for days; as if the two of them hadn't fought each other with fire and rain the day before that.

"It is," Minos replied. "And we must go there, to say farewell. All of us must do this." He smiled. "Lead us to the ship, Queen of Crete."

I don't understand them. The words circled in Ariadne's head as she watched her mother descend to the courtyard and walk across it and out, with Minos behind her and the crowd behind him.

"I'm fairly sure they're both mark-mad," Deucalion said

from beside her. Ariadne started and turned to him. He was staring down at the final few, hurrying people. "But at least they're not bringing fire and flood down on us all anymore."

She glanced past him at the stairway. Glaucus was there, of course, poised to follow his brother wherever he might go next. "Aren't you going with them?" she asked Deucalion. "To summon the wind that will bear the great Daedalus out of his long exile?"

"Yes. But you were up here, and you looked . . . I thought I'd see if you wanted company, on the way to the harbour."

"Yes," Glaucus said, "what *about* you? You going to come and say goodbye to your pet bird?"

"*Glau,*" Deucalion began, but before he could say anything else, Ariadne strode past him to the staircase. She slapped Glaucus so hard her palm tingled and scarlet bloomed across his cheek. Then she went down the stairs, quickly, her feet barely touching them.

"Ari!" Glaucus called, his voice cracking. "I was joking— I'm sorry. . . . Come back; come with us. . . ."

She walked faster.

I don't know where to go. Not to the cliff above the harbour— I'm sure of that—but where, then? Just away. Away from my brothers and my parents and all their chattering, dimwitted subjects. They'll miss me, surely—ask each other why I'm not there—but no: I won't go to wave at Daedalus's ship with them.

Her mind did nothing but chatter. Her feet took her to Daedalus's workroom.

——— · ———

An enormous crab's shell hung by a cord from the ceiling. There were things inside it—tiny levers and gears that whirred and spun and sometimes sparked. The shell glowed. When Ariadne sat down on a stool beneath it, the glow was light blue; eventually it shifted to pink; sometime after that it was a bruised purple scattered with golden specks. She watched the colours ripple on the pillars that separated the chamber from the corridor. No fire- or lamplight; just Daedalus's magic in the damp, silent dark.

Time passed. She thought that the shell's colours had been set to mimic the sky, and so it must be night. She wasn't hungry or tired. Her muscles weren't sore at all, though she held herself stiff and straight. She imagined that she was sitting on the throne at Knossos, flanked by images of scaled, beaked monsters and towering plants. She imagined priests and priestesses in lines before her, raising their hands in a new salute—one devised just for her. She would acknowledge them by bowing her own chin to her chest, just for a moment. . . .

"Princess," said a voice from the corridor, and Ariadne's head snapped up. Karpos was leaning against a pillar, his arms crossed. A lamp sat at his feet. "What are *you* doing here?"

"I . . ." She cleared the roughness from her throat and stood up. *Now* her back ached but she still didn't stoop. "I wished to think of Daedalus where he did so much of his work. Since I wasn't at the harbour to see him go."

"Weren't you? I didn't notice."

"Liar."

He shrugged and pushed off the pillar. "Now ask me why *I'm* here." She frowned and he chuckled. "You won't, will you, now that I've told you to. Though of course you're wondering."

"Hardly. You were Daedalus's apprentice—of course you wish to visit this place, too. To remember him, surrounded by his things."

"*My* things," Karpos said. He ran his hand over the spine of a sea creature that lay on one of the long tables.

He picked up a metal lizard and wound it. When he set it down, it squeaked and clanked its way in and out of the sea creature's ribs.

"Your father announced it to everyone, almost as soon as the ship was out of the harbour: I'm to have everything—the machines, the marble—everything, here and at Knossos."

Ariadne tried to shrug as casually as he had. "And so? You were his most talented apprentice. It's no surprise that my father wishes you to carry on in his place."

"Maybe not. But the king said something else. Something like: 'You, who have used your godmark to immortalize my son Androgeus, are destined to be more than just a master artisan. You may begin in the workshops, but the gods have told me that you will end in rooms far more grand than these.'" Three paces brought Karpos so close to her that she could have reached out and wrapped one of his dark curls around her finger. "You understand your father's thinking, Lady," he said, very softly. "Tell me what he meant."

She was dizzy, swaying; her head was full of whispers. "The gods spoke to him of this," she heard herself say. "Now you must wait for them to speak to you."

She fell sideways. He caught her; his hand was around her arm, and it was hot, which was strange—surely godmarked silver felt cool? "Princess," he said in a thick, far-off voice, and she wrenched her arm away and stumbled from the chamber as the lizard clacked and clanked behind her.

CHAPTER SIXTEEN

One night after the ship had gone, as the court was preparing for its return to Knossos, a messenger stumbled into the receiving chamber and fell to his knees before the king. Looking at him, Ariadne remembered the one who'd brought news of Androgeus's death. Many messengers had presented themselves to the king in the years since, of course—but this one, like that other, wasn't simply breathless: he was trembling and pale.

Minos rose, sweeping his arms out as if to balance himself on the air. He smiled, as Pasiphae twisted her hands in her lap. Her earrings tinkled in the silence.

"Speak, man!" the king said. The messenger coughed and retched, then pushed himself to his feet. His bare chest shone with sweat. Ariadne moved her gaze from it to his wide belt, cinched taut against the muscles of his belly. She glanced back at his face, which was unremarkable except for its wide-eyed fear.

"My King," the messenger gasped, "I bear news from the Chanian port. The ship—"

"Which one?" Minos said, turning his head to cast an amused eye over everyone assembled in the room. "I have several."

"The ship that carried the great Daedalus," the messenger said. His chest was still heaving, but he spoke more evenly. "The great Daedalus and all the men who laboured with him beneath the Goddess's mountain. The ship was lost, and all its passengers with it—pirates, my King. . . ."

For a moment Ariadne thought that the earth was shaking—the hard, stony earth that Daedalus himself had once told her was lined with fire. It rose and fell gently and she lurched forward, nearly into Minos's back.

"Princess?" her slave said, and she grasped Ariadne's arm just as Karpos had, only days before. When Ariadne turned to her, she saw that the slave's eyes were huge and unblinking, trembling with tears that had not yet fallen.

"Don't touch me," Ariadne snapped at her, as she should have at Karpos. She thrust at Chara's hand until it was gone. The earth's movements subsided. She stepped up beside her father and tipped her head so that she could see his face.

"How are you so certain?" Minos snapped.

"There were witnesses—fishermen close to shore who saw your great ship, and the other ship that intercepted it: a pirate vessel without paint or patterned sails. Men swarmed onto the deck. There was screaming—yet no treasures were thrown from ship to ship, and soon yours, my King, was set ablaze. The fishermen could do nothing, at first, except watch men jump into the sea. As your ship sank and the other moved away, the fishermen drew their own crafts closer, to see whether anyone had survived. In the end they pulled only one from the waves."

The king's eyes narrowed and he breathed a single, coiling stream of smoke. "A survivor." His voice was tight.

"Yes," the messenger said, "but he died too, just one hour later."

Minos smiled. His teeth flickered white and scarlet.

"Father," Ariadne murmured, "stop smiling; it is not seemly. . . ."

"Poor Daedalus," he said, still smiling. "Poor Daedalus, released at last from his long exile, only to perish at the hands of pirates seeking riches that did not exist. Except, of course,

for the ones contained within his great and complex mind."
He waved a hand. Cinders settled on Ariadne's left foot.

"Master Karpos shall drape his workrooms and
creations in cloth, to honour his master's memory."

Ariadne glanced sidelong at Karpos, who was leaning
against a wall. The paint on it was crimson and blue; his
skin was grey. As she watched, he put his hands over his
face. Behind her, the slave girl made a small, pinched sound.

"Yes," the king continued, "We shall mourn Daedalus
and his wife and their blighted bird-child."

Ariadne was too hot. Because of her father's heat—yes,
that—nothing else.

———— • ————

"My Lady." Ariadne groaned as the slave's voice murmured
again, into her left ear. "Princess. One of your father's men
is here—Theron. He says you must go with him."

Ariadne rolled onto her side and blinked at the girl's
shadow. "No," she snapped. The word echoed and faded in
the darkness.

"Yes, Princess," Chara said quietly. "Theron says that the
king demands it."

"Is that so?" Ariadne slid her legs off the bed and rose.
"Theron!" she called into the corridor. "Come here to me."

"But Princess," the slave hissed, "you are not dressed—
you should not—"

Ariadne waved her to silence. "Theron!" she called again.

A man stepped beneath the door lintel. His torch flame
guttered in a wind gentle enough to be Glaucus's.

Her pulse was suddenly racing. She held up her arms and
Chara drew a jacket along them and fastened it at her waist
and across her breasts. Theron's eyes roved across her skin. He
was as old as her father, and his cheeks were pitted with scars.

As ugly as the surface of the moon that Daedalus showed me once, through his long-glass, she thought. *I should have this wretch punished for staring at me*—and yet she smiled a little, as she slipped her legs slowly into her skirt.

"So," she said, "my father requires my presence."

Theron nodded slowly. "He does, my Lady." His voice was low and rough. He smiled back at her, just a little.

"Enough," Ariadne said to the slave, who was fiddling with her girdle, "I am ready."

At Knossos it would have taken half the night to get from the royal apartments to the underground storerooms, but here it was a matter of two short staircases and one long one. As she followed the wavering torchlight, she imagined Asterion here, casting his distended bull-shadow on the jars and the damp stone walls.

He must have felt the ceiling pressing down on him, in that first cave, she thought. *He must have thought it a prison. Maybe he's remembering it now, inside the mountain, and wondering at his own foolishness.*

Theron led her past a row of doorways, to three storage jars. They were twice as tall as he was, and bulbously round in the middle. A dark red-painted octopus writhed up one; a school of green flying fish leapt up the other two.

Theron knelt and traced his finger along a seam between two flagstones. "What you are about to see is secret, Lady. Your father the king will tell you: you must not speak of it. I have sworn a blood oath that I will not."

"Indeed," she said, her voice steady though her heartbeat, suddenly, was not. "And how can a row of jars and a wall be secret?"

He glanced up over his shoulder at her. The lamplight pooled in his scars. "Princess. Have you no faith in your father?" He smiled his small, insolent smile again, and bent back to the floor. She heard his fingertip dragging. His breathing was raspy, breathy, like an old man's. "Where are you, now," he muttered, and leaned forward until his head had nearly disappeared between two of the jars. "Ha!" he cried, and flicked his hand upward with a flourish. Ariadne saw a glint of metal—something protruding from the floor—and then gears ground, deep within the wall, and stone dragged against stone.

The wall opened.

Ariadne picked up the lamp and crouched behind Theron. Even in the light, she could see nothing but black, empty space. "Ah," she said. "So this secret is the work of the great Daedalus. May the gods grant him the peace he deserves."

The man laughed harshly. "May they indeed, Lady," he said. "Now, then. After you."

She drew breath to order him in first, but something in his narrowed, glittering eyes made her press her lips together instead. She crouched and moved past him. The edges of the opening tugged at her hair, and a dank, cool wind raised gooseflesh on her arms. She felt the stone beneath her become dirt, and tried not to recoil.

"Come on, Princess," Theron said. He was far too close to her, but she didn't command him to step back. "Can't keep your father waiting."

Once beneath the wall, she eased herself up until she was standing. He emerged beside her. The lamp's glow fell on walls that looked crumpled—unworked rock, not stone—and a ceiling strung with roots.

Ariadne plucked her calfskin boots out of the dirt, one after the other. *Don't stand still. Turn around—get back to the opening.* "No," she said, "I will not walk here. Take me to my father by another way."

"This is the only way, Lady. I am sorry for your discomfort." But he wasn't; he was leering at her in the part-light, leaning close.

She held her skirt as far above the dirt as she could without pulling it over her head. "Very well. Quickly, then, at least."

The passage twisted and rose and dipped and rose again, endlessly. *It must be as long as the road between Knossos and Amnisos,* she thought. Sometimes she had to rush to catch up to Theron and his bobbing light; once she stumbled over a root and into his back and he steadied her with damp, lingering hands.

"Tired?" he murmured. His breath stank of old wine. "Care to rest?"

Enough of this, she thought. She wrenched herself away and pushed him forward with a grunt.

"My father," she panted. "The king. Remember?" His laughter echoed around her as he led her onward.

This will never end. I'll starve, in here—and imagine that: even Asterion gets food, in his box! And then there's Theron. I'll have to kill him somehow. A rock? Yes: a knee to the groin and a rock to the back of the head when he goes down. . . . Maybe my father never did ask to see me. Maybe this was all Theron's doing from the start. Maybe I should just curl up now and—

"Here we are, Princess. Well, come on then. You've been slow; kept him waiting too long."

Theron slid his hands up the rock to the mossy roof and pushed. Dirt hissed down onto Ariadne and she shook her head, stamped to get it off her shoulders. When she looked up again, all but his legs had disappeared. She watched them vanish too, into a space of darkness and stars.

"Up you come." He was leaning through the trap door, his hands extended. She saw no way except these hands, which she took as her insides roiled. He hoisted her up and into air so fresh and clean that she breathed it in in great gulps that made her cough. She stood up very tall and tipped her face to the sky.

"Go on, then," Theron said. "Over that way, to the cliff. I wait here, by his command."

She tossed her head so that the glossy snakes of her hair slithered across her back. "A shame," she said. "I believe I was beginning to fall in love with you."

His eyes were slits. His hands tightened into fists. "Careful, Princess," he said softly. "Careful, pretty girl."

"No," she said. "*You* be careful. My father would punish you if I told him of your impudence."

She walked away from him, her strides long, as if she knew where she was. A wide swath of grass with jagged hills behind and a lip of cliff ahead. The sea below, stained with moonlight. She knew much of the land around the summer palace, but not this.

Minos was standing at the cliff's edge. At first he was nothing but a fire-veined shadow against the black sky, but when she saw him her pace and pulse quickened.

"Father," she said when she was close enough to make out his real, solid shape, "what is this—what do you want with me now, here . . . ?" She had meant to sound imperious, but as her voice trailed into silence she knew she was just a little girl, waiting in the dark for a king to turn to her.

He did, slowly. His eyes were orange, rippling circles with black embers at their hearts.

"You and I made a secret plan, once." She felt each word puff against her cheeks like steam. "Together. And then, because I wanted to, I made one by myself."

She swallowed. Her throat was tight. The wind felt cool on her skin, in the spaces between his words.

"I will show you what I planned without you, because I wanted to. There," he said, pointing down. "There is where you start."

She sat with her legs over the edge. Her heels kicked against the cliff face as she craned up at him.

"Yes," the king said, his smile red. "Just there."

Icarus would have loved it up here, she thought. *With his grasping toes and his ball of humming string . . .* She turned quickly around and lowered herself down, poking at the rock with her toes. She found the first foothold almost immediately but had to stretch to find the second. They were shallow and she slipped several times, clutching the indentations with fingers she could tell were bleeding. She didn't look down until she was standing on rock, not merely clinging to it. A ledge, she saw when she inched around to face the sea. Three steps forward would take her over.

Father, she thought as her teeth chattered, *what is this?*

A rope bounced off the cliff by her left shoulder. She crept right as Minos slid down to stand beside her.

"I am not so young and spry as you," he said. "Once was. Not now. Need a rope." She heard it sizzle as he unwrapped his hands, and held her breath so that she wouldn't smell its acrid burning. "Look at us, Daughter! Look at where we stand, above the vast, dark waters of our land. A rhyme!" he cried, and laughed mad, swirling sparks into the night.

She cleared her throat so that her voice wouldn't tremble. "You did not bring me here to gaze at the sea. Please tell me what we are really doing."

"Of course," he said, abruptly solemn. "Over there. To your right. Step carefully—yes, good—one more . . . now put down your hand. Do you feel it?"

She felt metal, rough with rust. Another door, she realized as she knelt and looked. At the level of her knees, if she had been standing; tiny and rounded, with rusted bolts and a rusted lock.

Her father leaned past her and inserted a stubby key into the lock. The door screeched as he pulled it open. "Close, now," he said. He touched her cheek with his palm. She didn't flinch at the heat.

She'd had to crouch to enter the tunnel behind the jars, but here she had to crawl. She couldn't remember the last time she'd crawled. On the ground of the ring, perhaps, when she'd been a child learning to bull-dance and had fallen and needed to scrabble out of the way of the beast's churning legs? But she'd hardly ever fallen, and the ring had been smooth and cool, not dirty and prickly with stones as this place was. Minos's glow from behind her flickered off a low, curving ceiling and root-encrusted walls—much narrower than the others had been, tonight—and an opening—thank Zeus, a space not that far ahead where she could stand and stretch and brush the dirt from her legs and hands.

It was a cavern, and it soared far, far above her, glittering with crystal veins and hardened drippings of something that looked gold in the godlight. She craned up at it as Minos straightened beside her. The light grew brighter and steadier then, and she shifted her gaze back down and saw bodies on the floor.

There were three of them, lying on their sides against the cavern's far wall. Their wrist and ankle bonds had been tied together so that their backs were bowed inward. They'd been arranged in a row with their faces all pointing the same way. They looked like three empty mussel shells. Minos gestured at them with one silver-red hand.

"Go closer, Daughter. Go and see this secret that is now ours."

She walked over to them. The king's light followed her. It played over their faces: Icarus's, Daedalus's, Naucrate's. Their skin was streaked with dirt and dried black blood. Their eyes glistened as they rolled their heads to look at her.

"Ari." Ariadne hardly recognized Icarus's voice; it sounded like cloth tearing. His twisted lips twisted even more, and a bead of fresh blood welled between them. The talons at the end of his fingers scrabbled weakly at the dirt.

Ariadne turned to her father. "The pirate attack," she said. "Was there one?"

He smiled down at her. "Oh, yes. The ship went down—after my men got these three off. Just before it burned. It sank, and everyone else with it. But these three . . ." He was smiling down at them, now. "They deserved more."

Daedalus lifted his head and spat. He'd probably meant the mucus to land on the king's feet, but instead it clung to Daedalus's chin. "And now," he rasped, "you have come to give us this 'more.'"

Minos's laugher echoed off the cavern's walls and up into the emptiness above them. "I have," he said. "And my daughter, who deserves to know this secret, will be here to watch."

A sour taste surged into her mouth—fear and anticipation; disgust too, because the prisoners' own fear stank so badly. *I told you: no more blood*, she thought. *I told you to send them away. Why this?*

Minos spun on his heel and strode back toward the cavern's opening. "I thought about starting with Naucrate," he said as he picked something up from the ground there, "but I have reconsidered. I believe I will start with the great and clever Daedalus."

He walked back. His hand was wrapped around a hammer—one that Daedalus or Karpos might have used to work their colossal blocks of stone. Minos's other hand closed around Daedalus's dirty collar and hauled him up and over to a low, flat rock that Ariadne hadn't noticed until now. Daedalus choked, and his bent-back body lashed like a snake.

"Now, then," said the king, and drew a dagger from his boot. He cut the rope that attached Daedalus's wrist and ankle bonds. "Let us get you settled properly. You are an artisan, after all; arrangement and order matter to you." He pulled Daedalus's bound hands onto the rock and pinned them there, pressing down on the rope around his wrists. Ariadne stared at his upturned palms. The lines in them looked so deep, in the dancing light. His fingers jerked inward as if he wanted to make fists, but Minos adjusted his hold and flattened them out.

"Little Queen," he said. "Come and help me."

Her feet felt heavy, but she forced them to carry her across to the rock. Minos took her hand. His skin was so hot that the sick feeling burst up inside her again, but she didn't flinch.

"Kneel behind him. . . . Yes. Now press here on the rope, as I did. . . . Good. He will try to move, in a moment. Use all your strength to keep him still."

She licked her dry lips. "Yes, Father," she said.

Daedalus turned his head so that one bright eye was on her. "Ariadne," he said, in a low, rough voice. "Minnow."

"No. Don't call me that. Do not." She tightened her grip on his wrists and looked up at her father.

Minos raised the hammer and brought it down on Daedalus's right palm.

His hands flapped and a tremor went through the rest of him—Ariadne saw it bend his spine, from buttocks up to skull. He hardly moved, otherwise. He screamed, but only once. As the hammer came down on his other palm and all his fingers, one by one, he dug his chin into his chest and shuddered. Bones cracked in skin and Icarus shouted and Naucrate wailed and Ariadne sucked in her breath with every hammer strike, but Daedalus was silent.

When Minos was done he laid the hammer down and crouched in front of Daedalus. "You will never make anything again, old friend," he said, shaking his head regretfully. Red light glowed behind his teeth. Cinders drifted between them and into his beard. "Surely this will be a relief: first exile, then endless seeking for things you could never quite touch;

your art has only ever caused you pain."

Ariadne let go of Daedalus's wrists. Her hands were slick with sweat. She rubbed her fingers together and didn't look at his. Her blood pounded in her head so loudly that it almost drowned out Naucrate's sobbing.

"Little Queen," Minos said, rising, "would you agree that it is not just the great Daedalus's hands that have caused unhappiness in our palaces?"

Ariadne swallowed hard. *Speak firmly*, she thought. *Don't let them imagine that you're afraid. And think*—think *what he'll want to hear.*

"I would agree," she said firmly. "He has also *spoken* wrongly—yes; I remember the feast at which he said my noble brother Androgeus's name over and over, in defiance of your command."

Minos nodded. A blotch of flame appeared beneath his flesh, at the hinge of his jaw. She watched it wriggle up past his ear to the pouch beneath his left eye, where it stopped and pulsed, perhaps in time with his heart. "Precisely, dearest. His words have wounded us. What else, then, might we do to him?"

The knife was in his hand. His fingertips stained the haft with coursing, molten orange.

She could feel Icarus's little round bird eyes boring into her back. She could hear his talons, still scritching at dirt and pebbles. She could hear Naucrate too, whispering Daedalus's name over and over.

"We might cut . . ." Ariadne's voice cracked. *Godsblood*, she thought savagely, *if you falter now you don't deserve to rule anywhere, ever.* "We might cut out his tongue," she said, and smiled at Minos.

The king smiled back at her and thrust Daedalus onto the ground and fell to his knees beside him and pried open his jaws—which stayed open, gaping, fish-like—and with that same hand he pulled Daedalus's tongue out between his teeth and with his other hand he raised the knife and set it to the tongue and sliced.

Icarus and Naucrate had gone quiet. The only sounds were a far-off, steady dripping and the low moan that bubbled from Daedalus's weeping mouth.

"Minnow."

Naucrate spoke softly, but the cavern's rock caught the word and made it louder.

Ariadne watched Minos drop the wet, dark tongue onto the dirt. She swallowed more convulsively than she had before, and turned to look behind her.

"*You* will not call me that, either." She sounded calm and threatening at once. This surprised her.

Naucrate was holding her head up as best she could, but it was trembling, bent at an angle. Tears had made clean streaks on her skin. "Princess," she said, "I loved you. Even as I watched you grow and change and scheme, I loved you, because when I looked at you I always saw the little girl who used to bury her face in my lap and cry. The little girl who ached for her life to be different."

Her dresses always smelled like lemon, Ariadne thought, before she could stop herself. *She kept oatcakes in an alabaster jar beside the doorway that led to the workroom with all those blocks of marble and the ivy and the tiny little Knossos made of wood.* . . .

"I do not know why you expect me to feel mercy." Ariadne heard herself speaking but didn't feel it. She was very far up, where the cavern's roof became a second sky. "I do not know why you even try. After all, I am my father's daughter."

Naucrate's head sagged back onto the ground. Her eyes were wide and fixed on nothing. A long, tangled strand of hair slid across her forehead and nose. It rose and fell gently, with her breath.

Minos pointed at her. Sparks hissed and fell from his forearm. "Look here: the beautiful, brave Naucrate does know how to fear!" He went to stand above her. More sparks fell. Ariadne watched them light and linger on Naucrate's hair; she smelled burning. "You have never feared *me* enough," he said, suddenly quiet. "Even when I took you as my lover, you never trembled. I would have killed you then, except that I grew too bored with you to bother. And I am glad. For this, now, will be far more pleasing."

Naucrate's head came up again. Her lips parted and the singed strand of hair sank between them, but she didn't seem to notice. "I have always hated you," she said in a cold, flat voice Ariadne hadn't heard before, "but I have never feared you. So do this pleasing thing. Do it quickly or do it slowly. It will not matter. And remember: I hate but do not fear."

Minos made a growling noise deep in his throat. The fire that had lit him from beneath throbbed brighter and higher until it leapt from his skin and out into the air. It fell on Naucrate like a sheet of rain. Her hair, her neck, the grimy cloth stretched tight over her back: all of it kindled and glowed. She thrashed until she was on her stomach. Minos chuckled as he bent down and cut all of her bonds. Ariadne covered her nose and mouth but the stench of filth and burning was still terrible.

She remembered another thing, though she didn't want to: Naucrate bending down to her, murmuring, *But even though it crackled and smoked and made me very hot, it never hurt me.* Now it was: now Minos's fire was turning her to sizzling hair and spitting fat and a high, broken voice.

Ariadne didn't see how Naucrate rose, but she did. She wrenched herself around and up, streaming, screaming. She reached her blazing hands out to Icarus, who curled himself away from her. She reached for Daedalus, who was crouching with his hands swollen and limp behind him, his mouth still dribbling blood. He tipped toward her but she was already past him, stumbling for the hole that led out to the sky. Minos held his hands up and sent flames after her. It didn't matter: she was gone, leaving smoke and skirling sparks in her wake.

Ariadne stumbled after her.

No. What are you doing? Go back; go, and attend to your father the king. . . .

She crawled until the tunnel opened onto sky. She rose and teetered on the ledge, her arms and mouth wide, grasping at air. She peered over the edge and saw a ball of fire, falling very slowly. She heard a long, high, warbling bird cry, swelling and dying over the sea.

When she ducked back into the cavern, Minos was waiting for her. Smiling.

"What now?" Icarus's voice was scratchy and stark. "How will you break *me*, great king?"

Minos didn't turn to him. Ariadne didn't want to, but she did. Icarus was lying still, his face turned up to the king. His pale eyes were steady and unblinking.

"Poor bird-boy," the king said, still smiling at Ariadne. "He cannot fashion anything—certainly not wings that fly, despite the mark his god has given him. I shall let him stay here to keep his father company." At last he looked down at Icarus. "Perhaps you will chirp while he gabbles?"

"Ari." She'd heard Icarus sound shy and awkward and unsure before, but she'd never heard him plead. It made her feel sick in a way that the sound of Daedalus's shattering hands had not.

"Ari, please. Your father listens to you. Don't let him do this."

She crouched beside him and reached for him slowly, with her steady hands. She watched him watch her. Watched his horrible beady eyes brighten a little, on her face.

The ball of string was where it always had been: wrapped up under his belt. He flinched when she put her fingers on the cloth, and again when she drew the hook out of the end of the ball and pulled it free. She sat back on her heels and tossed it up and down as if it were a child's plaything.

"Ari—no—leave me something. . . ."

She laughed. "Oh, Icarus: why would we leave you with this, when it might help you escape this cave? No: you have no more need of it. Not ever." The ball felt light and cool in her palm. Its hum vibrated from her wrist into her chest, which unsettled her—but she didn't drop it.

Minos said, "You will find that the walls, deeper in, run with fresh water. Do not imagine you will be able to follow it out; it comes from rock and returns to rock. One of my men will come, once a month, with food and wine. Take care not to eat and drink too much."

Icarus looked away from Ariadne at last. "My King," he said, "why not kill us and be done with it?"

Minos walked toward the exit. His feet left black impressions in the dirt. "I may yet have need of you," he said over his shoulder. "And also, gods enjoy the suffering of mortals. That is simply the way of things. Daughter: cut him free."

Minos tossed a knife to the ground next to her. She picked it up and set it to the rope around Icarus's ankles. They took a while to part, but the ones around his wrists were quicker. He shifted and writhed, and she stood and tucked the knife into the hem of her open bodice. Then she threaded the ball's hook next to it.

As she ducked out after Minos, Daedalus made a sharp, agonized sound behind her, and Icarus yelled, full-throated and raw. She heard him scrabble for the tunnel; she felt the air ripple behind her as he threw himself in behind her. She crawled faster, panting. Minos's orange glow bobbed and vanished briefly, as he reached the air. Something brushed the sole of her foot; she kicked out and crawled faster yet, whimpering now. When she reached the opening Minos leaned in and pulled her and she cried out at the burning of his hands but at least she was free, and he slammed the rusted metal door home with a clang that echoed over the sound of Icarus's scream.

———·———

"You fear that I am mark-mad."

Ariadne slid her gaze to her father. They were walking side by side, back along the tunnel Theron had led her through earlier. It seemed like an age since she'd been here. Theron himself was behind them—far behind, at Minos's command. (This had made her smile, despite the sickness that lingered in her gut.) The king wasn't looking at her now. His eyes were fixed on the way ahead—so fixed that she wondered whether he were seeing anything at all.

"Your godmark is terribly strong," she said slowly, "and I worry . . . We agreed, after Asterion wounded you, that you would send Icarus and Daedalus away—yet you made this decision without me! This is not like you. So, yes: I worry."

"I may well be mad," he said briskly. "But there is no cause for you to fear this. In fact, I call you 'Little Queen' for a reason!" His voice leapt. For a moment he sounded like an excited child. "For I will make you queen before I give myself to the fire."

She stopped walking. He continued on for a few paces before he realized she was no longer beside him. He turned: dark shadow, to shadow with silver-orange teeth.

"But I have no godmark," she said hoarsely. "It would not be permitted. The priests and priestesses—the people would never accept me."

She hadn't ever spoken these words aloud before; had

barely spoken them within her own head. *The people would never accept me.* As they echoed from the rock, she shrank even farther back, more fearful than she had been in the cave.

Minos shook his head as he walked back to her. "Sweet girl—how could you think this? Priests, priestesses, people—all will heed *me*. And if they do not, I shall unleash my madness upon them." He stroked her hair with both his hands. She leaned into them.

"But Deucalion—your heir, since Androgeus . . ." she murmured.

"No. He is not cruel enough. And it is not a matter of sequence, my dear—you know this. It is the reigning monarch who chooses the next one. This choice is mine, alone."

She nodded until her vision swam. "Glau—but of course not." She laughed unsteadily. "And you will not choose a husband for me and make him king, and me queen only through him?"

He chuckled. "And what husband of my choosing would be strong enough for you, Daughter?"

She pulled slowly away. Blinked against the heat that lapped at her skin like the breath of the Goddess's mountain. "Queen," she whispered. "Do you swear this?" The dank walls grasped her words and sent them back to her, over and over.

"I do. You shall rule. You may well take a husband of your own choosing and produce godmarked children—but this does not matter. *You*, Daughter, shall rule."

The chuckle was a laugh, then a bellow. Ariadne covered her ears. Fire streaked from the centre of his chest and out along his arms and blasted from his fingertips like molten rain. She ducked and felt sparks pattering on her neck and arms. Behind her, Theron gave a startled yelp.

When she looked up, Minos was walking away from her.

Though she hurried, he didn't glance at her again—not even when they emerged into the storeroom. Not even when they came to the staircase that led to the royal apartments. She put her foot on the lowest stair, expecting him to do the same; instead, he turned sharply and strode across the courtyard and out between the gate columns. She watched pulsing flame fade into darkness.

"Princess," Theron murmured. He was leaning against a pillar. The light from a brazier at its base flickered over his scarred flesh and his grin. She turned and walked up the stairs.

Chara was in her room, arranging food on a tray. "Go," Ariadne snapped.

"Princess?" The slave raised her eyebrows, which disappeared beneath the unruly thatch of her hair. "What is wrong?"

Ariadne lifted a hand as if she would strike the girl, but Chara didn't blink, let alone flinch. "Out," Ariadne snapped. "Before I beat you. Again."

Chara set a fig carefully on the tray. She lifted a tiny spoon from a tiny jar and drizzled honey over the fig. "Princess," she said, and bowed her head, and slipped from the room.

Ariadne waited until the sound of the slave's footsteps had faded. Then she removed Icarus's ball of metal string from her girdle pocket. She reached up and placed it on the shelf above her bed. Daedalus's maze box already sat there; she'd brought it with her from Knossos, knowing she'd exult, as she imagined Asterion in his own prison. She set the thrumming ball up against it. It rolled a bit because her hand was shaking.

"Queen Ariadne," she said. Her laugh shook too, at first, but then it rang from the painted stone, hard and cold and sure.

THREE

CHAPTER SEVENTEEN

Asterion,

This is silly, but I have to do it. I'm much better at writing now than I was when you were here—and this, if you can believe it, is due to your sister. She makes me write her letters for her, on long scrolls of Egyptian paper. (She says pressing lines into clay takes far too long, and the tablets are far too heavy. She's actually right about some things.) They're love letters, mostly. "Thalcion—if you continue to gaze at me with such fervour, I shall have you flogged. Come to my chamber tomorrow at moonrise." Sometimes hate letters too. "Diantha—you have been less than nothing to me for years. Stop flaunting your lovers or I shall have you flogged." I've become very good at writing. So, now that she's sleeping, all I want to do is write to *you*. It makes me feel as if I'm talking to you. As if you might laugh and reply.

For a very long time after they put you under the mountain nothing much happened. Ariadne made me write to her would-be lovers, especially Karpos (who never answered). Ariadne tried to talk to Minos, who kept wandering off with his limbs on fire, burning up the countryside. Ariadne tried to make your mother smile at her. She hardly ever succeeded at any of these things, but that didn't matter. She's a tenacious woman, your sister. (I learned "tenacious" from the physician, who was talking about Minos.) Glaucus still carried his stick-sword everywhere. Deucalion still defended Glaucus. Everything was the same—until the time for the second sacrifice came.

Notice that I didn't say *I'd* been the same, since they put you under the mountain. I'm sure I seemed the same. I'm sure no one saw me pacing, muttering about how I'd free you. I missed Icarus so much (still do). I imagined talking to him, instead of to myself—we used to listen very well to each other—but no, it was just me, and I couldn't stop thinking about the lava pipes and the great metal door with the littler one in it. I wanted to go back to the Goddess's mountain alone, but there just wasn't a chance. So I planned to find a way in at the time of the second procession. And because Icarus wasn't around to tell me otherwise, I swore I'd succeed.

Ariadne went on and on about how pathetic the second procession would be. "It was one thing when those first Athenians came. Remember that red-headed girl who wouldn't stop crying? And then Asterion, being pushed in there after them: that was wonderful and exciting, but it won't happen again. The people won't care, this time."

She was so, so wrong.

You used to tell me that I knew far more than any of the royal family did. And I'd tell you that this was because being a slave was like having a godmark of invisibility. It's so true, Asterion. I clear tables and wash Ariadne's clothes and scrub her floor and walls—and I hear people saying things, while I'm working. I watch them, even though my head is always bowed. So I knew, as the time for the second sacrifice came, that Karpos was making statues, some at Minos's command, some at the queen's. I knew that the priestesses' acolytes were stitching banners with Asterion's name on them. That children were learning dances, and that, while they danced, they wore bull masks just like the Athenians'. Somehow Ariadne was ignorant of all this.

The second group of Athenians looked like the first,

except that there was no girl with red hair. There was another handsome youth, whom Ariadne fed figs to, in front of everyone. He could weep silver tears that tasted like wine. Quite a godmark—and imagine the princess's delight as she stood, in front of everyone, and ordered him to cry, then licked the tears from his cheeks. Ugh.

She wasn't nearly so cheerful when the procession began. Because of the children and their bull masks, and the banners—but especially the statues. There were six of them: three of you (as boy, and bull-boy, and bull) and three of your brother Androgeus. They were Karpos's, of course, so they stood on their little wagons and seemed to breathe, and sometimes to blink. When the procession was underway, I touched the boy one on the hand and the fingers twitched, which was so strange that I nearly tripped. Anyway, Ariadne turned very pale and hissed at Karpos, "You didn't tell me about these," and he shrugged and said, "You've stopped visiting my workshops; I imagined you wouldn't be interested."

There seemed to be more people than the last time. More priests and priestesses, more Bull worshippers. Singers sang about you all day and night. (I admit that even I found this annoying.) Ariadne sulked in her tent. "How can he be more popular than ever? Why? Such fools!" She stared at the sky as the sacrifices were pushed into the darkness. I stared at the darkness. I'd half expected to see you standing there, when Phaidra unlocked the door. No, not half expected— less than that. And you weren't standing there.

It took ages for her to fall asleep that night. When she finally did, I crept out of the tent. I spent the night climbing—much easier to do this time, with the ground all hard and parched, not scalding and running with mud. I heard the lava pipes before I saw them: the wind was making music with them again. I remembered Polymnia and her own lovely silver voice, and wondered whether she was still alive, under all that rock. Whether you were. Whether, gods forgive me, you'd killed her and the others and were now hunting the newest ones. (I felt very sick, thinking about this.) I jumped and scrabbled as I had before and got no closer to touching the pipes. I looped down and around, looking for some miraculous crevice, some hole I could leap down into. There wasn't anything, though. Just as Icarus had told me. I missed him even more, just then.

I was so tired and sad the next day on the road home that Ariadne actually demanded to know what was wrong with me. Then she laughed and said, "Ah—you must be missing your dear little friend Asterion again." She didn't wait for me to answer; she was already striding ahead so quickly that children stumbled and bull masks fell onto the road.

She might have recovered from the humiliation of the procession, in time. But before she could, something even more horrifying happened to her: an announcement. Minos waited until we were all back at Knossos to make it.

(It's now the day after I began this letter. I can't believe I was able to write so much at once. I'm a little afraid of how long the whole thing will be, how long it will take to write. But I must keep going. I feel so *other* while I'm writing. Is that what godmarks feel like?)

"My people!" the king cried. He was standing on Ariadne's dancing ground with his hand on the enormous statue of Androgeus. (He'd ordered it moved a little, so that it would be in the very centre.) He'd been gone from the palace for at least a week, but someone called out, that day at dawn, that they saw a plume of smoke. It was Minos, staggering back from wherever he'd been. He didn't enter the palace. He stood there in the lovely circle Daedalus had made for Ariadne, and the people who'd been waiting for him listened.

"My people! I have been gone from you, but thinking only of you." He sounded drunk. He looked drunk. He slurred and swayed, and we all had to glance away from him because he was so bright with fire. "I have been thinking as a father thinks of his child. Pondering what will become of you when I am gone. Others have been pondering this, too, it seems." He gestured up at the High Priest and Priestess, who were side by side on the gallery above the gate. "Look at them: so fretful about the state of my mind that they have made peace with each other!" The priest shook his head slightly, his dark brows drawn. The priestess lifted her chin.

Minos staggered and groped for the statue's cupped hand. "At last I know what I will tell all of you. At last I know who will sit on that throne when I am consumed by flame."

I was standing beside Ariadne. I almost always am when some speech or other happens. Wedged between her and one of her brothers (though them I don't mind at all, not even Glaucus, who makes her mad with irritation). Phaidra's always close to Pasiphae, and she was that day, too, on the steps above the dancing ground.

"Godsblood," Ariadne hissed. "It's time. He's going to do it now. *Godsblood*." She took two steps toward Minos, then fell back to where I was. Her feet moved on the outermost arm of the shell spiral as if she was trying not to dance. Her lips smiled and trembled at the same time.

"Of course," the king said, "it should have been you." He was pressing both hands against the statue now, leaning on its hip, gazing up at its marble face. "You, only beloved— you were going to be king. Until the spawn of that other king took you from me." I could see the stone giving a little beneath his red-gold-silver hands. The stone was silver too, where he touched it. I craned to look for Karpos but couldn't see him. Maybe it frightened him or angered him to see his godmarked work touched this way? Or maybe mark calling to mark is a desirable thing? I find it all very strange.

Minos pulled away from the statue and turned again to the crowd. "Pasiphae. My Queen. I have not chosen you, for you are no longer young, and this land needs a young ruler."

The queen didn't frown or start, but her fingers started to glow silver, and within moments water was dripping from them. "Indeed," she said. Phaidra looked up at her mother and raised a slender hand, which her mother ignored. Pasiphae said nothing else. Just watched her husband as he crackled and shone.

"My sons: I have not chosen you either." I felt Glaucus stiffen. Deucalion bowed his head, smiling a little. He's never wanted power over anything but the wind, so I wasn't surprised.

"Yes," Ariadne whispered. She grasped my hand and held it so hard that it went numb almost right away. I didn't try to disentangle myself. I waited, hoping she'd let go.

Minos took a step. Black craters smoked where he'd been standing. "Ariadne. Daughter."

She drew herself up and dropped my hand. "Yes, Father." Her voice wasn't quavery at all. I tell you: your sister is impressive.

"Despite my promise, I have not chosen you."

I heard people murmur, right away. "Why would he have chosen her? She's unmarked!" said someone near me. "He is already mad, to have made such a promise!" hissed someone else. Ariadne blinked once, and again, and her teeth crept down onto her lower lip and fastened there.

"No," Minos called, holding up his hand to quiet the crowd. "Not you, for I love you too much. You are not as Androgeus was—you are too precious for the world I have known, these many years. No," he went on, sweeping both hands up, sizzling, as she drew breath to say something, "the throne needs someone who has toiled and failed and

221

toiled again. Someone who has strength and godmarked silver in his hands."

"What?" Ariadne said. This time her voice cracked. Pasiphae threw back her head and laughed as the crowd began to murmur again.

"Karpos," Minos cried. "Master Karpos: step forward."

Karpos did. He walked and everyone murmured and made way for him, but when he stopped before the king, silence fell. "Master Karpos, you are strong and godmarked. You have laboured to make my son Androgeus live in this stone, though he is long dead. You are my choice."

For a moment Karpos stood very still, staring straight into the king's molten eyes. Then he knelt—gracefully somehow, not fawningly—and smiled. He said nothing. He didn't need to. The silence shattered as the crowd cheered. Some of them fell to their knees, too.

Ariadne's shriek rose above everything else as she launched herself at Karpos and her father. She was stumbling, as drunk-looking as the king was. "No!" she screamed, over and over. She thrust herself past Karpos and into the shimmering space around her father. "How dare you? You promised. You *promised*!"

She battered at him with her fists. "Daughter," he growled. She didn't stop. "Daughter. Ariadne!"—and as he yelled her name a great gout of flame burst from his chest and blew her backward. She fell. She clawed at the earth, moaning, twisting her body around like a fish on dry land, seeking the sea. The flesh of her hands and forearms was bubbling. I could see it; I thought I could smell it. I remembered you, and thought that while your own flesh had often bubbled, you'd never grovelled and wept.

"Come, Karpos," Minos said, and Karpos rose smoothly. "I must teach you things before I give myself forever to the fire." They went up the steps and under the doorway into the palace. Karpos didn't even glance at Ariadne.

Glaucus took one pace toward his sister. "No, Glau," Deucalion muttered. "Leave her be." Pasiphae was already gone, and Phaidra, too. The crowd dispersed in bits and pieces.

Everyone left except me. I went over to her and said, "Princess." The smell was very strong, right beside her. No water from her mother's hands to soothe her, as you'd always been soothed.

Her head rolled around. One of her eyes gazed up at me. I don't know if it saw me. "Princess," I said, "get up. I'll see to those burns." I wanted to say much more, but had no idea what this much more would be. She was biting her lip again. She was bleeding.

"Get up. Please."

She heaved herself onto her knees. I put my hands under her armpits and pulled her up, very slowly, gagging at the stench of her. Blisters burst water all over my hands. We staggered up the steps and into the courtyard. It took us a very long time to climb the stairs to her rooms. I could feel people watching us. I could hear them whispering.

"He promised," she gasped when I had gotten her onto her own bed. "Tell me why. Why did he take this away from me?"

Because you're unmarked. Because you're almost as mad as he is. I shook my head. "No," I said. "I can't. I have no idea."

She cackled, then coughed and turned her face to the wall. "Just a slave," she said. "No wonder."

I dribbled olive oil on her burns and snipped her singed hair off. I wrapped her hands and forearms in clean dry cloth. I pretended she was you. That's the only way I managed it.

I thought she'd fallen asleep, or maybe fainted, when she said, in a soft, slurred voice, "The king of Athens has a son."

"Princess?"

"A fine and heroic son. Theseus. My father ranted about

him. Daedalus told me . . . other things. Theseus. He can speak straight into people's minds. He is a warrior who hates my father nearly as much as I hate my father."

I said "Princess?" again, though I didn't expect her to say anything I'd understand. She didn't speak. I leaned over her and made sure her eyes were closed. Then I squatted at the foot of her bed and thought that I would write to you. And look! Now I can't stop.

So.

I need a plan. I've known this for a while, but it's even more urgent now: I need to get to you and bring you out. Knossos is sunk in the madness of your father and your sister and everyone else, more unbearable than it ever was before. I'll get you out of your mountain box and we'll both get away. I'll read this to you, when that happens. Until then, though, I'll hide the scrolls with all this writing on them behind our favourite row of jars—the ones that look like stooping giants in the lamplight.

Asterion. Please wait for me.

"I miss you," clicked the crab
And the fishing crane clacked, "Me?"
"Why yes," crab said,
"You've shown me
That there's sky as well as sea."

——— · ———

To Theseus, Son of Aegeus, King of Athens,

Perhaps you will think that I am overly forward, writing to you this way. Perhaps Athenian women (even the princesses) are not so forward.

I am Ariadne, Princess of Crete, and I am supposed to hate you and your city, but I do not. In fact, I have nothing but admiration for you. Even here at Knossos, where Athenians are so reviled, I have heard of your exploits. The Great Sow who tore men's throats out, and the Spider Thief who clung to his cliffside and pushed men to their deaths, and the Wrestler, and the Stretcher who had cut off so many other men's feet—you killed all of these monsters, each at a door to the Underworld itself! Also the murderer who would tear people apart by tying them to two pine trees. And you wrested the club from the Epidaurus Bandit's hand and beat him to death with it! You did all this on your way to Athens, where you were determined you would claim your rightful place as the son of the King. (And that was not without its perils either, I hear, for your stepmother tried to poison you.)

These tales prove your manhood, your intelligence. The ferocity of your people's love for you proves your godmark. Apollo's, yes? You speak directly into their minds with your own. Surely this is a sort of poetry, a casting of light into dark places. Or perhaps your mark is Athene's? For you impart wisdom to those whose thoughts you touch with yours.

It does not matter who gave you your gift, my Prince: I simply need it. I need your strength of body and of mind. That is why I am writing now, sparing barely a thought for the punishment that would be inflicted on me if I were found out.

You know all too well the price my father the King exacted from Athens after my brother Androgeus was murdered there. I am sure it is a price that is always in the minds and hearts of Athenians, weighing them down like iron shackles. Seven youths and seven maidens, to be sent every two years over the sea to Crete and set loose in the labyrinth where a monster awaits them. Twenty-eight have already perished. Fourteen more will soon be chosen. This sacrifice must rankle.

Your pain is matched by my shame. Has my country fallen so low that the mad rage of its ruler must bring another great realm to its knees? Shame, yes—I am ashamed to be a Cretan. I no longer take any joy from the accomplishments and beauty of my home. I see only further weakening if we continue on this path, and I fear that we will soon be mocked more than we are feared. There is only one way ahead. You are this way.

You are already a hero to your people, and yet still you struggle to maintain your dominance (and your life!) in a palace crowded with other claimants to your father's throne. Imagine if you could do something even more spectacular than what you have already done. The Great Sow, my lord, would be as nothing beside the Great Bull.

You could kill the beast that lives within the maze. You could disguise yourself and sail with thirteen other youths; you could rid the world of the creature that brings grief to your country and shame to mine. You could do all this because I will help you. I will tell you about the beast, and give you the means to kill it.

In return for this knowledge, and the fame that will surely come to you, I ask only one thing: that you take me with you when you sail, triumphant, from Crete. I cannot bear my life here any longer. I would go wherever you deigned to take me—though I admit that the prospect of seeing Athens fills me with excitement. (Daedalus, our royal craftsman, used to tell me of your city—his words were all rich and honeyed, and they made my father's seem like weak, poisoned wine. I miss Daedalus terribly.)

I appeal to you—I beg and implore you: help me.

(I have enclosed a sketch of myself, done by Daedalus's apprentice, Karpos, at my command. I hope that my need will be as stark upon my face as it is within my breast.)

Humbly and hopefully yours,
Ariadne, Daughter of Minos, King of Crete

———— · ————

"Girl," Ariadne snapped, "why are you writing so slowly?"
She frowned, and cocked her head to one side. Her bandaged
hands twitched and she pressed them lightly together in
front of her. "Do my words upset you? I ask you to write of
Asterion's demise—does it make you miss him?"

Chara raised her head. Her charcoal was still poised
above the tray balanced on her lap. "No," she said, and
paused. "It makes me think of a time when I was foolish. It
makes me ashamed."

The princess smiled a full, satisfied smile. "Good," she
said. "Because if you were sad—if you did miss him and
thought to tell someone of what you know—I would kill
you."

Forgive me for lying, Asterion, Chara thought. *But the lies
will help me find you.* And she smiled, too, after she bent to
stroke Ariadne's name-lines onto the paper.

CHAPTER EIGHTEEN

Oh, Asterion. It's nearly time.

I've written many things to you, these past two years, just as I did in the two years before those, but I've saved almost none of them. If someone found my other writings behind our jars I'd be laughed at and probably banished for denigrating the royal family. But if someone found a record of my plan . . . Well, that thought frightened me so badly that I burned all the words I ever wrote about it. Now, though, I must write again. Nothing that will give me away. Just words to bring you closer, once more, before everything changes.

Prince Theseus arrived yesterday.

No one knew it was Theseus, of course. No one other than Ariadne and me. She'd cornered me earlier in the day, before we all went out to meet the ship. She pressed me against a pillar and said, "Remember: I'll kill you if you speak of what you know." I said, "I would not, Princess." She scowled at me. (She's lucky there weren't any burns on her face. She hides the ones on her arms with long, filmy sleeves that some other women in the palace are now wearing too, and she wears a closed bodice to hide the ones on her breasts, and her hands she shoves inside the folds of her skirts as much as she can.) After a moment she blew out her breath (and so did I, silently) and stepped back and we went with the others to the cliff.

Fourteen more Athenians for the mountain, and we Cretans were just as hungry to watch them arrive as we had been the other twenty-eight. Even the king made an appearance. He'd been gone for months this time, leaving your mother to rule. Your mother and Karpos, who's now far more likely to be found in the receiving chambers and money rooms of the palace than he is in his workshops. Your mother lets him hang about. He's very polite to her. She probably finds this a strange new thing.

Oh: Ariadne tried to get Karpos to marry her. She had me summon him, and I was in the corridor afterward and heard everything. She proposed that he make her his queen. He said no. She asked him why, because wouldn't they make the loveliest royal couple in the history of everything? He said he'd never love her. She said most royal couples didn't love each other, but that he could want her, and that that would be enough. No, he said, he'd never want her either, for he loved and wanted a young soldier in her father's army, and before that he'd loved and wanted a kitchen boy. Ariadne cried out that this was wonderful—she'd simply rule by his side and they could each take lovers. Karpos said he would have to like her for this to happen. "No, Princess," he said as she sobbed. "I'll take no queen." Right after that she had me write the message to Theseus. (I've wondered, since: why didn't she have Karpos killed? She probably would have got away with it, as she has so many other things. Maybe this island really has become intolerable to her. Maybe that part, at least, is true.)

Anyway: the king came back from wherever he was to receive the Athenians, and Karpos stood beside him. Karpos was clean and handsome and stood up very tall. The king was stooped. His loin cloth was soot-black and full of holes and his beard was long and matted. In several places on his cheeks it had burned away and you could see the skin beneath, all pink and puckered. His godmark's so strong that his body isn't able to contain it anymore. He's withering under the flame that's always dancing on his flesh. (The priestesses have been demanding that Pasiphae lock him up, but she keeps refusing—and not because she's afraid of what the priests would do. I think she enjoys watching her husband frighten his own people.)

His voice cracked as he called out. As usual, everyone looked afraid. Pasiphae didn't look anything. She lifted her hands and dribbled water over his arms and he smiled at her as the fire sputtered a bit.

I knew which one was Theseus as soon as the ship was in the harbour. My eyes skimmed over others—all the girls, obviously, and a skinny boy, and one so beautiful that the air around him shimmered with silver, and a dark-haired one who was on his knees, wailing—and found him. He's not all that tall, but he stood at the ship's side like a man who's accustomed to being seen. He has golden hair, wavy, not curled as Cretan men's is. Muscular arms and thighs. A face that's handsome but not unusual.

Ariadne gaped at him. No one would find this strange; she'd gaped at the handsome youths in the other two groups, too. She watched him as the priestesses' breathing, bucking craft brought him across the water. She watched him as he climbed the stairs. At this point I stopped paying attention to either of them—because I have a plan too. And I was looking for the girl I need just as much as Ariadne needs Theseus. I found her. She's not as tall as I am, but I can make myself shorter. I can make myself invisible. She's even got curly hair, though that won't be important, in the end.

Her name's Sotiria. She told me this as I knelt in front of her that night—last night—and held a cup of wine to her lips. Her eyes darted about when I asked her, but I murmured, "I'm just a slave. No one notices me, so no one will notice you. Tell me your name."

"Why?" she murmured back. I repeated what I said to

Polymnia four years ago, though this time it was a lie. "I don't know, but it seems important. Please tell me." And she did, staring into my eyes across the cup.

Theseus and Sotiria. Ariadne and me. You. I can't let myself think of any other people from now on.

This morning I went with Ariadne to the cells where the Athenians are being kept. I thought I might have to follow her secretly when she went to Theseus, but she told me I should come. She wanted me to carry a pitcher of water. "I wish to serve them myself," she said to the priestesses who guard the corridor where the cells (little storerooms, really) are. "I wish to do them honour before they die for Crete."

The wailing boy was first (though he wasn't wailing this time). Ariadne gestured, already glancing back into the corridor, and I filled a cup for him and held it to his lips. His wrists were bloody where they were rubbing against his bonds. His eyes were huge and pleading. I don't think anyone has ever seen me as clearly as he and Sotiria have. Anyone except you, that is.

Theseus was in the third cell down, in the middle of the room, as if he'd been waiting for Ariadne. Piles of clay tablets stood along the wall behind him.

"Princess," he said with a smile that lit his lips and eyes and the air around all of us, "you are lovelier than I expected."

Ariadne froze, halfway into a curtsey. "But surely Master Karpos's likeness prepared—" she whispered, glancing over her shoulder at the empty hallway, and Theseus's bound hands came up and waved her to silence.

"You are lovelier than any likeness, even a godmarked one."

I thought, *This begins well*, and wasn't sure whether to be frightened or excited.

"Forgive my haste," Ariadne said, stepping closer to

him, "but someone could come at any time, and we mustn't be found out. Your godmark—the way you open your mind to others. Try it with me now. I must know that I will be able to hear you, while you are under the mountain."

"Will you also wish to see me kill something, so that you will be certain I can slay the beast?"

She gave a low laugh. "I have no need to see that. But I *shall* give you something with which to do this slaying."

Theseus took another step. He was nearly touching her. "These youths were chosen for their godmarks; there may be no need of anything else. But show me how you would have me kill. Show me this before I use my own godmark, here."

I was the one who peeked out into the corridor, this time. I saw the priestesses at the entrance, standing still, facing away. *Don't move*, I thought at them. *Because I need to know this, too.*

Ariadne lifted the flap of her girdle. Beneath it, tied around her waist, were two things: Icarus's ball of string, and a dagger haft.

"Where did you get that?" I didn't mean to speak; the words just spilled out. Theseus and Ariadne turned to me. He looked mildly surprised, as if he were noticing me for the first time. She looked furious. I kept talking, though. "It's . . . it was Icarus's. Did he give it to you before he left?" This idea hurt me.

"Be silent!" she hissed. "There's no time!" She probably would have said more, or struck me, but she wanted to impress Theseus. So she looked back at him, smiling, a little embarrassed. "You'll let this out as you walk, in the maze. It's magical—never runs out, is as strong as iron and as supple as thread. When you've killed the bull, you'll follow the string back to the door. You'll let me know when you're there, with your mind-voice. And I'll open it for you."

Thank you, I thought. Because I hadn't been able to come

up with that part of my plan, and she'd just given it to me.

"And the killing of the bull," he said, one golden brow raised. "What of that? Surely you will not tell me that a dagger haft will be enough."

She held the haft in her palm. "Look," she said, and pressed down, and the haft grew a stubby portion of blade. She pressed again and another portion snapped out, then another and another, until she was holding a sword. "Daedalus was indeed a master, but even before that, he was an Athenian. He would be honoured to have his creations used by you."

A footstep sounded in the corridor. Ariadne pressed the sword back into a haft and put it and the ball of string back under her girdle. She leaned until her lips were against his ear and whispered, "They'll bathe you tonight, and shave your head, and dress you in a white robe. Tomorrow morning I'll come to you here and give the thread and dagger to you. They will be easy to conceal. No one will touch you again until they push you toward the maze's door."

More steps. "Princess?" called a voice, and I stepped nearly to the doorway and said, maybe a bit too loudly, "My Lady, this prisoner has drunk more than his share. We must go to the others now."

I know it's difficult to believe, but the glance your sister gave me was almost grateful. She said, "You are right. My tendency toward mercy makes me forget my task." We stepped out of the cell just as the priestess was reaching it.

"He was greedy," Ariadne said to her, "and he begged for his freedom with sweet, clever words, but I do not wish him punished for this. The Goddess will mete out her own punishment, or blessing, very soon."

The priestess peered past her at Theseus, whose head was bowed, but who still managed to look like a prince. "Very well, Lady," the priestess said, and we moved to the next cell.

Sotiria's—the girl I'd chosen for my part of the plan.

I've barely noticed anything since. I've walked and talked, served, cleaned and done everything else I usually do, but my mind's been on my plan. My bigger, better plan. I did pay attention when Ariadne said, in her chamber tonight, "I only wish there had been time for him to test his godmark on me." I didn't respond, because she hardly ever expects me to. "Imagine: they're probably shaving all that glorious golden hair off him right now . . ." I just kept pinning her own black hair into coils and hoped she'd fall asleep quickly so that I could slip back to Sotiria's cell and tell her what I had to tell her. And Ariadne did— thank all the octopus's arms (as you'd say). More than that I cannot write of here. (Except to tell you that Sotiria's godmark is being able to take other people's pain from them and suffer it herself. Not just being able to: *having* to. She has nearly as many scars as you do.)

"Nearly time" the small fish cried
And tickled bigger fish insides. . . .

I'm giddy. Sick. I should try to sleep; I need to sleep.

"Be brave," the starfish said, "and bold
I'll give you all my hands to hold. . . ."

CHAPTER NINETEEN

"Chara. Help me dress."

"I'm not well." Chara's voice shook—a fine touch, though she hadn't intended it. With heavy-lidded eyes she saw the princess's face, blurry and close. *Back up*, she thought. *Look away, just for a moment.*

"Get up and help me dress!" Ariadne cried. "The procession begins in two hours! And," she said, in a quieter voice, "I've just been to see *him*. I've given *him* the things. Though we still could not test his mind-voice. . . ." At last she turned—and Chara rolled onto her side, stabbed her finger deep into her throat and vomited the remnants of the previous night's crab dinner onto the floor. There was a great deal of it; she'd made sure to eat far more than she wanted.

She squeezed her eyes shut as Ariadne gave a cry of disgust. Chara heard her slippers tap as she retreated. "And I suppose you're too sick to clean up after yourself, too! *Gods*, but you try my patience. . . ."

"I know," Chara mumbled, "that you need my help today. . . ." It took her three tries to swallow over the acrid dryness in her throat.

Ariadne snorted. "Do you think I would let you help me with what must be done today? No—but I will probably miss you when I get thirsty." She made a choking sound. "You stink. This room stinks; I'll dress in Phaidra's. Get yourself to the bathing room. I'll send another slave in to clean this up."

The moment Ariadne's footsteps had faded, Chara pushed herself to her feet. Her throat stung and her mouth tasted of sick but she didn't stop for a cup of water. She ran. At first she ran through empty corridors, but soon she had to take a public one, which was full of palace folk. She slowed to a walk and tried to school her gasping breaths to silence. They were laughing and talking, holding garlands of flowers and shells, gesturing up at the brightening blue of the sky. "A glorious day for the sacrifice," one woman said as she adjusted a basket of bread on her hip. The man next to her said, "Indeed—the Great Mother will be well pleased," and the woman replied, "As will the Bull—though I suppose he doesn't care so much about the weather," and they both laughed as Chara slipped around them, unnoticed.

The collection of things she'd left in the darkest corner of the grain storeroom was still there. She knelt and picked up the knife. For just a moment she stared at its long, sharp edge. It glinted only a little because the light from the lamp in a far column bracket was so weak. But she wouldn't need light.

Come on, then, she thought. *Do this. Think of Asterion and do it.*

She'd chosen the sharpest knife in the kitchen, but it had been made for cutting fish and meat, not hair: it took ages to saw off all her curls. She was nearly panting by the time they lay in soft little mounds around her—but she didn't pause. She put the knife down and dipped both her hands into the bowl. The water was so cool that she shivered as it ran over her face and down her neck and back. The razor's bronze was cool, too, and she shivered some more. *Stupid girl. Be steady and firm or you'll cut your own throat.*

The sound of the blade scraping over her skull seemed terribly loud at first, and so did the gasping noises she made every time it caught on her skin. *Scriiiitch snick snick* scriiitch—like Icarus's taloned feet dragging on rock. She shaved the right side of her head, then the left, then the middle, then rinsed everything and bit her lip because the water stung her cuts. She ran her hands over the stubble that was left and found tufts she'd missed—and even though she was aching with the need to be away, she shaved them too. The Athenians' heads would be smooth and clean, glistening with oil.

When her stubble was as even as she could make it, Chara set the razor down beside the knife. She rose and dusted the hair off her thighs and the soles of her feet. She wound the cloth around her head the way her mother had, when they'd been going out into the olive groves; she tied the bundle of figs and cheese and bread to her belt and slung the waterskin across her chest. After that she took a few very deep breaths, clenching and unclenching her hands, which felt numb.

This time she took only shadowed, empty pathways that no one but slaves used. She passed some: a boy bent double beneath a bolt of scarlet cloth, an old woman with shell garlands strung over both her arms, a younger woman carrying nothing, but nearly running. They all nodded to Chara; the hurrying woman smiled a tired, resigned smile that seemed to say, *Such a life we have, no?*

Chara turned and watched her until she vanished around a corner. *This is my home*, she thought, *or one of them, anyway—and I'm leaving it, and I may never see it again.* Tears prickled her throat and eyes, and she thought, *No, Freckles—you have no time; just go.*

The sun was already high in the eastern sky when she walked out onto the road that led up to the peaks. The procession would take this road, very soon. She would not. She made for the clumps of rocks and cypresses that hid the rising slope. Her bare feet were almost as tough and sure as a goat's on the rough ground; thank the gods she'd so often refused Ariadne's demands that she wear boots. Chara ran steadily, even when the sun was directly above and there was no shade to cool her.

I'm a deer, she thought, as her feet rose and fell. *I'm a deer, a hare, a hound. I'm not tired. I'm not afraid.* She stopped a few times to drink from the waterskin and stretch out her tight calf muscles and retie the cloth around her shorn head. She looked back when she stopped, and saw only the empty mountainside falling away behind her, in waves of silver-green olive leaves and burned red earth.

The sun had edged into the west when she stopped for the last time. She craned up at the great metal door and the peak that soared like jagged horns above it. The door seemed bigger and darker than it had those other years. She unwound the cloth from her head and tilted her face into the wind that always blew here—the breath of the Goddess, warm and sweet on blistered skin. She closed her eyes and saw bright orange spots dancing beneath her lids. When she opened them again, she walked straight for the door. Its metal was hot under her palms and brow. She traced her fingers over the lock and the lines of the smaller door. She bent and set her ear to the door-within-a-door and heard a dull, bottomless roaring that was somehow deeper than silence.

"Asterion," she whispered, "I'm coming."

———·———

The procession arrived at sunset. Chara heard drums and flutes first, then a distant babble of talking, and singing that scattered on the wind. Suddenly the figs she'd eaten felt like stones in her belly. She pressed herself even farther into the shade of the thick, squat rock she'd chosen, which hunkered on a rise to the west of the labyrinth's mouth. As the procession's sounds grew clearer, she imagined what she'd see if she dared to look: the brilliant scarlets, blues, and greens of flowers and dresses and the marble statues on their rolling platforms; the iridescent glinting of shells; the stark white of the Athenians' shifts; the dark brown of their masks and the bull faces stitched into the golden banners.

She crouched, nearly motionless, until the red sky filled with black and stars. Only then did she ease her cramped limbs straight and peer around the rock. She blinked at the torchlight and godfire that streamed and twisted in the Goddess's breath. People-shadows were moving among the flames, but she wasn't interested in them—only in the ones who wouldn't be moving. Her sharpening vision found them swiftly; after all, she knew where to look. Fourteen of them, bound and still, kneeling in two rows before the door. The boys were in the front, the girls behind. If the girls' arms had been free they would have been able to reach back and touch the metal. Chara wondered briefly whether it would be hot, even at night.

Theseus, she thought as her eyes sharpened and she made out the shape that had to be him—the one that was straighter and broader-shouldered than the others, *are you ready? Am I?*

As in those other years, there were no guards: just two priestesses, standing at either end of the boys' line, facing the throng. Chara had watched them, last time; she knew that they wouldn't glance back at the Athenians unless one of them cried out or caused some other sort of disturbance. None of them did, as deeper night fell. They knelt without moving. The shapes of their mask-horns wavered on the ground, caught in the light.

Eventually all the lights dimmed and died. A flute trilled a last, fading line of notes. A baby whimpered and coughed and went quiet.

Chara slipped out of her clothes and into the white shift

a priestess had given her. She had told the sister that one of the Athenians had soiled hers. Fear caught her when she was halfway down the slope. She didn't falter. She kept crouching low, kept angling toward the line of girls.

Sotiria, she thought. *Sotiria's all you're after. Don't even try to glance at Theseus—look only for her.*

She was at the very end, as Chara had known she would be: the priestesses liked to arrange the sacrifices with the smallest at either end and the tallest in the middle.

Chara dropped to her stomach and pulled herself over the stone-nubbled dirt. *Not a deer, a hare, a hound: an invisible snake . . .* She slithered until the girl's bound, crossed ankles were right in front of her. Chara lifted herself onto her elbows and whispered, "Sotiria."

The masked head snapped up.

"Shhh," Chara murmured. "Gently. I'm right here, just like I said I would be. Everything's fine. The priestesses can't see or hear us."

Sotiria nodded. Chara was close enough to see that her lips were cracked and her skin was caked in dust that made her look very pale, in the starlight. Chara tugged the mask off. Sotiria made a hissing sound and squeezed her eyes shut. When they opened, they were black and steady on Chara's. Her eyebrows looked very thick and dark beneath the polished nakedness of her head.

"Good," Chara mouthed. She smiled. Sotiria didn't.

Chara eased the razor out of her belt and moved behind Sotiria. It took only a few minutes to saw through her wrist bonds, which were thickly knotted and slippery with blood. (And long: thank the Goddess, long enough to re-tie, even after they'd been cut.) Sotiria shuddered but made no sound. The ankle bonds were even thicker, and they creaked as Chara was working at them; the girl beside them shifted on her knees and turned.

Chara froze. Sotiria, who'd been flexing her arms in front of her, craned to look over her shoulder, her black eyes even wider than they had been. Chara put her finger to her lips and smiled again, even though her insides were crawling with dread. She watched the masked girl wet her own lips with her tongue, as if she were about to speak. Instead she slumped farther back onto her heels and dropped her chin to her chest. She made a low, keening sound that lasted for the space of one long breath out. No one else stirred.

Chara set the razor to Sotiria's ankle bonds again, and they parted in a few cuts. She pressed the girl's shoulders until she sat back, shuddering more violently than before, her eyes gleaming with tears. "There's no time," Chara whispered. "You have to bind me right away."

Sotiria swallowed and nodded. Her hands trembled as she picked up the lengths of rope. She shuffled behind Chara and slipped the rope around her wrists.

"No," Chara murmured, as soon as Sotiria had made the first loop. "They made their knots tight. You have to make yours tight, too, or they'll wonder."

Sotiria pulled, hard. Chara had been expecting this, but she chewed at the inside of her mouth anyway, to keep from gasping.

"Now the mask," she said.

This time the girl's hands were firm right away: they slipped the leather over Chara's stubbly head and pulled it sharply down, almost to her upper lip. Chara tried to suck a breath in through her nose but the mask pressed against both her nostrils.

"Stop," Sotiria hissed. "Breathe only through your mouth. And don't be afraid if you feel like you're not getting enough air: you will."

Chara drew in another breath, and another. "Thank you," she said at last. "Now listen: there's a rock just up that slope—a big one shaped like a tooth. There's a waterskin there for you, and a bag with some food and a few coins, and my old clothes."

The silence that followed seemed so long that Chara thought Sotiria had slipped away without speaking, but then she said, "I shouldn't. I take people's pain away; I *promised* to do that, in there. I promised them, and they're my countrymen, my friends. . . ."

Chara shook her head and wriggled her bound hands. "I'll be more help to them. I will, though I don't have any godmark at all, let alone one as powerful as yours. I'll be the only one who knows what they'll be facing. *Who* they'll be facing. Trust me with this, Sotiria. And go—quickly."

After a moment fingers brushed her cheek, below the mask, and then her throbbing hands. "May all my gods and yours protect you," Sotiria whispered. "Farewell."

———— · ————

Ariadne had slept fitfully, beneath the whispering cloth of the royal tent. Now, an hour after dawn, the words of her mother's speech sounded like the buzzing drone of bees, even though Pasiphae was standing only a few paces away. Ariadne fastened her eyes on Theseus, bald and masked like the commoners but standing a little too tall, a little too proudly. His eyes swivelled, behind the holes of the mask, and found her. She felt a thrumming in her head, so sudden and powerful that she clutched her own hair convulsively.

::Don't . . . afraid.:: The words crackled and stung and she winced. ::This is how I . . .::

She frowned at him, and even though he'd told her that she wouldn't be able to respond to his mind-voice, she thought, *I can't hear every word, my Prince—should I be able to? Is this how it is with everyone?*

His lips curved. ::*You will . . . from me soon . . . this,
Princess.*:: He spoke no more words into her head, but the
thrumming was still there, like a pulse far beneath her
own heartbeat. It stayed, even when she tipped her head
back and watched a hawk turning in the pink-blue air far
above all of them. Even when she closed her eyes, Theseus
of Athens was still with her.

When the great door screamed open behind her she felt
the motion through her shoes and up her legs and gritted
her teeth, just as she had the other times. She opened her
eyes and didn't move them from the hawk, but even so, she
pictured the lock coursing with the same silver that would
be streaming from Phaidra's hands. Minos's hands would
be dribbling sparks and gouts of flame—but he might, at
least, stay silent.

Pasiphae's voice stopped. The priestess's began; when *her*
droning ended, with a cry of "Accept our gifts, Great Mother!
Accept our obeisance, Bull Prince!" Ariadne finally lowered
her gaze to the place directly before the door. She saw the
first bull mask come off. Saw the first young man roll back
on his heels, reeling as the light struck his eyes. He flailed
his just-freed arms and twisted around so that he was facing
Ariadne. He opened his mouth in a soundless cry.

The priestess raised her snake staff. The gold trim on
her bodice arms flashed. "Go with blessings," she called.
The two guards grasped the youth's arms and walked him
to the yawning black emptiness of the doorway. They bent
him forward and thrust him inside.

He disappeared immediately, just as all the others
would. Four years ago Ariadne had thought a great deal
about this vanishing. Two years ago she hadn't—but now
that Theseus was there, everything was different. He was
next. He was throwing his shoulders back, the fool—and
when one of the guards wrenched his hood off he tossed

his head as if he still had a golden mane. He, at least, didn't seem blinded; his eyes swivelled to Ariadne's once more, then away, before she had time to glower at him.

May you be as strong as you are bold, she thought. *For only you are good enough to take me from this place. Only you, someday-king of Athens.*

"Go with blessings!" the priestess called. Theseus pretended to stumble, as the guards turned him toward the door, but even so he looked graceful and coiled; a warrior, disappearing before anyone knew he was one.

:: *In* :: said his mind-voice, and she shivered as the word plucked at her veins. ::*In . . . beautiful and deep and . . .* ::

No more words came. Ariadne wrenched her eyes away from the place where he'd been and concentrated on the hawk again. While the guards sent one sacrifice after another into the darkness, she pretended that there were no onlookers, no banners; nothing but this bird alone in the sky.

Then she heard a rising murmur beside her. She glanced sideways at the people before the door. The priestess and guards were clustered around an Athenian girl. She seemed to be the last one: a slip of a thing, awash in her loose white robe. Her mask was off. The priestess was running a hand over the girl's head, which was all Ariadne could clearly see of her. It was far stubblier than the others' heads had been. Stubbly, and crisscrossed with angry red cuts. "No," Ariadne heard the priestess say. "This cannot be. Something is not—"

The Athenian took a step back and turned so that Ariadne could see her profile. At first she saw only a slender girl who wasn't as smoothly, flawlessly bald as the others— but a moment later she saw something else: another girl, overlaid atop this one. A girl whose nose was familiar. Her nose and her freckles. A girl whose sea-grey eyes, roaming wildly up and around, found Ariadne's and went still.

Ariadne moved forward slowly. She thought slowly, too; the new pulsing in her head was so strange, so relentless. "No," she managed to whisper. "No!"—louder, so that her mother and the priestess and all the people in the throng would turn to her, at last.

They did. And as they did, the slip of a girl sprang silently out of the guards' grip and sprinted for the labyrinth's door.

"No!" Ariadne cried, one last time. "Stop—Chara: *stop!*"

Chara bent and leapt into the darkness.

"'Tiria?"

The child was skinny and brown, perhaps eight years old. During the three days he'd known her, he hadn't left her side.

She'd run, as Chara had told her to. She'd run all day and all night and then most of the next day and night, through passes that took her farther and farther from the Goddess's mountain—and at last she'd fallen. The child's shepherd father had found her, sprawled unconscious on his highest pasture, and taken her back to his hut to set her broken ankle bone.

"What's your name?" he'd asked as his hands gripped and twisted.

"Sotiria," she'd stammered, twisting herself, as if she might be able to wriggle away from the pain. She'd borne so much pain—other people's, mostly, thanks to her godmark. But this was her own, and it was strange and raw, not silver at all.

The child had put out a hand and laid it on her burned, bald head, and his father had snapped, "Let her be, boy."

And Chara had said, "No, no, it's fine," because the child reminded her of her brother.

When she'd woken the next morning, the child had been crouched beside her pallet, his eyes wide and solemn. This should perhaps have alarmed her, but it didn't. She'd smiled at him, though she'd wanted to cry—because she wasn't, now, at a port, trading Chara's coins for passage away from Crete. Because the boy was like her brother. Because her ankle throbbed, and the shepherd was kind, and had asked her no questions.

"'Tiria?" the boy said again. He was sitting with her against the broad, tangled bole of an ancient olive tree. The shepherd had carried her here at her request, and commanded his son not to bother her with talk. "Why did you fall?"

"Because I was running in the dark, and I'd been running for too long."

"Why were you running?"

"Because I was trying to get away from the mountains. Because people might have been chasing me."

"What people?"

She didn't answer. She watched the shepherd, who was standing on a hillock below them. He was gazing down on his flock, scattered across the bright green of the pasture and among the trees around its edges. The mountain's red-brown flank rose above them all, stark and shadowless in the midday sun.

"You talk funny," the child said.

She took a deep breath. "I'm not from this island."

"So were you trying to get home?"

"Yes." She bent forward and fiddled with her bandage so that he wouldn't see her tears.

"When your ankle's better will you try again?"

"Yes," she said, remembering seagulls wheeling above the port at Athens, and the columns atop the Acropolis glowing at sundown as if they were on fire, and her brother's eager, cracking voice.

"Are you *sure* you want to go home?"

Many peaks away, a plume of black smoke rose into the cloudless sky. *The Goddess's breath, or King Minos's mark-*

madness? Sotiria imagined Melaina conjuring a blackness to match the smoke's, and Tryphon crying out in fear. She imagined Adrastus laughing, and a beast stirring in the dark. And even as she imagined these things, she felt Theseus's mind-presence in her blood and bones and veins and up behind her eyes. He was many peaks away, where the smoke was. All of them were there, together.

"No," she said, as her godmark grasped at her with its gentle, tireless, silver claws.

The boy nodded emphatically. "Good," he said, and leaned his head on her arm.

The shepherd whistled and thwacked his staff against his leg. One sheep bleated, then several more.

The gods have given you this chance at peace, Sotiria told herself. *Be still, now; don't think at all. There's nothing more you can do for them.*

And for a time, she almost believed it.

GIVE US A TITLE AND WIN!
WANT TO NAME CAITLIN SWEET'S NEXT BOOK?

— · —

Read the prologue and first chapter
of the exciting sequel to
The Door in the Mountain
And help us avoid calling it something boring
like *"The Door in the Mountain II"* or
"The Door in the Mountain: The Sequel" . . .

— · —

Just send us an email at
doorcontest@chizinepub.com
with your suggestion for a new title!
If we use it, you'll get a special mention in the book and
win a copy of all 2014 and 2015 ChiTeen titles!

— · —

Worldwide Release October 2015 in Paperback and eBook

PROLOGUE

The sky above the Goddess's mountain was on fire. Manasses saw it first.

"Papa!" he called from outside the hut. "Come and look!"

Alexios set down the bowl of curds he was holding and stepped out of the lamplight and into the night. His godmark always turned darkness to silver-tinged day, for him—but *this* darkness was different. A sheet of red-orange threaded with silver lightning hung to the south. It rippled slowly and silently, blotting out the stars.

"It's fire," Manasses whispered. He was tipping his head back, and his eyes were wide and nearly unblinking. "Godmarked fire: I can tell, because of the silver in it."

Alexios put his hand on Manasses's shoulder; the child backed up and leaned against him. Below them in the paddock, a sheep bleated and quieted.

Alexios felt Manasses draw a deep breath. "Is that where 'Tiria was running away from?"

After a moment, Alexios said, "I imagine so"—though she hadn't told him much more about that than she'd told his son.

"Is it where she went back to, when she left here?"

"Child," Alexios said, too roughly, "enough questions." He remembered how she'd tried to calm him, when he was hard on the boy. How she'd squeeze his hands and make funny faces until he smiled. *I only knew her for two months,* he thought, as he already had so many times before. *How can I love her?*

"I don't know," Alexios said again, as gently as he could.

She'd put her slender, scarred arms around him, the night she left with the bird-man, and said, "Someone needs me. An Athenian. I have to go to him."

"Come back," Alexios had said, his lips moving against hers with every word. "When you've healed him." His godmark showed her to him with such beautiful, helpless clarity, in the dark.

"Tell Manasses goodbye for me," she'd said, and kissed him, and slipped away.

Manasses squirmed around to face him. The lamplight from the hut played over his forehead and cheeks. "I want her to come back, Papa. I want her here."

Silver lightning spread like a spider's web across the flame. *Godmarked fire*, Alexios thought, and fear froze the breath in his chest.

"So do I," he said.

CHAPTER ONE

"Princess."

Ariadne started up from her bed. The first thing she thought was, *Theseus—oh, thank the gods, I hear you; it's been far too long.* . . . But even before she opened her eyes she knew it wasn't Theseus—for the word had been spoken aloud, not in her head; because he'd been silent for ages, and something was definitely very wrong.

The second thing she thought, as her vision wobbled and cleared, was, *Chara. Chara, thank the gods you're back—* but it wasn't Chara, either. Of course it wasn't: Chara had run into the labyrinth months ago, along with the Athenian sacrifices and Theseus.

All Ariadne had heard of her were some garbled words Theseus had sent her at the very beginning: :: *Chara is here and says you . . . Chara knows the . . .* ::

No: this would be the other slave, who hardly ever said anything and lurked in corners, staring with her dull, close-set eyes. The other, whose name she didn't know.

But it wasn't the other slave.

"Ariadne," Queen Pasiphae said. "Get up and follow me."

Ariadne remembered another night when her mother had needed her; just the one, so many years ago, when Ariadne had been six. Pasiphae had been in the Goddess's altar room, naked, straining to birth a baby. Ariadne's half-brother: Asterion, who was half-bull, half-boy. Asterion, marked from the beginning by his god, when none (not gods, not goddesses) had given Ariadne anything.

"Mother," she said now, sitting up, reaching for skirt and jacket, "what is it?" She couldn't help it: her voice shook with eagerness or anger or dread or curiosity—one, all of these.

"Your father," Pasiphae said. *Her* voice was steady and hard. "His mark-madness is worse."

Ariadne stood up. Her vision was entirely clear, thanks to the moonlight that streamed down through the roof of the corridor beyond her chamber. She could see the painting on the wall behind the queen, though the green plant spirals looked black, and the brown fauns and hares were blurry, as if they were moving. She could see her mother's eyes glinting, along with the gold at her ears and throat. She could see her long fingers, curling and uncurling around the flounces below her girdle.

"Why do you care?" Ariadne said, steadily this time. "You haven't cared about him in years. About either of us. It's Phaidra you favour—why is *she* not helping you?"

Queen Pasiphae turned and took a step toward one of the pillars that framed the doorway. She looked over her shoulder at Ariadne. A coil of dark hair slid across her back and over her shoulders and settled against her neck like a snake on marble. "Minos is a danger to all of us, now more than ever. I am thinking only of my people." She looked away. "He refuses to speak to anyone, including me, of course. And he used to listen to you. Never to Phaidra."

Ariadne smiled and stretched her arms above her head, because her mother was gazing at her again. *You stupid woman*, the princess thought as her heart stuttered and sped. *He promised to make me queen. He broke his promise. He burned me when I protested. How can you possibly imagine that I'd help him? And yet . . .* She smiled again, a true smile, this time. *There just may be some new thing to find out.*

"Very well," she said, running her fingertips lightly over the scars on her arms. Puckered, pink ropes, scored by godfire. "Take me to him."

———— · ————

Minos was standing between the stone horns where Ariadne had stood, years ago, the day he and his army had returned from the war in Athens. He was leaning out into the air above the gate, just as she had. She remembered how he'd looked that other night; the flame-bright lines of him sharpening as he drew closer. The loincloth, hair, beard and skin that hadn't burned, because his mark had protected him, even as it seared holes into the earth.

He was naked now. The loincloth, Ariadne knew, had long since blackened, curled and fallen away. His jaw and cheeks showed in livid red patches through the remnants of his beard. His skull was blistered and smooth, though there were wisps of charred hair just above his ears. His godmark, consuming him because he could no longer contain it—or perhaps because he no longer wanted to.

"Husband!" Pasiphae called. He strained even farther into the wind, which whipped the flames in long, streaming lines behind him. Ariadne saw a knot of people on the steps far below, craning, staring. High Priest Hypatos; another, shorter priest; a man with a bow in one hand and an arrow in the other. "Husband, I have brought someone. Turn around. Come down from there."

He didn't. Ariadne stepped up level with the horns and laid her fingertips on one of them. It was as hot as sunbaked sand. She eased her head around the front of it and saw his face. She'd imagined he'd be smiling, exulting in mark-madness as she'd seen him do before—but his eyes and mouth were holes, black and gaping and wild with pain. *Ah*, she thought, pressing her hand against the pillar. *Good.*

"Father," she said, over his crackling and the wind.

He turned to her. His hole-eyes didn't blink—no lids, she saw. His raw, oozing lips shaped her name, though he made no sound.

How long has it been since I saw him? she thought. *How much longer can he possibly live?* "Come down," she said. "Please."

He gave a whoop and she stumbled backward. As she steadied herself, she saw the guard below nock the arrow to the bow and raise them both.

"Ariadne!" Minos bellowed. Gouts of flame spewed from his mouth and into what was left of his beard, and Ariadne choked on a waft of burned hair and flesh. He leapt down from the horns' pediment to stand before her; he seized her hands and she gasped, though she wanted to scream—*Not again, not again; no more burns!*

Pasiphae was between them both, suddenly. Her own hands were silver and running with water, and she wrapped them around Minos and Ariadne's. Ariadne felt the godmarked moisture drip and seep and numb; she moaned with relief and then with anger. *Why didn't you do this for me when he hurt me last time? And why did you tend to Asterion's burns whenever he changed from bull back to boy? You hateful, cruel woman . . .*

"Minos," Pasiphae said in a low, urgent voice. "One of your men is below us with his bow trained on you. Others will join him soon, if you do not come down—all the way down, to the ground. We will talk more there."

He stared at Ariadne with his empty eyes. They were weeping a thick, yellowish fluid, she saw, and drew her hands away from her parents so that she could wrap her arms around herself.

He stared and stared, until she said, "Yes. We should get down now." The moment the last word was spoken he was past her—two long strides and a leap, and a hissing plume of flame that faded to smoke as Pasiphae and Ariadne gazed at it.

Ariadne fell to her knees and peered over the edge of the roof. She'd never seen anyone jump, or jumped herself; had always clung to a pillar with her hands and feet and eased herself up or down with her dancer's muscles. Minos was beneath her, facedown, his limbs outstretched.

"Do not fret, daughter," Pasiphae murmured at Ariadne's shoulder. "He will get up."

I'm not fretting, Ariadne thought. *And I don't care if he gets up.*

He did, of course. His limbs twitched and snapped, and he raised his head and stared up at her. His blistered lips moved. She heard nothing but wind, and her mother's breathing, but she understood.

Ariadne. Come down to me.

She slid down the column, unaware of muscles or effort or care. She knelt at his head. Tendrils of smoke wove through her fingers. He laughed a spray of sparks.

"Your mother . . . wishes to speak to me of weighty . . . things."

"I do," Pasiphae said, above Ariadne's left shoulder.

Minos wrenched himself up—a molten caterpillar on a leaf, hovering and clinging at the same time. "Speak, Wife. It has been a long time . . . after all."

Ariadne glanced up at her mother. The queen was bending down, her green eyes even greener, in the light from his fire. "Minos. Minos King. Even your priests are demanding that you be put out of the palace. Exile on an island, they say, and my priestesses agree. Karpos is begging me to summon the kings of Phaistos or Mallia, to get their advice."

"Karpos?" He was panting. His lower lip was dripping blood slowly onto the ground. "Who is that?"

Ariadne bit her own lip so hard that there were bits of skin between her teeth, when she let go. She didn't make a sound, though, which pleased her.

"Daedalus's apprentice," Pasiphae said, her voice suddenly very low. "The young man you have made your heir, thereby humiliating your own two sons, and me."

And your daughter, Ariadne thought. *Your daughter most of all.* All of her scars seemed to throb, suddenly: on her arms and hands, her chest and belly. Her hands twitched to touch them but she kept them still.

"Karpos," Minos said, his breath whistling as he panted. "How odd. What does Daedalus . . . think of this?"

Pasiphae sucked in her own breath and coughed. Ariadne dug her fingernails into her palms. "Daedalus is dead," the queen said at last. "Are you truly so far beyond this world? Do you not remember? He and Icarus and everyone else who worked on the altar within the Great Goddess's mountain—they all died in a pirate attack more than *six years ago*."

"Did they," he said, in a low, smiling voice. "Did they . . . indeed—Daughter?"

He swung his sightless eyes toward Ariadne, whose head spun with words: *You and I and that horrible Theron are the only ones who know they didn't die, and you know it very well: you'd be* winking *at me now, if you had eyelids—gods, no one else must know! Not my mother; not anyone. It's* our *secret and I've been keeping it close, waiting to make use of it . . . soon, perhaps, if Theseus's silence continues. . . .*

As she waited for her voice to stir in her soot-thickened throat, he waved a hand. "Never mind, my dear, never . . . mind. And what of you, my water lily, my seahorse, my . . . queen? What do *you* think . . . should be done with me?"

"I think," said Pasiphae, "that you are a king, not a lizard. I think that you should get up and come with us to your Throne Room, where we will continue this discussion."

Minos sat up, very quickly. Ariadne heard a wet ripping sound, saw gobbets of what had to be flesh glistening on the dusty ground. She tried not to look at his chest and thighs. "I will speak with Ariadne now," he said to Pasiphae, so sharply that he almost sounded like his old self. "And I will speak with her here. Leave us."

Pasiphae lifted her chin so that she was not looking at either of them. Water flowed from her hands—from all her skin, Ariadne knew, because the queen's jacket and skirt had begun to cling to her, and because her curls had straightened flat against her neck and back. Her moist lips parted; Ariadne saw the tips of her perfect teeth before her lips closed again. She whirled and walked away from them, toward the staircase that would lead her to the royal apartments.

Minos growled a laugh, and it, too, sounded so terribly familiar.

It's just the two of you, Ariadne thought. *Just like before, when he loved you and promised you the queenship, and you loved him. Only it's not. Remember: he betrayed you, and he is mad, and you* do not love him.

When his laugh had faded into tendrils of silver smoke, he said, "They are all right—the people who worry about me. I *am* mark-mad. And my god and father, Lord Zeus, no longer wishes me to live in the world of men."

He wasn't breathing hard, anymore. His words slid out of his cracked, blistered, bleeding mouth and he could have been sitting on his throne, leaning toward Ariadne with his fists on his knees, as he had so many times before. She closed her eyes to quell this image, or to pull it closer; she didn't know which.

"So I am going to give myself to my god."

She opened her eyes. "When?" she whispered, when he said no more.

"In two months, on the festival of his birth."

"Where?" Though she knew, of course.

"The place of his birth, child. The Great Goddess's mountain." This time his laugh trembled a bit, and a tongue of silver-blue flame slithered out between his teeth. "Since Daedalus built his box inside it, the mountain has belonged more to your mother's god than it has to mine—and more to Athenians than Cretans. It is time that the people remembered Zeus. And they will, as they watch me burn myself to ash for him."

He stood up so quickly that Ariadne had to scramble to rise with him. He moaned and doubled over. His flesh seemed to fade and thin, until it looked transparent. Rivers of fire branched and boiled and overflowed; he was Zeus's lightning and Apollo's sun, silver and gold, red and white. She felt the heat of him pulse against her own scarred skin.

"What of the Athenian sacrifices, when you go?" Her words rushed out as if she'd planned them. "King Aegeus will no longer fear us—it's you he's feared. He'll stop sending the youths of his city here—and then the priestesses will demand that Asterion be freed. Who will do that? Where is the key?"

Thick, rank-smelling fluid dribbled from Minos's mouth when he smiled. "Your sister is the only key," he said. "I commanded Master Daedalus not to fashion any other."

"What?" Ariadne forced herself to press her lips together, so that she wouldn't gape. "But that's . . . that's ridiculous! I—"

"My King?" High Priest Hypatos was standing between the pillars of the gate, the bowman behind him. Ariadne blinked at the priest, and saw that his honey-coloured eyes looked like tiny, unlit coals. His beard, wrapped in golden thread, was so slick that Ariadne imagined she could see the olive oil dripping from it to the front of his black tunic. He could summon lightning and earth-cracking thunder, when Zeus wished it. Even when Hypatos wasn't using his godmark he was storm, lowering and dark.

Minos's bald head spewed flame as he turned. He lowered himself into a crouch as if he meant to spring, but he didn't; he shimmered, still and silent.

"My King," Hypatos said again, stepping forward. "Please. Let us escort you somewhere—a place where you will be able to rest, beyond the range of the prying eyes of your people."

"They fear me." Minos spoke so quietly that even Ariadne, who was so close to him, had to strain to hear him. "You fear me. Perhaps even my wife fears me. None of you will *make* me go; none of you would dare provoke my god or me that way. Isn't that right, Hypatos?"

Minos's light reflected off the priest's eyes and turned them from coal to liquid gold. The two men stared at one another for what seemed like a very long time, until Hypatos blinked and looked down at his feet. "It is," he said. Such short words, but it took them a while to rumble into silence.

"My Lord King," Minos said, as if instructing a child.

Ariadne fell back a pace, dizzy with heat and dread and even excitement, because this almost always came with dread. Just as Hypatos opened his mouth to say something, though, her head filled with another voice.

::*Princess! Listen . . . see what we . .* ::

Suddenly it was not just Theseus's words, throbbing behind her eyes and along her veins: it was images, too. This had never happened before, in all these long months, and he'd never warned her that it would, and she felt herself fall as the pictures came: *a vast cavern ringed with pillars and gaping corridor mouths and no ceiling; a girl—no, a woman who was a girl, the last time Ariadne saw her, but who was now changed, except for the wild fall of her red hair; and Chara—Chara, by the gods, her own hair just a dark fuzz; Chara, crouched with her dirty, bleeding hands held before her . . . And something, down a corridor. Something enormous and distended, with horns that shone bronze in a strange, rippling light . . .*

Asterion, some part of Ariadne breathed.

Theseus said ::*We can't keep him a . . . why did you not tell me what you did to . . .*::

Chara was crying; her freckles looked smudged and blotchy. The red-haired woman was screaming, though Ariadne couldn't hear her: just Theseus, shouting words that crackled and hissed and fell away as the bull-boy—the bull-man—who was her half-brother lowered his horns and charged—

"Daughter? Ariadne? Little Queen?"

She was curled on her side. She heard whimpering and knew it had to be from her, because Theseus's voice was silent and Minos was talking—talking, talking as his godfire lapped at her skin. She didn't open her eyes, which were full of wavering, dying lines that might have been a pillar or a horn.

"Princess? Ariadne? Can you hear me, little love? I heard you—heard you cry out and fall—Ariadne?"

I must get into the labyrinth, she thought. *I commanded Theseus to kill Asterion and he hasn't—he may fail. So I must save the great Athenian hero, because only he can save me. He promised to take me away with him. He promised. I need him. I need to get in—and I need to get* up, *right now.*

She opened her eyes as she pulled herself to her knees. The world tipped and steadied. Sickness bubbled into her throat when she stood, but she swallowed it down. Her father gazed up at her with his black, unblinking eyes; Hypatos and the bowman gazed at her.

"I am fine," she said loudly, so that they would all hear her. "It was just the heat, making me weak. Your godmark, Father—it is a powerful thing. You know this."

No, she thought, *oh, no indeed: I was listening to Theseus. Theseus, son of Aegeus, king of Athens, whom you blame for your own son's murder. Theseus, who will get me off this island. Would you kill me, if you knew? Would you burn me to ash, then yourself?*

"Yes," Minos said gently. "I know this. I have hurt you in so many ways, and do not deserve your forgiveness. When I am gone, you will no longer have to endure it. The gods will soon grant all of us peace."

I'll be gone long before then, you miserable man, she thought. "Yes," she said. "I am sure they will." She smiled at him, though he wouldn't be able to see this, and she smiled at Hypatos, who would, and then she walked away from them.

ABOUT THE AUTHOR

Caitlin Sweet has written three other novels: *A Telling of Stars* (2003), *The Silences of Home* (2005), and *The Pattern Scars* (2011). *The Door in the Mountain* is her first book for young adults. Its yet-to-be-named sequel will be published in 2015.

When not writing, Caitlin teaches writing at U of T's School of Continuing Studies. When not writing or teaching, she works for the Ontario Government. She lives with her family in a Magic Bungalow, which (in addition to cats, fish, a disabled rabbit, a hamster and a mouse) supports an enormous number of raccoons, a couple of opossums and one large groundhog.

Find her online at www.caitlinsweet.com.

FLOATING BOY AND THE GIRL WHO COULDN'T FLY

P.T. JONES

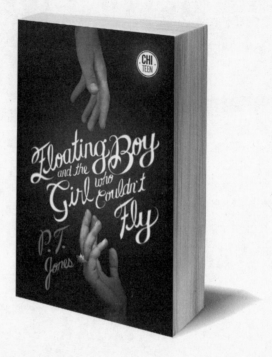

Things Mary doesn't want to fall into: the river, high school, her mother's life. Things Mary does kind of want to fall into: love, the sky. This is the story of a girl who sees a boy float away one fine day. This is the story of the girl who reaches up for that boy with her hand and with her heart. This is the story of a girl who takes on the army to save a town, who goes toe-to-toe with a mad scientist, who has to fight a plague to save her family. This is the story of a girl who would give anything to get to babysit her baby brother one more time. If she could just find him. It's all up in the air for now, though, and falling fast. . . .

AVAILABLE MAY 2014 IN CANADA/OCTOBER 2014 IN U.S.

ISBN 978-1-77148-173-1
eISBN 978-1-77148-174-8

CHITEEN.COM

DEAD GIRLS DON'T
MAGS STOREY

Liv might be in love with a serial killer. You'd think the fact she can talk to the dead would make it easier to discover who's really been slicing up her high school bullies. But all the clues have been leading back to Adam—the oh so hot fugitive she's been hiding in the funeral home. As the bodies pile up, she'll have to risk matching wits with the ghosts of her freshly dead clasmates— some of whom have deadly agendas of their own. Was the cute guy with the wicked grin really framed for murder? Or will Liv just end up the latest bloody victim at Rosewood Academy?

AVAILABLE OCTOBER 2014 IN CANADA/MARCH 2015 IN U.S.

ISBN 978-1-77148-306-3
eISBN 978-1-77148-307-0

ALSO AVAILABLE FROM CHITEEN

PICKING UP THE GHOST
TONE MILAZZO

Living in St. Jude, a 110-year-old dying city on the edge of the Mississippi, is tough. But when a letter informs fourteen-year-old Cinque Williams of the passing of the father he never met, he is faced with an incomplete past and an uncertain future. A curse meant for his father condemns Cinque to a slow death even as it opens his eyes to the strange otherworld around him. With help from the ghost Willy T, an enigmatic White Woman named Iku, an African Loa, and a devious shape-shifter, Cinque gathers the tools to confront the ghost of his dead father. But he will learn that sometimes too much knowledge can be dangerous—and the people he trusts most are those poised to betray him.

AVAILABLE NOW

ISBN 9781926851358
eISBN 9781926851990

WESTLAKE SOUL
RIO YOUERS

All superheroes get their powers from somewhere. A radioactive spider bite. A science experiment gone awry. I got mine from a surfing accident in Tofino. The ultimate wipeout. I woke up with the most powerful mind on the planet, but a body like a wet paper bag . . . .

Meet Westlake Soul, a twenty-three-year-old former surfing champion. A loving son and brother. But if you think he's just a regular dude, think again; Westlake is in a permanent vegetative state. He can't move, has no response to stimuli, and can only communicate with Hub, the faithful family dog. And like all superheroes, Westlake has an archenemy: Dr. Quietus—a nightmarish embodiment of Death itself. Westlake dreams of a normal life—of surfing and loving again. But time is running out; Dr. Quietus is getting closer, and stronger. Can Westlake use his superbrain to recover . . . to slip his enemy's cold embrace before it's too late?

AVAILABLE NOW

ISBN 9781926851556
eISBN 9781927469064

THE CHOIR BOATS
DANIEL A. RABUZZI

London, 1812 | Yount, Year of the Owl. What would you give to make good on the sins of your past? For merchant Barnabas McDoon, the answer is: everything. When emissaries from a world called Yount offer Barnabas a chance to redeem himself, he accepts their price—to voyage to Yount with the key that only he can use to unlock the door to their prison. But bleak forces seek to stop him: Yount's jailer, a once-human wizard who craves his own salvation, kidnaps Barnabas's nephew. A fallen angel—a monstrous owl with eyes of fire—will unleash Hell if Yount is freed. And, meanwhile, Barnabas's niece, Sally, and a mysterious pauper named Maggie seek with dream-songs to wake the sleeping goddess who may be the only hope for Yount and Earth alike.

AVAILABLE NOW

ISBN 9780980941074
eISBN 9781926851761

THE INDIGO PHEASANT
DANIEL A. RABUZZI

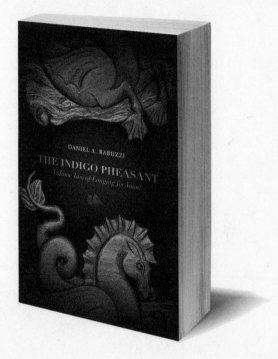

London 1817. Maggie Collins, born into slavery in Maryland, whose mathematical genius and strength of mind can match those of a goddess, must build the world's most powerful and sophisticated machine—to free the lost land of Yount from the fallen angel Strix Tender Wurm. Sally, of the merchant house McDoon, who displayed her own powers in challenging the Wurm and finding Yount in The Choir Boats, must choose either to help Maggie or to hinder her. Together—or not—Maggie and Sally drive to conclusion the story started in The Choir Boats—a story of blood-soaked song, family secrets, sins new and old in search of expiation, forbidden love, high policy and acts of state, financial ruin, betrayals intimate and grand, sorcery from the origins of time, and battle in the streets of London and on the arcane seas of Yount.

AVAILABLE NOW

ISBN 9781927469095
eISBN 9781927469170

NINJA VERSUS PIRATE FEATURING ZOMBIES
JAMES MARSHALL

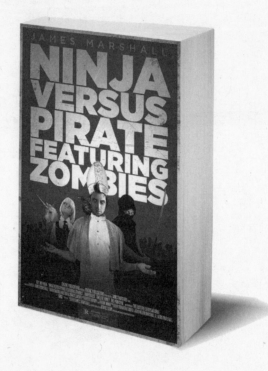

In a world where ZOMBIES control banks and governments, only one young man sees the way things are and emerges from the CHAOS and destruction: GUY BOY MAN. While he tries to end human suffering worldwide and in his high school, Guy Boy Man meets a cute PINK-HAIRED girl named BABY DOLL15 who has a UNICORN that follows her everywhere. An EPIC ROMANCE begins, but forces BEYOND THEIR CONTROL are intent on keeping the young couple apart. One of those FORCES may—or may not be!—Guy Boy Man's closest friend, a handsome African-American NINJA named SWEETIE HONEY; another could be four EXOTICALLY BEAUTIFUL, genetically engineered and behaviourally modified EASTERN EUROPEAN girls; yet another, the principal of their HIGH SCHOOL ... not to mention an impending standardized test known as the ZOMBIE ACCEPTANCE TEST! Will Guy Boy Man find a way to be with Baby Doll15 in a WORLD WHERE EVERYONE IS DOOMED to become either zombies or zombie food??!!

AVAILABLE NOW

ISBN 9781926851587
eISBN 9781927469088

ZOMBIE VERSUS FAIRY FEATURING ALBINOS
JAMES MARSHALL

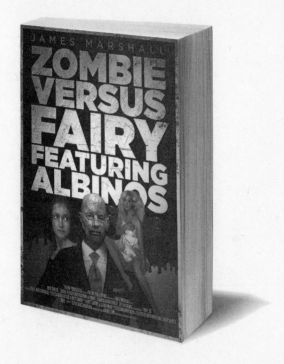

In a PERFECT world where everyone DESTROYS everything and eats HUMAN FLESH, one ZOMBIE has had enough: BUCK BURGER. When, he rebels at the natural DISORDER, his marriage starts DETERIORATING and a doctor prescribes him an ANTI-DEPRESSANT. Buck meets a beautiful GREEN-HAIRED pharmacist fairy named FAIRY_26 and quickly becomes a pawn in a COLD WAR between zombies and SUPERNATURAL CREATURES. As Fairy_26 flies him between her tree-branch apartment in FAIRYLAND and an aircraft-carrier PIRATE SHIP in a zombie-infested DYSTOPIA, Buck Burger struggles to make sense of it all and remain FAITHFUL to his OVERBEARING wife. Does sixteen-year-old SPIRITUAL LEADER and pirate GUY BOY MAN make an appearance? Of course! Are there MIND-CONTROLLING ALBINOS? Obviously! Is there hot ZOMBIE-ON-FAIRY action? Maybe! WHY AREN'T YOU READING THIS YET?

AVAILABLE NOW

ISBN 9781771481410
eISBN 9781771481427

NAPIER'S BONES
DERRYL MURPHY

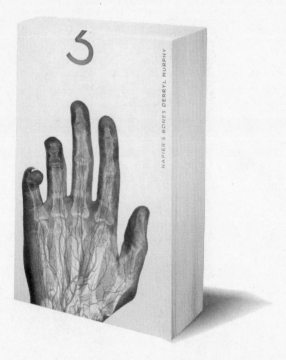

What if, in a world where mathematics could be magic, the thing you desired most was also trying to kill you? Dom is a numerate, someone able to see and control numbers and use them as a form of magic. While seeking a mathematical item of immense power that has only been whispered about, it all goes south for Dom, and he finds himself on the run across three countries on two continents, with two unlikely companions in tow and a numerate of unfathomable strength hot on his tail. Along the way are giant creatures of stone and earth, statues come alive, numerical wonders cast over hundreds of years, and the very real possibility that he won't make it out of this alive. And both of his companions have secrets so deep that even they aren't aware of them, and one of those secrets could make for a seismic shift in how Dom and all other numerates see and interact with the world.

AVAILABLE NOW

ISBN 9781926851099
eISBN 9781926851938